W9-DEG-045

the long walk home

Will North

the Long walk home

a novel

Three Rivers Press

NEW YORK

This is a work of fiction. Names, characters, places, and incidents either are the product of the author's imagination or are used fictitiously. Any resemblance to actual persons, living or dead, events, or locales is entirely coincidental.

Copyright © 2007 by Will North

Reader's Group Guide copyright © 2007 by Three Rivers Press, an imprint of the Crown Publishing Group, a division of Random House, Inc., New York.

All rights reserved.

Published in the United States by Three Rivers Press, an imprint of Crown Publishing Group, a division of Random House, Inc., New York.
www.crownpublishing.com

Three Rivers Press and the Tugboat design are registered trademarks of Random House, Inc.

Crown Reads colophon is a trademark of Random House, Inc.

Originally published in hardcover in the United States by Shaye Areheart Books, an imprint of the Crown Publishing Group, a division of Random House, Inc., New York, in 2007.

Library of Congress Cataloging-in-Publication Data
North, Will.
The long walk home : a novel / Will North. — 1st ed.
1. Married people—Fiction. 2. Middle-aged persons—Fiction. 3. Widowers—Fiction. 4. Americans—Wales—Fiction. 5. Wales—Fiction. I. Title.

PS3614.O778L66 2007
813'.6—dc22   2006102143

ISBN 978-0-307-38303-7

Printed in the United States of America

Design Lynne Amft

10 9 8 7 6 5 4 3 2 1

First Paperback Edition

To Miss P,
who is with us always

december 18, 2005

prologue

She was upstairs cleaning the last of her three guest bedrooms when she heard the crunch of automobile tires in the gravel forecourt. It surprised her. It was early Sunday afternoon. The weekend bed-and-breakfast guests had long since departed and it was too early for new ones to be arriving—not that she expected any; no one had booked. What with Christmas coming, and the winter gales roaring in off the Irish Sea, almost no one came to this remote valley in northwest Wales. The break was welcome; it had been a busy summer and fall. At middle age (she had turned fifty this very day), she had to admit it was nice to have things quiet down for a bit. In fact, the only reason the house had been full this weekend was because rich old Bryn Thomas, who'd been pestering her to sell him her farm ever since her husband, David, had died, had dropped dead himself. He'd married three times and there weren't enough beds in Dolgellau to accommodate all the relations who'd flocked to the funeral—probably, she thought uncharitably, to find out what was in the will for them. Truth be told, Thomas had been after more than just her farm, but she was having none of that, either. She didn't need Bryn Thomas's money and she didn't need his attentions. She knew what love was, even though she'd learned it late, and she wasn't settling for anything less ever again.

She hurried down the low-ceilinged upstairs hallway to the guest room overlooking the forecourt and peered out the window. It was a foul day and the gusting northwest wind hurled rain and sleet against the windowpanes. Below, a small, new-looking silver car—she never had been any good at recognizing models—had pulled up to the house. The driver's door opened and a man in a hooded anorak unfolded himself, arched his back as if he was stiff from driving, then bent into the car to retrieve a cane. It was hard to see much through the streaming window, but she thought he seemed an older gentleman. He closed the car door, put the cane in his right hand, hunched his shoulders against the wind, and walked out of view toward the front door.

She gathered the dirty sheets she'd left piled in the hall, glad she'd made up the rooms already, descended the back stairs, left the sheets on top of the old scrubbed pine table in the middle of her big, warm kitchen, and hurried to the front hallway. She could hear the man stamping the water off his shoes on the flagstones outside.

"Goodness, forget that, and come in out of the weather," she scolded gaily as she threw open the door. "You'll catch your death!"

The man was bent over and turned slightly away from her, slapping the rain from his shoulders. He straightened, turned back, pulled back his anorak hood, and pushed a mane of silver hair from his forehead.

Fiona froze, transfixed by his clear blue eyes. His weathered face crinkled into a smile, and a voice she had thought she'd never hear again said, "Happy birthday, Fiona."

Her right hand flew to her mouth. She staggered back from the door, groping with her left hand for the wall behind her. Reaching it, she gripped the arm of the old chair she kept there for guests to take off muddy boots, dropped into it, and closed her eyes.

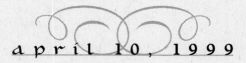

april 10, 1999

one

*i*n a life lived long enough, there are strange symmetries that we recognize only later, if we recognize them at all—moments when an experience or a perception has a parallel moment in another time, a balancing echo, years in the future, or perhaps years in the past, a moment when it feels as if a circle is closing, encompassing and completing something infinitely precious.

Often this circle begins, or ends, or sometimes begins anew with a slight disturbance in the world of the senses—a sound, a smell, a glimpse of something, an inkling vibrating just below the level of conscious thought. This is a world we civilized people have been taught to dismiss. When the French philosopher René Descartes wrote "Cogito, ergo sum" in 1637, those three words of Latin—*I think, therefore I am*—ushered in an era historians call the Enlightenment. In a sense, we still live in it today; it is a world in which the mind is elevated above the senses, where rational thought is judged superior to feelings. And yet, and yet . . . things happen in our lives that challenge this conceit: slight shifts occur in the firmament of everyday existence, the turning world hesitates imperceptibly, the known constellations of experience inexplicably blink—and everything is changed. These are moments that do not lend themselves to rational thought; they are entirely sensual.

For Fiona Edwards, this is how the circle began: out of the corner of her eye one Saturday evening in early spring, Fiona, who was standing at her kitchen sink at the time, sensed a flash of color—blue—down at the main road, by the gate leading to the long, sinuous lane that wound up the hill to Tan y Gadair Farm. The farm had been named, centuries earlier, after the mountain whose cliffs reared up from its back pasture: Cadair Idris—"the chair of Idris," a mythological Welsh giant. The window above the sink faced away from the mountain and offered a panoramic view of the pastoral vale far below the farm. This April evening, with the setting sun low in the west, the meadows glowed a nearly neon green, and the ancient stone walls that edged Fiona's lane seemed burnished with gold. This was her favorite time of year, the long-awaited end to the dreary, wet days of winter, a time of possibilities. Besides the view, though, Fiona liked the fact that she could see her guests coming and be outside to greet them when they arrived.

Ah, she said to herself, *that will be the Bryce-Wetheralls, at last.* Year after year, Fiona Edwards's sixteenth-century stone farmhouse bed-and-breakfast had won awards from the Welsh Tourist Board, the Royal Automobile Club, and the Automobile Association, and one reason was the warmth of her welcome. Guests at Tan y Gadair often wrote in her guestbook that she made them feel as if they'd "come home" to a place they'd never been before.

The Bryce-Wetheralls were a couple from Manchester. They'd called earlier to say they were having car trouble and might be late. Her other guests had already checked in, had tea, and gone into town for supper. An unusual patch of warm weather at the end of March had started the tourist season early this year.

Fiona didn't hurry. The farm lane was nearly half a mile long. It rose and dipped and twisted around granite outcroppings and through oak copses and was out of sight from the farm for much of its length. She finished tidying up the afternoon tea dishes, put aside her apron, and walked through the old house toward the front hall. In the mirror above the sideboard in the dining room, she checked her appearance and frowned. A petite forty-three-year-old, she still had her looks, but there were unmistakable wrinkles now—especially since David's illness: two worry furrows between her brows, crow's-feet at her eyes. And there were random, coarse strands of gray hiding in the naturally blond hair that fell just to the base of her neck. She parted it in the middle and had it cut so that it curved around toward her chin on each side, a little trick to hide the fact that her jaw was losing a bit of definition. On this particular evening, she was wearing a simple white cotton blouse tucked into a pair of snug blue jeans her daughter had nagged her to buy. Her husband hated them; made her look like a hussy, he'd said. *Good,* she'd thought, *maybe you'll be more interested.*

Reaching the front hall, she retrieved a pair of garden shears from the basket on the floor by the umbrella stand, threw a paisley wool shawl around her shoulders, and stepped out into the fading evening light to cut narcissus and grape hyacinth from the border garden while she awaited her late arrivals. The garden was her pride and joy. The house stood on gently sloping ground, facing west. In the far distance, between two rocky foothills, you could see a sliver of the Irish Sea and the reed beds and sand of the Mawddach estuary. She'd had fill hauled in to create a level forecourt and had it surfaced with pea gravel so guests could park close to the house. The new forecourt was supported by a low stone retaining wall and it was just three steps down to a broad lawn and the gardens she'd created from a former sheep meadow. A gnarled old apple tree anchored one corner. The western exposure wasn't ideal, but in the summer the southern sun got high enough that it cleared the crest of Cadair Idris by midmorning and her flowers flourished. Because of the warm spell, the crocuses had bloomed and were already fading, but the daffodils and narcissus were thriving, the hyacinths were out, and the tulips would soon bloom as well. In a few more weeks, if the weather kept on like this, the border garden would be a riot of herbaceous flowers: spires of delphinium in several shades of blue and white; pastel columbine; multicolored lupines; pale pink oriental poppies, their blossoms like crepe paper at a party; ground-hugging tufts of alyssum and dianthus; clusters of scarlet Sweet William; sprawling clouds of lavender, and much more. Behind them all, where now there were only bare canes, there soon would be vigorous, old-fashioned ivory-pink "New Dawn" roses, intertwined with the saucer-sized blue blossoms of clematis, clambering over the stone wall that surrounded the garden and protected the tender plants from storms off the Irish Sea.

It took only a few moments for Fiona to gather a bouquet for the table. While she waited for the Bryce-Wetheralls in the garden, she looked back at the house. When she and David moved in—what, nearly a quarter century ago now—her father-in-law had let the place run down. Hard not to, really: one old man trying to keep a hill farm going. The original farmhouse had been built with massive oak timbers. The beams holding up the ceiling on the ground floor were more than a foot thick and blackened with age. The exterior was built of huge blocks of hard, igneous rock, quarried from the slopes of Cadair Idris. The second story huddled under a steeply pitched slate roof punctuated by three gables. Squat stone chimneys were attached at the south and north faces of the original building like bookends. The inglenook fireplace in the dining room was so big you could stand up inside it—at least she could—and even with your arms fully spread you still couldn't touch its sides. Afternoon sunlight flooded through the big casement windows set into the thick stone walls of the front rooms. Smaller windows nestled under the three gables on the upper level.

Running a bed-and-breakfast had been her idea. David had the
farm and she wanted something of her own to manage. David balked
at first, but raising hill sheep is a marginal existence, even with the government subsidies, and Fiona's business started making money right
from the beginning. The first thing she'd done was have all the leaky
old windows replaced with double glazing; there was nothing atmo-
spheric about drafty rooms. Then she upgraded the bathrooms and
managed to rearrange the upstairs so that her two spare bedrooms had
their own bathrooms. A few years ago, they'd been able to build a two-
story addition on the northern end of the house, creating a luxury bedroom and bath upstairs and a new sitting room for her guests
downstairs. Then, as they were able to take in more guests and charge
more for the luxury of the accommodations, she'd had the new kitchen
built in a one-story shed addition overlooking the valley and the approach to the house. She'd had the masons use old stone for the walls of
both additions and oak for the lintels above the windows, to match the
old part of the house. Another winter or two of weathering and you
wouldn't be able to tell old from new.

She had been standing there, feeling a bit "house proud" for several minutes, but still no car had arrived. Odd, she thought; probably
just someone turning at the gate. People were forever getting turned
around coming out of Dolgellau, the small market town a few miles
down the valley. It was situated at the point where the Mawddach and
Wnion rivers joined before meandering west to the estuary and the sea.
A seven-arch stone bridge was built in 1638 across the Wnion, and the
town's growth was fueled first by the wool industry in the eighteenth
century and then by a brief gold rush in the nineteenth. The town re-
vived again in the Victorian era when vacationers flocked to the mountains to pursue a new fad, hill-walking.

The name Dolgellau, a typical Welsh tongue twister, baffled English speakers: "How do you pronounce this place?" they'd ask. The
answer, roughly, was "Dol-geth-lie," though even that wasn't quite

right. Welsh is a Celtic language full of consonant pairs and combina-
tions that don't sound anything like they look. Awkward-looking on
the written page, Welsh is musical when spoken; it sounds a bit like
water flowing over rocks in a fast-moving stream. It had taken Fiona,
who was English, years to master it after she married David, who had
been born and raised in this valley. Even now, she sometimes had to
struggle to keep up with native speakers.

Almost as twisting as the town's name were its narrow, one-way
streets and alleys, squeezed between old stone town houses, shops, and
hotels built long before anyone envisioned cars or buses. Strangers
often found themselves heading west up Cadair Road toward Fiona's
farm when they meant to be going east toward England.

Fiona gathered up the flowers and returned to the kitchen sink to
trim them . . . whereupon the blue color reappeared beyond the window, not as a car but in the form of an enormous royal blue knapsack
attached to the shoulders of a lanky, middle-aged man who was now
striding up the lane toward the farm. Fiona was used to seeing walkers;
one of the tracks to the mountain's summit went right past the farm.
But most British walkers and climbers didn't carry backpacks as big as
this one, and anyway Cadair Idris was a day hike. What's more, while
the mountain was within the boundaries of Snowdonia National Park,
it wasn't really on the way to anywhere, so she didn't imagine he was a
through-walker. That the man had fetched up here was puzzling—all
the more so when he ignored the signpost for the trail to the mountain
and carried on right into her courtyard.

She finished arranging the flowers, placed the vase on the table in
the breakfast room, and went to the front of the house, arriving just as
the walker knocked. She opened the door to a man who filled the doorway, and then some. He was well over six feet tall, lean, and very fit.
She could tell this because, given the warm weather, he wore very little:
sturdy and well-worn hiking boots, abbreviated khaki hiking shorts,

and a sleeveless black T-shirt made of some lightweight material. His longish brown hair was sun-streaked blond, and he was very tan. Sweat drenched his shirt, and he looked like he hadn't shaved in several days. Despite this, he was arrestingly handsome.

He bent slightly at the waist, leaned on his walking stick, which had a curved handle made of ram's horn, flashed a shy grin, and said, "Hi. Are you Mrs. Edwards?"

"I am, yes . . ."

"I saw a picture of your farmhouse in the window of the Tourist Information Center in Dolgellau and I wondered if you might have a single room available tonight? Well, actually, two nights."

"I'm afraid I don't," Fiona said. "Didn't they tell you?"

"The Information Center was closed when I got there. Wasn't supposed to be, according to the posted hours."

"That Bronwen!" Fiona said, shaking her head. "Whenever she has marketing to do, she just closes the Information Center early and off to the shops she goes. It's disgraceful." And it was; she had caused Fiona trouble more than once. Because of all the awards Fiona had won, the Tourist Information Center featured her farmhouse in their window, but the truth was that once the season started, Tan y Gadair was almost always booked solid. She'd had to turn a lot of people away.

Fiona was trying to place the man's accent. Clearly not British. North American, she guessed, but where?

"You're Canadian, then?" she asked.

"American."

"Really! We don't get many Americans way out here."

"Been here before. Stayed across the river, at Ty Isaf."

"With Graham and Diana? They've moved away now, you know."

"So I discovered."

"Only to be further misled by our esteemed Tourist Information

Center. Look, I'd love to have you, but I'm completely booked. I have a room available tomorrow night—Sundays are often slow—but not tonight."

"I understand," the walker said.

"Look here," Fiona said, "why don't you step inside and I'll just call Janet, at Rockledge. Perhaps she has a room tonight; then you could come here in the morning."

"That's very kind."

"No trouble at all; I'll just be a tick."

The man watched her go. She was nearly a foot shorter than he, but she carried herself in a way that made her seem taller. Her hair swung like a silk curtain across the nape of her neck as she walked. He guessed her to be several years younger than he, and he noticed, with an ache of longing that surprised him, how good she looked in those tight jeans.

Fiona scurried into the kitchen and dialed her neighbor, a mile back down the road. After several rings, Janet finally picked up.

"Dolgellau 531," Janet said, using the old way of answering. Janet was getting on in years and hadn't taken to all-numerical telephone numbers. She was also hard of hearing.

"Janet!" Fiona shouted into the phone. "Fi here. Look, I've got an American walker chap at the door who needs a room, but I'm booked solid; have you one free? No? Well, yes, I know: the season's started early this year. Yes, I'm busy, too. No, Bronwen's gone and closed early again and this fellow's walked all the way here. I know, I know; it's just not right, is it? Okay, Janet, must run. Thanks awfully; thanks. Bye!"

Fiona returned to the front hall. "I'm afraid Janet's booked as well. I'm so sorry."

"I heard. Thanks anyway. Sorry to have troubled you."

"No, no trouble at all," Fiona replied. "Look, may I at least offer you a cup of tea?" She realized she was drawing out the exchange.

Though the man had few words, his voice was a soft and rumbly baritone; she had the curious sensation of being warmed when he spoke.

"No thanks. It's getting late. I'd better find someplace to stay tonight."

He turned, paused, then turned back to her again with that same shy smile. "Lovely meeting you, though," he said. And then he was off.

Fiona returned to the kitchen and watched him as he turned down the lane. The man had beautiful legs—long, hard, and muscular, but in the way a dancer's legs are muscular—articulated, but elongated, not massive. Like many Welsh farmers, her husband was dark, fairly short, and big-boned: a strong, sturdy man well suited to raising hill sheep, but also, she had often thought, rather coarsely made. David plodded when he walked; this American chap, now; he was graceful. No, that was too feminine, she corrected herself: *lithe,* that was it. He moved smoothly and easily despite the heavy pack.

As she watched him leave, she realized there was something else about her visitor that had affected her, something she struggled to pin down. Though he seemed a cheerful sort, Fiona couldn't help but sense something beneath the easy smile. Sadness—that was it. It was just the most fleeting of sensations, barely perceptible. But it clung to him like a fragrance.

two

*a*lec Hudson was tired. Bone tired. Soul tired. Tired in that way you are when you think you've reached your destination at last but discover there's yet another hill to climb. He'd been walking all day. In fact, he'd been walking for nearly three weeks, all the way from London's Heathrow Airport to this remote valley in North Wales.

He thought of it as a pilgrimage, this walking; each day was like a prayer, each step a kind of incantation. It was as if the horizon toward which he walked, and which kept advancing ahead of him, was an ideal he strove for but could never attain. He was not entirely sure what ideal the horizon represented, but he thought it had something to do with love, with duty, with keeping faith. Maybe he was doing penance.

From Heathrow, he had walked a few miles south to the river Thames and then followed the footpath along its banks upstream to the west, halfway across England. When the river turned north toward Oxford, he kept his heading, climbing up to the edge of the rolling Berkshire Downs. Here he followed the Ridgeway, a track cut into the brilliantly white chalk soil of the downs by ancient feet more than five thousand years ago—before Rome, before Greece, at the dawn of recorded history. By the end of the first week, he was in the southern Cotswolds, roughly halfway between the once-Roman cities of Cirencester and Bath. At the Tormartin interchange above the M4 Motorway, a truck driver picked him up and carried him across the older of the two bridges spanning the broad mouth of the Severn River. Alec had been standing in the sun with a handmade sign that read JUST ACROSS THE BRIDGE.

"Not supposed to do it," the driver said, "but Reg, I says to myself, a bit 'ard for the bloke to fly across the river wot wit that bloody great thing on his back, innit?"

Alec tried to pay the bridge toll but the driver wouldn't hear of it. He dropped Alec off on the other side of the Severn, near Chepstow Castle, before driving west to Cardiff to deliver a load of kitchen cabinets from Devizes. Alec turned north to follow the twisting valley of the river Wye, which for part of its length serves as the border between England and Wales. He stopped briefly at Tintern Abbey, the picturesque ruin Wordsworth had immortalized, and then walked on to Monmouth. From there he headed west to the narrow and peaceful Llanthony Valley, and followed a single-track road north all the way to the crest of Hay Bluff, high in Wales's Black Mountains. A few miles farther along, he rejoined the meandering river Wye and followed it to Builth Wells, reaching the town at the end of his second week and marveling at how much landscape one could cover simply by putting one foot in front of the other, mile after mile, day after day. He'd calculated that he averaged between two and three miles an hour, depending on the terrain. Up most days with the sun, he put eight to ten miles behind him before lunch and another eight or ten, sometimes more, before calling it a day. From Builth Wells, he pressed north and west up into the bleak moorland of the Cambrian Mountains, reaching Machynlleth, on the river Dovey near the Welsh coast, toward the end of the third week. He'd been lucky; with the exception of a few misty mornings, he'd had clear and exceptionally warm weather the whole way. As he strode north, spring advanced with him. Daffodils bloomed in cottage gardens and along the roadside. Wild garlic sent up plumes of delicate white umbrels. Primroses burst lemon yellow from the chinks in stone walls. He noticed that in many species of plant, the yellow-flowered varieties seemed to blossom first, as if to add more light to the dun-colored landscape and heat to the weak spring sun.

When evening came on, Alec alternated between bed-and-breakfast accommodations and camping out. Often there wasn't a choice. After ten or more hours of walking he stopped wherever he ran out of steam. Sometimes it was a village with a place to stay; sometimes it was in the middle of nowhere and he pitched his tent. During the day, he'd stop in a village to shop so he always had a picnic dinner if he needed it: some salami, a chunk of farmhouse cheddar, a small loaf of chewy brown granary bread, an apple, sometimes even a bottle of red wine.

The people he met asked him where he was going. That was easy: North Wales. They asked him why he was walking, and that was a harder question to answer. "It just felt like the right thing to do, under the circumstances" is what he usually said, and when he told them the story, people seemed to understand.

"There's something I need you to read," Alec's ex-wife had announced from her hospital bed a year earlier.

He and Gwynne had been divorced for years, lived on opposite sides of the country, in fact—he in Seattle, she in Boston—but they had never quite managed to fall out of love. Alec had tried, but it didn't work: Gwynne Davis was the kind of woman who lit up rooms when she entered. Part of it was sheer presence: she was six feet tall in her stocking feet and another three inches taller in her signature stilettos. Part of it, too, was spirit. She radiated an almost childlike joy of life. She wasn't just lively, she effervesced. In the early days, at least, it had been magical, as if he were being showered with fine particles of delight.

They had met in the mid-1970s, in New York—the city where he was born and raised. His friend Karen, whom he'd known since high school and who, it seemed to him, had been matchmaking for him ever since, had decided he spent too much time alone writing his books and announced one day that she had arranged a double date. There was no denying Karen; she assumed capitulation. Karen had met Gwynne while shopping at Bergdorf's on Fifth Avenue, where Miss Davis, as she was known, worked in the fashion office. *Well,* he'd thought glumly, *at least she'll be well dressed.*

"You'll like her," Karen had said. Then, employing yet another of her endless supply of non sequiturs, she added, "She's tall."

Then the day had come and he was standing, somewhat uncomfortably, in the designer lingerie department, which was just outside the fashion office. Karen had left him there while she went to find his date. Alec was idly thumbing through one of the racks, wondering how the prices for things so flimsy could be so breathtakingly high, when a slightly husky female voice behind him said, "Don't you think those will be a little small for you?"

He turned to respond, tilting his head down to the place where women's faces generally were, and found himself staring directly at the woman's chest. He raised his head slowly, his jaw dropping as he did so, until he was almost certain he was actually looking *up* into the woman's hazel eyes. Uncharacteristically, he was speechless.

"Alec," he heard Karen's voice say, "meet Gwynne."

Anticipating the usual question, she put her hands on her hips and said, "The answer is, six feet even. Six-three in heels." Then she flashed him a dazzling smile.

Still trying to recover, Alec blurted, "It's just that I've never . . ."

"No, I don't suppose you have," she said. Then, opening a little window into herself, she leaned a little closer. He could smell her perfume—something earthy—as she whispered, "Relax; it's really nice to meet a tall man for a change, even a speechless one."

Then she turned to Karen and said, "Are we having dinner or are we all going to stand here and starve to death in the lingerie section?"

While Karen and Gwynne talked over the evening's plan, Alec registered what his date was wearing: over a pair of tight black jeans, which he had trouble believing anyone made that long, she had tossed an old, award-bedecked Boy Scout shirt she'd found in a secondhand store on the Lower East Side. She'd sewn in dramatic shoulder pads and replaced the khaki buttons with red ones to match some of the award patches. The oversized shirt was cinched tight at her narrow waist with a thin red leather belt. Several of the top buttons were unbuttoned and she wore a modest black silk camisole beneath. Wrapped several times around her swanlike neck and then draped carelessly over both shoulders was a long, black silk crepe scarf that echoed the jeans. Her high heels matched the red belt. Her long, softly wavy, light-brown hair had reddish highlights and fell to her shoulders. She wore no jewelry, which, given her professional position, surprised him. The only makeup he could detect was a hint of color on her lips and possibly a blush that highlighted her cheekbones.

Later he would realize that the whole outfit was classic Gwynne: creative, mischievous, unpretentious, and yet—on her, at least—stunning. The fact that she could put things together in a way that looked fabulous but cost almost nothing drove the other women in the fashion office crazy and delighted Bergdorf's president. She was his "golden-haired girl" and he had plans for her.

Alec fell for her immediately. A few weeks later, his mother asked, as mothers do, "Is she pretty?" He thought about this for a moment and answered, "No, not pretty, Mom . . . striking. Beautiful in a handsome sort of way—the way Katharine Hepburn is beautiful." What was captivating about Gwynne, what galvanized nearly everyone she met, was the energy she radiated. She was luminescent.

Now, more than twenty years later, she was dying and Alec was at her side. The doctors thought they'd caught her breast cancer but the malignancy had spread. Alec had come east to care for her. She hadn't eaten anything solid in two months. For more than a week, she hadn't been able to drink anything and keep it down. The veins in her arms, hands, and legs, through which she'd been receiving fluids, had collapsed. Her skin had become mottled—a sure sign, the nurse told him, that she was dying. And yet her spirit seemed undiminished, even as her body withered. Each morning she'd wake up, flash Alec that searchlight smile, and say, "Well, I guess I'm not dead yet!" The nurses adored her. One said, "She's incredible: we go in there to care for her but she ends up making *us* feel better."

On this particular morning she gestured to a manila envelope on her tray table. The label said "Last Will and Testament."

"Ah," he said, making light of the situation the way they always did, "instructions for distributing your vast fortune." It was a joke; Gwynne was not wealthy.

"Read it carefully, love," she said. "You're my executor."

Alec read the will. The terms of her bequest were pure Gwynne: both generous and mischievous. Her modest assets were to be equally divided among the members of her family and his—she had always said his zany family felt more like hers than her own. But there was a catch: the money could only be used to do something that the beneficiaries had never felt they could afford to do. And it had to be fun.

Alec leaned across the hospital bed and kissed her. "That's perfect," he said. "That's you."

"Keep reading," she ordered, smiling as if she had a secret. A few paragraphs later came this: "I direct that my ex-husband and executor shall scatter my cremated remains atop Cadair Idris in Wales."

He looked up, dumbfounded. True, Gwynne was part Welsh, and they had climbed the mountain together years earlier, but still he was stunned. "Why there?" he asked.

"Because," she said, "climbing it was the hardest thing I've ever done physically and the thing I'm most proud of."

Alec had never known. Gwynne was secretive about many things.

The next day, when the doctors confessed there was nothing more they could do for her, Gwynne asked Alec to take her home to her own bed. A week later, after a terrifying descent into dehydration-induced confusion and paranoia, she slipped into a morphine haze and quietly died in his arms. She was fifty years old, a year older than Alec. They'd always joked about him being her "toy boy."

It had taken him a full year to book a flight to England to honor her request. It felt so very far away. He thought that by taking her there he was somehow abandoning her. This was selfishness on his part, he knew: even in death he wanted her close to him. The box holding Gwynne's ashes sat on a shelf in his bedroom, admonishing him. "I know," he'd say to it. "I will. Soon. I promise."

When spring came again he knew it was time. Gwynne loved springtime in Britain—the sheer range of greens splashed across the landscape, the emerging wildflowers, the hawthorn hedgerows in frothy bloom, the exuberant birdsong, the tiny lambs bouncing stiff-legged across daisy-dappled meadows.

Gwynne hadn't asked him to walk; that had been his idea. It seemed only fitting: the two of them had spent so many magical days walking through the English countryside during their marriage; it was where they'd always been happiest, a place where the troubles between them vanished, at least for a time. Yet Alec also knew the long walk was something he had to do to save himself. The divorce had been hard enough—something both of them later agreed they should have been smart enough to avoid. But they had always been able to pick up the phone and hear each other's voices, listen to each other's troubles, poke fun at each other's foibles, those quirks and habits only someone you've lived with a long time ever truly understands. They could laugh, and they did, often.

Now there was no more laughter. The finality of Gwynne's death, its unfairness, the incredible velocity of it, had left him stunned and numb. Then again, numbness was a protective device Alec had developed early in life. His father had been the kind of alcoholic who dealt with his own inadequacies by being verbally abusive to his family, tearing them down so as to make himself feel bigger. If you let it get to you, the viciousness was corrosive. His mother, who worked to support them, lived on tranquilizers to lessen the hurt. His younger sister simply withdrew into a world of her own. Alec, who was often the target of his father's tirades, learned to go numb. It can't hurt you if you don't feel it. He also learned how to cope with chaos, the everyday condition of his family. In a crisis, Alec became icily calm and coolly rational. He could be counted on when everyone else dithered, ducked, or collapsed altogether. But he was not an automaton; he had inherited a big heart from his mother and fell naturally into the role of caretaker. Years earlier, he and Gwynne had agreed that this caretaker characteristic was one of the things that had drawn her to him, like a flower turning to the sun. But it had burned them, too; her need for care and his eagerness to provide it eventually drove them apart. When cancer struck and she was dying, she joked that at last her need for his care was legitimate.

"No, Gwynne," he'd said, "it's a gift you've given me."

In the year since her death, he'd felt perpetually adrift. It was only in her absence that he realized how much—despite their divorce a decade earlier—she had been an anchor in his life. He struggled with verb tenses now when he thought or spoke about her: Gwynne is, Gwynne was; she will, she would have.

Gwynne had made him the beneficiary of a small annuity and he lived on that, writing poetry, none of which he liked. His heart, his emotional condition, seemed controlled by the changing seasons, the darkness increasing as summer slipped into fall and fall into Seattle's notoriously bleak winter. Weeks became months and his friends advised him, gently and with affection, that it was time he "moved on." He didn't know how. Thinking about it rationally didn't help.

And then one day it came to him: he needed to do it physically. He needed to carry Gwynne home to Wales, like a pallbearer. He needed to walk. The effort, the pain, the weeks spent moving toward the mountain at walking speed would be the cure. When he got there, he knew he would be able to let her go.

Alec reached the bottom of the long lane from Tan y Gadair and stopped where it joined the paved road. He leaned on his walking stick—"Hazel," he called it, because that was the wood from which it had been made, long ago, by a craftsman in England's Lake District, a man who'd also died of cancer. He thought about the long walk back to Dolgellau. Then it dawned on him: it wasn't that the walk back to town was long, it was that it was wrong. He had reached the end of his pilgrimage. He'd known it the moment he'd seen the Tourist Information Center photograph of Tan y Gadair, with the mountain behind it. This was where he was meant to stay.

He turned around and began the climb back up to the farmhouse beneath the mountain. He had a proposal to make to Mrs. Fiona Edwards.

iona stood at her kitchen window, as if by staring at the place where the lane descended out of sight she could cause the American walker to reappear. She had felt an uncanny sense of recognition when she'd opened the door to the stranger, as if she'd known him all her life.

It was silly. And besides, she was a married, middle-aged woman, for heaven's sake. She never looked at other men. For one thing, she was simply too busy. Running the bed-and-breakfast—caring for guests, cooking, baking, doing laundry, making up rooms, keeping them clean, doing all the paperwork the Welsh Tourist Board and the Inland Revenue kept thinking up—consumed most of the day. What time and energy were left went to helping David on the farm. She didn't even get to town much, except to shop for food.

She didn't mind the work; it filled her life. True, in the years since David had taken sick, life with him had become much more difficult. David had never been the most attentive or romantic of men—the very thought made her laugh. Still, even after he'd become ill and had to move away from the main house and the barns to an isolated building in a distant part of the farm, she spent many nights with him, as man and wife. As the illness wore on, however, he'd become first distant, then moody and unpredictable. The smallest things would turn him black with fury. The doctor had warned her he might have such spells and she had resolved to weather them. But it was getting harder. There were times now she feared him. It had emerged slowly, this fear, the way aphids sometimes attacked flowers in her garden: the changes were so small you didn't notice them and then, suddenly, plants began losing their vitality. That's how the fear felt: like it was sucking life from her marriage.

At bottom, though, she knew David was a good soul. That mattered, certainly. He was a good father, too. He and their daughter, Meaghan, had a closeness that she sometimes envied. This surprised her, because David often said that he "didn't understand women." Sometimes she thought this was an excuse for not even trying, but he had, after all, grown up without a mother or sisters. His mother had died giving birth to his brother, Thomas, and the two of them had been raised on this very hill farm by their father—a good man, too, people said, until his wife's death turned him as bitter as bolted lettuce. As the boys grew, David senior made it clear he expected one of them to take over the farm. Thomas made it equally clear that he wanted nothing to do with it. He had excelled at school, especially in maths, and had gone on to university. Today, he was an architect in London designing posh office buildings around the world—about as far away as you could get from Tan y Gadair.

David, on the other hand, struggled through school. It was years before the school authorities determined he was dyslexic, and by that time the pattern was set: he hated to read. Words swam on the page and made no sense. He struggled to spell simple words. As he grew, though, it became clear he had a special affinity for animals. His father's milk cow followed him around like a pet. He could sit on the ground in the farmyard and the chickens would gather around him, clucking and cooing softly, and eat from his hand. He seemed to know instinctively where the wide-ranging hill sheep would be found when it was time to bring them down to the winter pastures. At lambing time, he could tell which sheep would have difficulty giving birth. And he ran his father's border collie brilliantly, using the subtlest whistles and calls to guide her in herding the skittish sheep. As a boy he won so many ribbons at the annual sheepdog trials that the authorities moved him up to the adult class to give other youngsters a chance.

And he loved the hills. You'd have thought he'd had enough of them working in the mountains every day, but even before he and Fiona married, David had taken up fell-running, a particularly arduous form of footrace in which otherwise sane men competed against one another by running up and over the treacherous ridges and mountain ranges in North Wales. He was a founding member of the Eryri Harriers, a fell-running club, and had competed elsewhere in the United Kingdom—in the Lake District, Yorkshire, even Scotland. Fiona thought the whole thing was daft and feared he'd break a leg or fall off a cliff somewhere, but David was thickly muscled and well suited to the sport and won a number of trophies. Finally, though, his knees gave out from the punishment, and he'd had to stop competing.

Although Fiona knew David was clever—that was obvious from the farm's success—years of failure at school had left deep scars. He tended to disparage Fiona's passion for books, preferring to limit his reading to farm magazines. He wasn't much for conversation, either. Most days before the illness—how often her thoughts began with that phrase now—he'd come in from the hills in the evening, bathe in their big claw-foot tub, wolf down whatever was for supper, and collapse in front of the television while she read her books in the kitchen. She appreciated how exhausting it was to run a hill farm, but she had hoped for something more. Even as a girl she'd dreamed of a marriage in which the dailiness of life was shared in the evening, around the table, perhaps, or before the fire. Fiona had thought somehow that by marrying a farmer, someone who didn't have to go away to work the way her own father had, she'd have that kind of togetherness. It hadn't turned out that way. As for more physical forms of intimacy, well, though David had courted her ardently when they'd met, after they married his interest in lovemaking had faded more quickly than hers. Since his illness it had vanished altogether. To tell the truth, she didn't much miss the sex; even in the beginning it had been perfunctory at best. And after her doctor told her she'd be unable to have any more children, David had become even less interested, as if without the opportunity to create a son and heir to take over the farm, sex had become pointless. Fiona thought about her daughter, about how her whole life lay before her, and wondered what shape her own private dreams were taking. Meaghan had turned into a beautiful young woman with the slate-black hair and dark features of her father but her mother's delicate proportions. Even in a place as small as Dolgellau, the girl had no shortage of boys calling on her. Now that she was off at university, Fiona could only imagine what she was getting up to. *That's the problem,* she thought, almost wistfully. *I can only imagine it.*

Fiona shook herself out of her reverie, turned away from the window, and went upstairs to turn down her guests' beds. She had taken to leaving a small, locally made chocolate truffle in a paper doily on each pillow and her guests seemed to appreciate it, along with the individually packaged soaps and toiletries in the bathrooms. These things increased her operating expenses, but the costs were more than offset by the number of return visitors.

Over the years Fiona had redecorated the interiors of each of her guest rooms. One had an old oak four-poster bed in it, and the other two had double beds with luxurious drapes that swooped down from the ceiling and gathered at each side of thickly padded and tufted headboards. Taking a cue from *Country Living* magazine, she'd got rid of the busily patterned, rather gaudy carpets that were customary in Welsh houses and replaced them with wall-to-wall carpets in a muted sage green. The windows were draped in a contrasting dusty rose velvet, and the floral-pattern coverlets on the beds picked up both colors. She painted the walls the color of buttermilk and the windows and trim a brilliant white enamel. She sent away to London for fine sheets and pillowcases in the same warm cream color as the walls. And because she loved to read and assumed that others did as well, each room had upholstered chairs, books lined up along the deep windowsill, and antique reading tables with lamps that shed a soft and flattering light. There were also candles, and matches to encourage guests to use them. On top of the dresser in each room, Fiona placed a tray with a decanter of dry sherry and two small glasses. Romance, she felt, was important, no matter the age of her guests.

She'd just turned down the last bed when she heard a knock at the door.

Finally, she thought.

But it wasn't the Bryce-Wetheralls. It was the American again. Behind him, in the fading light of the day, she noticed clouds building over the sea.

"Oh! You've come back!" she said. She was slightly unnerved to find him there again, and secretly delighted.

"I have an idea," he said, as if their earlier conversation hadn't ended. "You have a lot of pastureland, and I have a tent. How about if we invent a new form of accommodation? We could call it 'tent-and-breakfast.' You get an extra paying guest and I get to stop walking."

Only an American, she thought, could think up something so unconventional. She looked at him for a moment, speechless, and then began laughing, with a richness that seemed to him to come from someplace deeper than her petite frame could possibly produce.

"Brilliant!" she said at last.

He looked directly into her eyes and what she suddenly saw was utter exhaustion.

"You have no idea how good that is to hear," he said softly.

"But look," Fiona said, leading him out into the garden, "you don't need to disappear into one of the pastures; why not pick a nice flat spot over here on the lawn . . . by the apple tree, perhaps? Yes, I think that will do. It's quite private; no one will be able to see you from the house. What do you think?"

"Sure," he said. "Thanks."

She rattled on: "Right, that's done then. Pitch your tent or whatever you need to do and I'll put on tea. Come in when you've got yourself sorted. You'll be wanting a bath, too, I shouldn't wonder."

"That would be great," Alec said, groaning a bit as he dropped the heavy pack to the ground.

Fiona turned to go and then stopped. "I have no idea who you are," she said, looking back to where he stood.

"Alexander Hudson. Alec."

"Fiona," she said, walking back to the house. "My friends call me Fi."

And then she was gone. Alec stood looking across the garden to the entrance to the stone farmhouse. It had been his idea to walk back up the lane, and to suggest this odd arrangement, and yet somehow he felt this woman had taken charge. After weeks of solitary decision making, he felt comfortably cared for.

He pulled the tent out of his pack and attached the two telescoping ultralight poles to their grommets and clips, bringing the tent almost instantly from a flat expanse of nylon to a taut dome. Then he attached the waterproof fly that arched over the tent. He'd done it so many times that it took only a few moments. He slung the backpack into the tent and climbed in after it. In another few minutes he'd blown up his inflatable pad and laid out his sleeping bag. He pulled some clean clothes out of the backpack, crawled out of the tent, and walked back to the house. Leaving his boots at the door, he entered the hall.

"Hello?" he called.

"In here!"

He padded through her formal dining room, noting it had already been set for breakfast, and stopped at the entry to the kitchen.

"Well, come in, come in," Fiona said. "I'll just put the kettle on." She'd been cooking.

"I was wondering if I might have that shower first," Alec said.

"Of course you can," she said. "I should have thought of that. But you'll have to settle for a bath. The guest rooms all have lovely new baths with showers, but of course they're all taken, so I'm afraid you'll have to use the old tub in my bathroom."

She led him back through the dining room, to the entry hall, and then through a low oak door with a small sign that said PRIVATE.

"Mind your head, now. This is the oldest part of the house and they didn't grow them as tall as you back then." They'd entered a small but cozy sitting room with its own fireplace. There were two high-backed wing chairs on either side of the hearth, and the wall opposite was lined with books. The wide-planked oak floor was covered by a worn but still beautiful Persian carpet, and a creamy sheepskin rug lay directly in front of the fire. Curled up on the furry sheepskin, as if anticipating a fire in the grate, was a black cat. The cat looked up.

"That's Sooty," Fiona said. "He thinks he owns the place. Not the friendliest cat in the world, but he's company."

As if to prove her wrong, Sooty hauled himself to his feet, stretched, yawned, sidled over to Alec, and began nuzzling his ankles, weaving in and out of his legs.

"Well, well," Fiona said, genuinely surprised. "That's a first."

"I don't know what it is," Alec said, reaching down to stroke the animal, "but cats seem to take to me."

When he stood up again, she had a bemused look on her face.

"Bath?" he said.

"Oh. Right. This way."

She led him through a bedroom with an enormous and very old and richly carved four-poster bed hung with forest-green velvet curtains at each corner, into a small bathroom with an old claw-foot tub. She pulled fresh towels from a corner cupboard.

"I hope you won't mind; I haven't got round to updating this bathroom. A bit like the shoemaker's children going barefoot, I suppose."

Alec smiled. He hadn't fit into a tub since he was a child. "I'll be fine."

For just a fraction of a second, Fiona visualized him trying to fold his naked body into her tub. She shook the vision away.

"Right, then. I'm off to take supper to David, so when you're finished, just come through to the kitchen."

"David?"

"My husband. And I'm running late. Take your time."

"Thanks," he called after her as he turned the handles.

Alec had camped the previous two nights, and now, as he slid down into the steaming tub, he thought about how healing hot water was and how odd it was that after the fall of Rome the magic of hot-water therapy, which the Romans had developed to an art form, had been completely forgotten in western Europe for centuries. It was almost inconceivable.

When he stepped out of the tub some time later, he felt newly born. From his shaving kit, he pulled the old wooden-handled brass razor Gwynne had given him years ago, slipped in a new blade, slathered on his shaving cream, and scraped off his three-day beard, dismayed at how gray it was. As he looked in the mirror over the pedestal sink he realized the three weeks of hiking had melted away the softness around his waist that had appeared, like an unwelcome party guest, after his fortieth birthday.

"Not bad for an old guy," he said to himself, but his gaunt face told a different story; he had aged visibly from the ordeal of Gwynne's death.

He was putting away his shaving gear when he realized there was something odd about the bathroom: it was entirely feminine. There were small, round French-milled soaps, powders, bath salts, a candle in a tarnished antique silver-plate holder, and, on the windowsill, two small bottles of perfume: Amarige by Givenchy, never opened, and another, half full, called—comically, he thought, for this part of the world—Rain.

But there was no razor, no shave cream, no heavy-duty soap for a farmer's grimy hands. There was only one toothbrush, standing upright in a delicate glass by the sink. Fiona was married. She'd said so; her husband's name was David. But in this bathroom at least, there was no evidence of him at all.

He put on a clean white expedition shirt, black wrinkle-free trousers, and a pair of lightweight black loafers, and threw a charcoal gray sweater around his shoulders. Then he went back out to the entry hall and took his boots, hiking clothes, and shaving kit to the tent. He noticed that the wind had picked up and the temperature had dropped. It was nearly dark.

Fiona was pouring hot water into the teapot when he came back into the kitchen. She turned around and exclaimed, "My goodness! You certainly clean up nicely!"

She wanted to stuff the words back down her throat, but it was too late.

Alec smiled. "I have to admit I was surprised you took me in. I looked like a hobo."

It wasn't that, of course, and Fiona knew it. With the salt-and-pepper stubble shaved off his jaws he looked ten years younger. With his white shirt and his deeply tanned skin, Alec Hudson was—in Fiona's experience at least—well, rather nice to look at. And though he was dressed very simply, there was a sort of casual elegance about the way he'd put the pieces together. All of this had taken only milliseconds to register; she felt like she was still trying to catch herself in midfall.

"Tea! How do you like it? White? With sugar?"

"Yes, please."

"Yes, please what?"

Alec chuckled. "Yes, please both."

He pulled a chair out from under the scrubbed pine kitchen table and sat. Leaning back against the wooden slats, he stretched out his long legs and crossed them at the ankles. It felt good to sit.

"I hope you like China black tea," she announced as she bustled around the room, "because that's what I've made. I can't stand that herbal stuff. This is a fifty-fifty blend of Kemun and Yunnan, with just a touch of Earl Grey, which I think is a nice addition in the evening. I take my tea seriously, mind you; only use loose leaf, not tea bags. You'd think that in a country that seems to run on tea, people would be choosy about what they put in the pot, but they're not. These days, most people just throw in a couple of bags of whatever the Tesco's or Safeway has on special offer and call it tea, but I think that's disgraceful. Not to mention that the tea in those bags looks and tastes like floor sweepings."

Fiona knew she was babbling. She desperately wanted to stop, but she didn't know quite how to go about doing it. Words tumbled from her mouth; they always did when she was flustered. While she chattered on another voice, an internal one, was scolding her: *You are a grown woman! You are a married woman! This is ludicrous!*

It was Alec who brought her back to earth.

"Fiona, why don't you sit down and join me."

And so she did. With relief.

He'd been marveling at her antic activity. Here was a woman who positively radiated competence. But he also sensed a deep well of something volatile within her—it was passion, he realized, but it was held in check, banked like coals in a fire grate overnight.

And she was beautiful, too, though in an unstudied way. Her features were delicate, but more athletic than fragile. There was none of the plumpness he'd seen in most British women her age. Her nose was strong and her cheekbones well defined. He noticed that one of her gray-green eyes had a tiny wedge of brown in it and he found this imperfection intriguing. Her lips were not full, but the upper lip was slightly feline, curving down gracefully, then up toward the corners. It was a mouth that broke into a smile easily, and when it did the corners of her eyes crinkled. She had a habit of tilting her head to one side when she was considering something and he found this quirk charming.

He watched her as she poured the tea. Her hands were slender but strong, with prominent veins. Her fingernails were clipped short and unpainted. They were hands that worked hard. He had the queer sensation of wanting to cup them in his own.

For the first time in the year since Gwynne's death, Alec Hudson felt himself uncurling. It was as if he'd been holding his breath a very long time and was, at last, breathing again.

She asked him what he did and seemed intrigued when he told her he was a writer. She asked if she would know his work and he said, "No, I don't think so," but nothing more.

They were quiet for a moment, and then she said, "That's some backpack you're lugging; have you come far?"

Farther than you can imagine, Alec thought to himself. But he said instead, "Just from outside Machynlleth today; I camped on the moors to the east of the town last night."

"No, I meant where did you start?"

"London. Heathrow Airport, that is."

"Heathrow!" Fiona's eyebrows shot up. "You walked all the way from there? Good Lord, you must be daft! How far are you going?"

"Just to here. This is where I was going."

"What, here? This valley?"

"Yes. I need to climb Cadair Idris; I promised someone I would."

Fiona waited for him to say more but he was looking away, lost in thought. She didn't press.

Alec was suddenly very tired. Maybe it was the hot bath. Maybe the days and weeks of walking had finally caught up with him. Maybe it was the warmth of the kitchen. Or of the woman across the table.

He turned to Fiona and found her smiling. There was a softness in her gaze that felt like a balm.

"I'm sorry, Fiona, but I'm bushed. Time to hit the tent. I really appreciate the bath and the tea."

"My pleasure . . . but wait, you haven't eaten anything! I have some of David's supper left over, a nice vegetarian stew. I could warm it up in no time."

"Thanks, but I have something in my pack if I get hungry."

Fiona smiled. "Well, I suspected you were a red meat man; I'm not much for vegetarian, either."

"No, that's not it, really. I'm just done in."

Fiona stood up. "Right, off you go."

Alec began carrying the tea things to the sink but she shooed him away. "Go on, then; that's what you pay me for."

When they got to the front door he turned and extended his hand. She took it and he placed his other hand on top of hers, holding it for a moment.

"Thank you."

"You are most welcome."

He opened the door and they were hit by a gust of cold wind and spitting rain.

"Oh dear, I'm afraid it's going to be a bit damp tonight. Will you be all right?"

He was already across the forecourt.

"Tent's waterproof; sleeping bag's warm," he called over his shoulder. "I'll be fine. 'Night, Fiona."

"Breakfast between seven and nine!"

Alec climbed into the tent, stripped, and slipped into his down sleeping bag. He didn't eat anything. He didn't hear the Bryce-Wetheralls when they arrived, or the other guests returning from town. He was asleep in an instant.

Fiona Edwards sat awhile in the ladder-back wooden chair in her entry hall. She could still feel the warmth of Alec's hands around hers. It was simply a gesture of thanks, an expression of gratitude, but it felt sweetly intimate. She couldn't decide whether it felt good or unsettling. Or both.

april 11, 1999

four

It was the sound of car doors slamming and engines starting that awakened Alec the next morning. Even then, he struggled to become conscious; he felt as if he was swimming to the surface of the ocean after a very deep dive.

It had been a rough night. The wind had continued rising and he was awakened at what he guessed was a little after midnight by the gunshot crack of the rain fly snapping in the wind. He'd crawled out into the darkness to check the tent pegs, getting wet in the process, but found them secure. Back in his down bag he'd had trouble getting to sleep again. Whenever he closed his eyes his mind ran a loop of disjointed images—places he'd walked through in the previous weeks, Gwynne lively and joking in the hospital, Gwynne's inert body after her spirit had departed, the looming cliffs of Cadair Idris, Fiona Edwards. Sleep finally came again, but it was often disturbed.

Now the wind had dropped. He unzipped the tent flap and saw a shredded sky, bits of torn cloud racing beneath an arc of deep blue. From the sun's position, he guessed it might easily be after nine. He sat up and pulled out the last of his clean clothing from the pack: a charcoal-colored lightweight pair of hiking trousers with zip-off legs and his other expedition shirt, this one olive. He put on his boots, thankful they were dry, and crawled out of the tent.

The front door was unlocked and he entered, leaving his boots in the hall. The breakfast room had already been cleared and he could hear Fiona moving around in the kitchen. On the sideboard, Alec noticed a photograph in a polished silver frame and stopped to examine it. A short, stocky, middle-aged man with closely cropped, slightly receding salt-and-pepper hair stood beside a red Volkswagen Golf. His arm was extended and he was handing what looked like the car keys to a beaming and darkly beautiful young woman with Fiona's slight frame. David, he guessed, and a daughter. He put the photograph back and entered the kitchen. Fiona was wearing an ankle-length floral skirt and a cream-colored hand-knit cardigan in a cable pattern. She looked up as he came through the door.

"Well, good afternoon, Mr. Hudson; nice of you to favor us with your presence!"

"Afternoon?"

She laughed. "No, I'm teasing. It's just gone ten."

"Sorry about missing breakfast."

"Nonsense! I've kept some warm for you in the cooker. Sit yourself down here at the kitchen table; I'm not about to go setting a place for you in the breakfast room again. There's a Spanish frittata with mushrooms, tomato, and oregano; local sausages from Lewis the butcher in town—very famous for them, he is; fresh fruit, yogurt, scones, jam, and so forth. Coffee?"

"Just tea, please."

"I thought you Americans had to have your coffee in the morning!"

"Not me."

She set a heavy earthenware teapot on the table and then took his breakfast from the oven.

"This is very kind of you. Thanks."

"Don't thank me, thank Jack; if you hadn't shown up, he'd have got it."

"You have a son?"

She tilted her head to one side.

"Jack's our sheepdog who doesn't like herding sheep. David thinks he's useless and lazy, naturally, but I like his company. Funny thing is, he's brilliant with the sheep when he's working with Owen."

"Owen."

"Owen's our hired man. Local, he is. Fresh out of agricultural college and wants his own farm, though I can't imagine why. It's hard work and pays practically nothing. He helps David in the meantime. We're lucky to have him."

There was a creak in the direction of the back door and Alec turned to see a long-haired black-and-white dog shamble in.

"It's no good, Jackie, you slept in too long, I'm afraid," Fiona chided.

"Not at all," Alec said. "Come over here, Jack."

The dog looked at him for a moment, sniffed the air, and sat beside him. Alec held out a piece of sausage and the dog took it gently from his fingers. Fiona was surprised. She didn't think it was just the sausage; it usually took awhile for Jack to accept someone new. She thought about Sooty's response the night before. Although Alec seemed almost withdrawn, there was a gentleness about this man that both animals had understood instinctively and that she was only now beginning to comprehend.

"Is that your daughter in the photo in the breakfast room?"

"It is. That's Meaghan, and my husband. She'd just got her learner's permit to drive. Very chuffed about it, she was. She's at university now, up in Leeds, studying graphic design."

"Lovely young woman."

"Yes, I'm afraid she is," Fiona sighed, staring off into the distance. "A mixed blessing."

"Meaning?"

"Boys. She attracts them like flowers attract bees."

"Doesn't surprise me. Except for the dark hair, she looks just like you."

Fiona laughed. "Would that be in the manner of a compliment?"

Alec looked at her.

"Yes. It would."

She cocked her head to one side again and smiled.

"The latest one's called Gerald, a city boy. She says he's more sophisticated than the others. I'm not sure that's the sort of thing a mother wants to hear."

"Gotta watch out for those city boys."

"That's what I mean. Where did you grow up?"

"New York City."

Fiona burst into laughter. Alec grinned.

"Will you go up the mountain today?" she asked, changing the subject.

"Yes."

"Did you climb it when you were here last?"

"I did."

"What month was it?"

"June, I think. Or July."

"I just need to tell you that at this time of year the weather on top of Cadair is often much worse than it is down here. It's because it's right on the Irish Sea. The weather can turn nasty in no time."

Alec looked out the window. "I'm not exactly a novice."

"On this mountain, everyone's a novice—including the Mountain Rescue. One of their own died up there just last year. Cadair's unpredictable, and a bit mean-spirited . . ."

Alec smiled. "I appreciate the warning. Tell me: is there still a bus that goes around to the other side of the mountain, toward Tal y Llyn?"

"There is, yes, a little local bus, why?"

"I'd like to start there. Then I could just come back down on this side."

"That bus runs about every two hours or so from Dolgellau. It goes on to Machynlleth. I could drop you off in town; I have to go in anyway." She checked a schedule tacked to the wall by the back door.

"There's one in a little over an hour. In the meantime, why don't you bring in your things. Your room is the one to the right at the top of the stairs. You can hang your tent in the boot room behind the kitchen to dry; it's warm there. Oh, and I'll bet you have clothes that need washing; just leave them there, too."

"I usually just wash them in the bathroom."

"Don't be silly; I have to do the sheets anyway. It's no trouble."

"Um . . . okay. Thanks."

He seemed nonplussed and it dawned on her that he wasn't used to anyone doing anything for him, that he was the kind of fellow who took care of others. But who took care of him?

"Shall I pack you a lunch?"

"I have some cheese and bread in my pack. I'll be fine."

"I'll bet that's fresh," she said, laughing. "All right, have it your way. Meanwhile, I'll go make up the bedrooms while you sort your things."

And then she was gone.

Jack had flopped down at his feet, and he reached down and idly scratched the dog's head, to appreciative dog noises. Outside, the only sound was the distant bleating of sheep.

He took his dishes to the deep porcelain sink and decided to wash them, along with the baking dish and frying pans Fiona had used to make breakfast.

When he crossed the kitchen to go out to his tent, Jack looked up as if considering whether to accompany him. Apparently he thought better of it and dropped his head back to the floor with a sigh.

When he'd finished stowing his wet gear and laundry in the back room, Alec climbed the stairs to his room and found Fiona had already made it up. He was a little stunned by how luxurious it was. The carpet was thick and felt good beneath his stocking feet. There was a semicircular wooden framework attached to the ceiling above the headboard of the double bed from which drapes that matched the duvet cover fell to the floor, pooling on the carpet. They were pulled back toward the wall with thick, braided satin roping. French doors opened to a little balcony with a view south toward Cadair Idris. Two easy chairs flanked the doors. But the high point of the room was the wall opposite the bed: it was made entirely of dark, richly carved oak, and very old. He thought it might be an original part of the old house, but when he saw the angels carved into the wood he decided it had to be a rood screen salvaged from some long-abandoned chapel. Etched glass panels were set into the wall, and a low door that filled the central part of the screen opened into a narrow but beautifully appointed bathroom. There was a long, deep tub with elaborate brass fixtures and a hand-held shower attachment, a pedestal sink, also with brass fittings, and both a toilet and a bidet. The thick Egyptian cotton towels matched the creamy porcelain.

Gwynne would have loved it.

He unfastened the top of his pack, which had hidden straps and doubled as a day pack, and set it on the bed. He put on a white sleeveless synthetic T-shirt that matched his black one and shoved the olive expedition shirt into the bottom of the day pack, along with his first aid kit and a plastic bottle that he'd filled with water at the sink. Then he reached into the big pack and withdrew the sealed, gray plastic box that held Gwynne's ashes and set it between the bottle and the kit.

"Soon, Gwynne," he said quietly to the box.

When she finished the last room, Fiona gathered the dirty linens and returned to the kitchen to start the washing. Along the way, she noticed Alec in the guests' sitting room, writing in a small bound notebook. When she started the wash, Jack bestirred himself, padded over to the back door, and slipped out through a flap.

It was then that she noticed Alec had washed the dishes. She put them away and walked into the sitting room. He looked up.

"I see you are a man of many talents," she said, "including washing up. I'm not sure I've ever had a guest treat me so well!"

"Would that be in the manner of a compliment?" Alec said, echoing her own words earlier.

"Yes. It would." Fiona said, gently mimicking his earlier answer to the same question.

Alec smiled.

"I'll just bring the car around from the barn," she said. "Meet you at the back door."

Alec laced up his boots and stepped out the door just as Fiona drove up. It was the same red car that was in the photograph in the dining room.

"Should I lock the door?"

She laughed. "No, city boy, we don't do that here."

He climbed in and set the day pack gently between his feet.

She gunned the engine, shot out through the farm gate, and sped down the twisting lane toward the main road. Alec was impressed; she drove like a pro.

They rode for a while in silence, passing a reed-edged lake, an isolated pub, and several other hill farms, the road sometimes squeezing down to a single lane and then widening again. The road engineers seemed to have favored old trees and stone outcroppings over a wide, straight strip of macadam. Alec liked that.

As she turned into the square in Dolgellau, Fiona cried, "Quick!

That's your bus!" She spun the steering wheel to the left and pulled the car in front of the parked bus to keep it from leaving.

"Nicely done," he said as he jumped out. "I figure two and a half hours up the mountain and one down. See you this afternoon. Three or four o'clock is my guess."

"Be careful!" she called after him as she pulled out of the way. He gave her a wave and climbed onto the bus.

"You'll be wanting Minffordd, I reckon," said the driver, a wiry fellow in his sixties at least.

"You reckon right," Alec said, surprised.

"It's the boots." The driver grinned as he slipped the bus into gear and pulled out of the square. "I get a lot of walkers going there. Rock climbers, too. But not this early in the year, usually."

Alec sat behind him so he could see through the front window. There was only one other passenger, a few rows back: an elderly woman who smiled at him sweetly when he nodded to her.

The little bus corkscrewed up the long hill out of Dolgellau and turned onto the A470, heading south. The road climbed steadily for several miles, leaving the lushly wooded river valley behind. As it ascended, Alec watched the landscape change from tidy village gardens to broad, sloping, daisy-dotted meadows edged with finely crafted dry-stone walls, and then to steeper, more rugged open moorland furred with thin grass and tough pale green bracken fern. The bus stopped at a remote junction high in the hills marked by the lonely Cross Foxes Inn. The old woman got out.

"Same time, Mrs. Thomas?" the driver asked.

"Same time, Fred," she chirped.

The driver closed the door and turned to Alec. "Does cleaning at the inn. Bloody shame someone her age has to do that kind of work, but there you are."

Then the bus turned onto the A487 and kept climbing, the landscape becoming more barren and weather-blasted. A couple of miles beyond the inn, the bus pitched over the crest of the pass and plunged into a gap in the mountains. Towering ramparts of rock loomed above the narrow road on both sides, blotting out all but a sliver of sky. The road itself clung to a nearly vertical cliff wall on the left. Huge blocks of rock littered the floor of the pinched gorge far below. At one point a mountain stream hurled itself off the high crags to the right, breaking into mist as it plunged, then re-forming as a stream again at the bottom before rushing downhill through the crease of the valley. The road itself was so steep the driver had downshifted to one of the lowest gears to save the bus's brakes, and the transmission groaned against the force of gravity. A few minutes later, the slopes of the valley eased open. In the distance Alec could see a lake, slender as a finger.

When the road leveled out, the bus swung right across the oncoming lane into a lay-by with a small bus shelter. Alec recognized the place immediately. He was out of his seat before the driver came to a stop.

"Been here before then, have you?"

"Long time ago."

"Then you know you're going up the hard way?"

"Yes, but it's the most beautiful way."

"It is that," the driver agreed, "but mind you don't have a nap by the shore of Llyn Cau, now."

"Why's that?"

"Legend has it that if you fall asleep at Llyn Cau you'll wake up blind, mad, or a poet!"

Alec laughed. "Too late for the middle one!"

The driver looked out his side window at the mountain. "Might get a bit of weather up there today; clouding up again, it is."

Alec followed his gaze. Sure enough, though the skies to the south were clear and sun flooded the valley, a turban of cloud wrapped the summit of Cadair Idris.

"Thanks for the lift," Alec said as he climbed down.

"Best of luck," the driver called after him as he closed the door.

The bus's horn gave a friendly toot and Alec turned away from the road, entering a dirt lane lined with neatly parallel old chestnut trees, obviously planted as an approach to someone's home at some point in the past. After a few hundred yards he reached a wooden footpath sign pointing uphill. MINFFORDD TRACK, it read.

The path became steep immediately, scrambling over rocky outcrops beside a merry cataract and entering an oak wood that Alec realized must be a remnant of the forests that had cloaked this part of Wales for millennia. The trees were weather-twisted, stunted, and gnarled. Their roots snaked across the ground among the rocky outcrops searching for a soft spot through which to penetrate the earth. Some of the trees looked as if they were growing directly out of the granite itself. The hillside and boulders were carpeted in mosses of every conceivable variety of green. He stooped to look more closely at them and found they looked like Lilliputian forests themselves. Sunlight cut through the canopy here and there, creating shimmering shafts in the damp air.

After perhaps forty-five minutes of climbing, he passed through a wooden gate set into an old stone wall. The trees gave way to a steep slope of dormant heather, yellow-flowered gorse, early pink campion, grasses, sedges, and bracken. Ahead, the footpath curved off to the right, following the shoulder of a foothill called Craig Lwyd.

After another half hour of climbing, Alec stopped to catch his breath and drink some water. Already, the view behind him was spectacular: the flat valley of Tal y Llyn spread out far below in a stone-walled patchwork. The lake glittered in the midmorning sun. Across the valley, the rampart walls of Craig Goch rose so steeply over the southern shore of the lake that he wondered if the ground there ever saw the sun.

Ahead, the path and the stream parted company, the stream clattering down the hillside to the right, the path climbing steadily up to the left. Here and there, sheep picked their way among car-sized, lichen-encrusted boulders, and complained to each other, like old people in a nursing home.

With the stream's racket behind him, the world now was uncommonly still and the low hum of bumblebees filled the fragrant air. Ahead, a ridge a few hundred yards wide blocked his way to the mountain. Ten minutes later, he crested the ridge, and spread out before him was a vast and silent mountain amphitheater with a sapphire blue, mirror-smooth lake for a stage—Llyn Cau. The lake was imprisoned by nearly vertical cliffs rising over a thousand feet in some places. The cliff faces were deeply etched with fissures and gullies and laced with waterfalls, some of them free-falling hundreds of feet. Shattered hunks of the mountain lay scattered about the scree slopes beside the lake— the weapons of winter, broken free and rained down by the insidious forces of frost. Far above and out of sight beyond the cliff rim, he knew, was the summit.

Alec slipped off his pack and sat on a ledge beside the lake. He and Gwynne had picnicked here on a warm afternoon many years earlier. They'd eaten too much and then laughed and groaned all the way up to the summit, with Alec often behind Gwynne with his hands on her rear, pushing, when she protested she could go no farther.

He took a sip of water and smiled.

Shortly after they married, Alec was offered a position as a speechwriter for Jimmy Carter. The president had read the political opinion articles Alec had written while he was teaching at Columbia University. Carter liked his straightforward style. When the president's chief of staff called with the job offer, he said that Carter had decided it would be better to have Alec with him than against him. The job was a huge opportunity and he and Gwynne jumped at the chance, moving to an apartment in Washington, D.C., within walking distance of the White House. Gwynne left Bergdorf's and got a job managing a luxury women's clothing store in D.C. that catered to the diplomatic crowd. They both knew it was a step down, but she promised him it was what she wanted; she was tired of the pressure in New York.

The next three years were a whirl of long days and glittering nights at White House receptions and at charity benefit fashion shows Gwynne organized at foreign embassies and the Kennedy Center. He'd even bought his own tuxedo. When Ronald Reagan defeated Carter in the 1980 election, Alec was promptly removed from his position, but they stayed on in Washington. Gwynne's star had continued to rise and, having dragged her away from New York, he decided it was only fair for him to take a backseat and let Gwynne soar. He negotiated a publishing contract for a book on his experiences in the Carter White House, stayed home working on it every day, and had dinner waiting for Gwynne when she came home. When they could squeeze the time from her schedule, they traveled—often to England, a place they both loved. They never stayed in London, preferring instead to drive from village to village, hike in the countryside, and dream of having a place of their own there. On one trip, they'd brought her parents, so her father could visit the place in the coal-mining valleys of South Wales where his own father had been born. But the mines were long closed and the valleys were ravaged and bleak, so they headed north to the scenic wildness of North Wales. It was on that trip, while her aging parents rested at the bed-and-breakfast where they were staying, that he and Gwynne had climbed Cadair Idris, on a brilliantly clear and warm summer day.

• • •

Alec replaced the water bottle, stood, and hoisted the pack onto his back. Not for the first time, he thought that whomever it was who first called cremated remains "ashes" should be taken out into a field and shot. They were not ashes. They had the consistency of fine-grained sand. They were not light and fluffy, as the word *ashes* might suggest; they were stunningly heavy. His back hurt.

In Washington, people talked about what a striking couple they were. Alec had a New Yorker's quick wit and, despite having been raised in a poor family, he moved easily through the diplomatic crowd. With her beauty, commanding physical presence, outrageous sense of humor, and hearty, unself-conscious laugh, Gwynne drew people to her the way light draws moths. And the affection between the two of them was obvious to everyone they encountered. They worked so well together at these events, someone once described the two of them, admiringly, as "the Gwynne and Alec Show."

But there was trouble backstage. What no one knew was that Gwynne, despite her obvious talents and radiant facade, was terribly insecure. Her hands trembled every morning as she did her makeup. She was often sick. It wasn't that Gwynne was failing at work or in any other aspect of her life. It was that she feared failing. And somehow the more she succeeded, the more she feared failure. Over time, Alec took on more and more of the responsibilities of their marriage. At first he didn't mind. Given his own family, he was used to being relied upon: if something needed doing, he did it; if there was a void, he filled it. It had always been that way; it was what he did. He felt that if he kept telling Gwynne that he loved her and believed in her, she would come to believe in herself.

But it didn't work out that way. Instead, his belief in her, his encouragement, his cheerleading, only added to the pressures she felt.

And they added a new fear to her list: the fear of disappointing him. She didn't say anything about this, and he didn't see it.

The years passed and Alec began to resent the burden of this care-taking. He talked with Gwynne about taking some responsibility for her own life, but her response was to become even more dependent, creating situations from which he'd have to "save" her. It began with small things, like repeatedly being stranded at work because she'd misplaced her car keys. In time, it grew to acts of self-sabotage—"forgetting" important appointments, delaying dealing with troublesome employees, failing to deliver important reports to the store's owners. At one point, Alec realized he could no longer trust his wife to tell him the truth about even the smallest things; instead, she told him, and others, whatever she thought they wanted to hear.

It was when she began drinking heavily that his frustration changed to fear. He wanted to be understanding and patient, he wanted to love her into wholeness, but he found himself becoming angry and hypercritical. And then one day he realized he had nothing left. He was empty. It stunned him. He thought his love and his determination were unlimited. He thought the energy he could pump into their relationship would never be exhausted. He was wrong.

They separated. Alec's White House memoir had sold well and he went off to the Pacific Northwest to write poetry, thinking that perhaps he could write himself clear about what was happening to them. A few months after he left, Gwynne was fired. She never gave him a candid explanation, but he suspected it was because of her drinking. Then, miraculously, an up-and-coming New York designer who had decided to open his own retail boutiques asked her to manage them. Alec returned to Washington. They would move back to Manhattan, where she said she had found a "fabulous" apartment in a brownstone on the Upper East Side. They would start over.

When he got to D.C. she hadn't even begun packing; she was paralyzed by the task of organizing everything. He sent her on to New York and, in two days of furious work, packed up their belongings, loaded them into a rented truck, and hauled them north. He met her at the new apartment.

The place was dark and filthy.

"It's New York," she said when she saw his face. "What did you expect?"

"I don't know, someplace habitable?" he'd replied. He wasn't even angry; he was heartsick.

In the coming weeks, after cutting a deal with the landlord to split the cost, he renovated the apartment, replacing the antique appliances, and installing almost-new kitchen counters and cabinets he bought cheap in New Jersey from a demolition contractor. After a couple of months, it looked like a place someone might actually want to live in.

Except he wasn't the someone. One day, he left for good; he had come to feel he was going crazy, that he had to leave to save his own sanity . . . and maybe Gwynne's as well. He knew he was part of the problem; it took the two of them to do what they did. He thought that if he left she'd have to take charge of her own life at last. He drove to Seattle, got a small apartment overlooking Puget Sound, watched the sunsets, and wrote poetry that he knew he'd never publish. They agreed to divorce. They also agreed to remain friends.

Alec trudged up the mountain, these memories heavier even than the container in his pack. The footpath now followed the razor-sharp southern edge of the amphitheater. The route had become a relentless series of jagged rock shelves and eroded gullies. At one point, he paused on the vertiginous rim and looked over the edge. A thousand feet straight down lay Llyn Cau. Its surface had changed from blue to black. It looked like a tiny onyx gemstone caught in a tarnished silver clasp. Then he looked up and was dismayed at what he saw. The tight turban at the summit had unraveled and now the entire upper plateau was swathed in dense cloud.

He reached the top of Craig Cau, a secondary peak, descended a shallow swale, and had just started up again when the cloud engulfed him. The temperature dropped immediately but the coolness was refreshing. The route ahead climbed through a bleak world of weather-shattered granite. There was no footpath to follow now; a series of cairns—pyramids of piled stones left by previous climbers—marked the way upward, assuming you could distinguish them from the rest of the rock in the thickening mist.

Alec was glad he knew this mountain and was one of those lucky people with a built-in compass. It was as if there were iron filings in his brain that lined up with Earth's magnetic field. It had always been this way, so he wasn't worried; he climbed though the cloud without pause. At each cairn, he added another stone; it was a climbing tradition, one designed to ensure that the cairns were always there. The hair on his arms and legs raked moisture out of the mist and left him sequined in silvery droplets. He had a rain jacket in his pack but he was still too warm to wear it.

The boulders over which he now clambered were wet and slippery. Often as not, he was using his hands as well as his feet. The higher he climbed, the worse the visibility became. He had never climbed in a cloud before and it was denser than any fog he'd ever encountered. There were times when he could see only three feet ahead. Finding the next cairn was becoming more and more difficult.

He was also hungry and guessed it was after noon. He sat down in the lee of a massive block of granite, put down the day pack, and pulled out the cheese he'd brought.

"Not exactly a walk in the park today, is it, Miss Davis?" he said to the box of ashes in the pack. He'd always called her that; she hadn't taken his name when they married.

* * * *

After he and Gwynne had separated and finally divorced, he'd kept to himself. He found the solitude suited him. He remembered a snatch of a Wordsworth poem he liked: "When from our better selves we have too long been parted . . . how gracious, how benign is solitude."

A year passed and Gwynne called one night to say she'd been re-cruited to be the chief designer for a small but imaginative clothing manufacturer in Boston. Alec had always believed that Gwynne was meant to be a designer, not a merchant, and he was delighted for her. It didn't surprise him at all that in this new job she excelled, designing clothes that doubled the company's business every season. Nor did it surprise him when, two years later, she was fired again.

This time though, she broke the pattern. She entered a treatment program and got sober once and for all. Then she started her own busi-ness, as an interior designer. The business flourished and she reveled in her independence. She'd found her niche. Things were going right for her at last. So it came as a shock when she called—was it only two years ago?—to tell him she'd just gotten out of the hospital after having two malignant lumps removed from her breasts. He'd had no idea she had cancer. She hadn't told him.

After the surgery, she went through the usual cycles of chemother-apy and radiation. The prognosis was very good, even if the process was brutal. The chemo made her terribly sick. Her hair fell out. They were in touch every day. He kept asking if she needed him to come to Boston, and she kept saying no. "If I need you," she promised, "I'll call." He was proud of her. She had finally taken charge of her own life.

Alec finished the cheese, shouldered the pack, and kept climbing until he reached a point in the increasingly impenetrable fog where every other direction was downhill. It felt like the summit, but he knew instinctively that it wasn't. There should have been a short concrete pillar at the summit—a surveyors' trig point—but it was nowhere to be seen. There should have been a low stone shelter as well, but he couldn't find it. The world around him was missing most of its usual dimensions; left, right, and up had vanished into a miasma of gray. There was only down; he could see his feet and a bit of the ground around them. That was all.

He pulled out his Ordnance Survey map, but without a good idea of where he was, the map was useless. He closed his eyes and put his internal compass to work. When he opened them again, he walked perhaps fifty yards and found a ladder stile that climbed up and over a barbed-wire livestock fence. Beyond it he found a caïrn. So far so good. He descended a few hundred yards, following a succession of cairns. Then he seemed to run out of markers. He went back to the last one he'd seen and began circling it in ever-widening rings, like the sweep of the band of green light on a radar screen searching out a blip that would be the next cairn.

Suddenly, his left boot slipped on a wet boulder and for a split second he was airborne. He landed hard on the rocks. The fall knocked the wind out of him. His ribs hurt. He lay still and took a deep breath. The pain didn't worsen with breathing. *Good,* he thought. *Bruised but not broken.* He rolled over . . . and found himself staring straight down into the yawning nothingness of the sheer thousand-foot drop to Llyn Cau he'd passed earlier. He scrabbled away from the edge and sat very still, waiting for the adrenaline to stop pumping in his ears. Suddenly, his bruised ribs seemed trivial. A few steps farther and he would have joined Gwynne in whatever it is that comes after life on this earthly plane. Moments later, he retrieved his walking stick and crawled back to the last cairn, stood, and retraced his steps to the ladder stile.

He was angry. In all his years of hiking, he'd never become disoriented, never been lost. He hurt and he was tired. He had a duty to perform, and he was failing at it. What's more, the weather had turned nasty; the mist had changed to a hard, cold rain and the wind was rising. Once again he closed his eyes to connect with his inner compass.

"Down," he heard a voice say.

His eyes flew open and he looked around.

"Hello?"

Nothing. Maybe it had been a crow's caw, distorted by the fog. Maybe not.

"I need to get off this mountain," Alec said aloud. He hunched on the pack with Gwynne's ashes, picked up his walking stick, and struck off in a new direction, determined to descend to wherever it led him.

five

e never did come across another cairn. Instead, Alec followed a faint, gradually descending track through the billowing cloud. He was like a boat cutting through dark water, the bow of him parting the deep, the deep re-forming itself again behind him. How different this climb was from the day he and Gwynne had been to the summit—a day of cobalt blue skies, warm wind, and isolated, slowly drifting puffball cumulus clouds. *And yet, maybe the gloom is only appropriate,* he thought. *Funereal.*

The last time Gwynne called was only two months after her final chemotherapy treatment.

"Hiya, toots, it's me. Any chance you might be able to make a visit? I've been in the hospital again," she said with a heartiness he knew from long experience was artificial. That's the thing about long-term relationships: you learn to hear what's meant, not just what's said.

Alec's heart lurched. "What's happened?"

"Oh, you know me; I like to do things the hard way. Seems like there's been complications. I think I could use a hand."

"I'll be there tomorrow night," Alec said. "Count on it."

Alec heard her voice break. "I was hoping that's what you'd say."

He dropped everything, flew east, and spent the next two months at his ex-wife's bedside. Although the doctors initially had been confident of her recovery, the cancer had spread to the fluid in Gwynne's brain. She only lived a block from the hospital; it was a short walk, and he and Gwynne walked there together, daily, for more chemotherapy.

Alec slept on a single bed in the guest room in her Boston condominium. He tried to cook for her, as he had years before, but the smell made her nauseous.

"It's the chemo," she explained. "It makes the smell of cooking disgusting."

Still, her spirit never flagged.

"Let's have takeout," she'd say brightly, and off he'd go to a Mexican place she loved. When he returned, she'd have a bite and then lose interest.

"A salad! I need a salad," she suggested another day. "That way you don't have to cook anything." But she ate almost none of it.

Next it was "Let's have sushi! No smell!" And of course he got it, but he ended up eating it all himself.

After a couple of weeks of this, on their way down the block to the hospital for another treatment, Gwynne stopped and said she felt dizzy. Then she collapsed to the pavement. Alec and a passerby lifted her and half-carried her to the emergency room. A nurse took her blood pressure, then took it again because she couldn't believe the result: it was only 70 over 20.

"Hell," Gwynne wisecracked, "I've known cantaloupes with higher blood pressure!" Then the orderly wheeled her upstairs to a private room. Surgeons installed a shunt directly into her skull and pumped neon green chemicals through it every other day. Alec sat with her from morning till night, went out for a quick supper, then returned and stayed with her until after midnight. They told each other favorite stories from their life together. No one told him to leave, which he took as a bad sign. And in fact it soon became clear that the new chemo was having no effect. Her chief oncologist, a young woman with a faintly German accent, was both caring and refreshingly candid: they could keep her on chemo, but it was unlikely to help. Gwynne's condition was terminal. Gwynne listened to this latest diagnosis calmly and Alec realized she'd already come to the same conclusion.

"Okay, Doc," she said, "here's my take on this: I think you should spring me from this joint and spend your time with somebody who's gonna make it. If I'm gonna die, I want to do it in my own bed. Besides, I've got work to do to get my house ready to be sold. You know what Oscar Wilde's dying words were?"

The doctor shook her head.

"Either this wallpaper goes, or I do."

Gwynne started laughing. Then Alec did, too. It was a story they loved. The doctor nodded quietly and left; Alec found her in the corridor, crying.

"I try to maintain a degree of emotional distance from my terminal patients," she said, "but I can't with Gwynne. She's beyond anything I've ever experienced before."

Alec arranged for a hospice nurse to visit every couple of days. Gwynne's decline was rapid. He was amazed that having eaten or drunk nothing for weeks, Gwynne still had bodily functions, but he cleaned her gently when she did and she accepted his help with grace. It was, he realized, perhaps the most intimate thing they had ever done together. He read funny books to her. He massaged moisturizer into the mottled, papery skin of her arms and legs. As her dehydration deepened, Gwynne's world filled with delusions and fear. Only semi-conscious but longing for the inevitable, she would suddenly sit bolt up-right in her bed, look at him, and plead, "What else do I have to do?" The hospice nurse increased the morphine dosage and Gwynne slipped peacefully into a coma. Alec bought an infant monitoring device so he could listen to her when he was in the kitchen. She breathed like some-one with sleep apnea: sharp intakes of breath, slow exhale, and then ag-onizingly long periods of silence. He spent hours at her beside, listening, telling her it was okay to let go. Finally, the hospice nurse took him aside and suggested that even though she was unconscious, Gwynne was willing herself to live so as not to disappoint him. It was common with the dying, she said; she saw it all the time. That evening, he sat in the kitchen listening to the ragged stutter of her breathing. The gaps between breaths lengthened. He went to her room, climbed up onto the bed, and held her in his arms, telling her, as he knew she al-ready knew, that he had never stopped loving her. Moments later, her breathing stopped. He closed her eyelids, kissed her forehead, and pulled the sheet over her body. Then he called the funeral home.

After perhaps an hour of picking his way downhill, Alec finally dropped below the level of the cloud wreathing the mountain's sum-mit. In the distance, sunlight shimmered on the lower pastures and cloud shadows raced across the hills. Able to see landscape features once again, he checked the map and discovered that he had walked far to the west of where he wanted to be. He followed a shoulder of the mountain downhill and reached a high saddle that ran south to north. There he picked up an old farm track and followed it around to the north, threading his way through high moorland thick with sedges and spongy wet ground. Here and there, he came upon the ruins of old farmsteads. Alec marveled at the artistry with which their thick stone walls had been built, intact and sturdy still, long after their roofs had collapsed. He marveled, too, at the optimism—or the desperation—of anyone who would go to such trouble to scrabble sustenance from such a harsh landscape.

He continued north, gradually curving around the flanks of the great mountain until he reached the edge of the boggy plateau. Off to his left, the sun was sinking toward the Irish Sea, and directly ahead he recognized the gentle features of the valley in which Tan y Gadair sat. He was still descending when he came upon a pasture filled with sheep and saw a young man struggling to control one of them.

Alec slipped through the gate and shouted, "Need a hand?"

The young man looked up sharply; he'd been so intent on helping the birthing ewe he hadn't seen Alec coming down off the mountain.

"Know anything about lambing?"

"Not a thing," Alec said as he reached the fellow. The ewe was on its knees, its neck arched backward, obviously straining. The young man was leaning against her side, pressing her gently against a stone wall to keep her still. He looked to be in his midtwenties and was of medium height, broad-shouldered and powerfully built. He had tightly curled short hair, nearly black, and his eyes were green with sparkles of amber, as if they'd been sprinkled with gold dust. On the ground was a plastic carryall loaded with tools and bottles.

He smiled. "Reckon you're about to learn. She dropped her water bag more than an hour ago and she's fully dilated. Nothing's happened, though. My guess is, she's breached.

"Usually, by this time," he continued, "the front hooves will have appeared and, after the ewe pushes for a bit, the head will appear and then the rest of the lamb will slip out. That's not happened. D'you suppose you could hold the ewe steady while I reach in and try to turn the lamb around in the uterus? Straddle her and hold her with your knees."

"Um, okay," Alec said, taking his position.

The young man disinfected and lubricated his right forearm, kneeled by the ewe, and looked at Alec.

"Ready?"

"As I'll ever be."

Alec watched as the fellow tucked his thumb and pinkie finger inward, streamlining his hand, and then gently inserted his hand, and then his arm, into the ewe's birth canal. His eyes were focused far off across the fields and Alec realized the shepherd was "seeing" with his hands. The ewe had stopped thrashing—whether from gratitude or exhaustion, Alec couldn't tell.

"There's the answer," the young man said, removing his hand and sitting up.

"What is?"

"Twins. Ewes are bred for multiple births nowadays. Good for the farmer but a bit hard on the sheep, I think. Especially young ewes like this one. These lambs are both facing to the rear, which is good. But they're jammed up behind her pelvic bone. Not good. I'll need to pull one out, and then we'll see if she delivers the second on her own."

He reached into his carryall and pulled out a short rope with loops at each end. He slipped the tip of one loop over the last knuckle of his forefinger and held the rest of the loop in his palm. Then he inserted his hand into the ewe's birth canal again.

"I'm slipping this loop over the back of the first lamb's head. Its legs are facing forward so we shouldn't have much trouble. Now here's where you come in," he said to Alec. "I need you to lift the ewe's hindquarters upward a couple of feet."

Alec did so, and groaned.

"You okay?"

"No problem," Alec lied, his bruised ribs complaining. "Why am I doing this?"

"It'll make the other lamb slide back down into the uterus. Right then, here we go," he said. After a few moments of fishing, his hands held the lamb's forelegs and the rope secured its head. Steadily, but very gently, he pulled. The ewe did not struggle. After what Alec guessed was about three minutes, two tiny hooves appeared, followed by a wet head. The young man stopped, pulled a cloth from the carryall, and wiped mucus away from the newborn's nose. Then he gradually pulled the gasping lamb into the world. The creature was inexpressibly small and vulnerable-looking, its eyes squeezed tight against the light. Instinctively, it struggled to stand.

"Okay, let the ewe down," he said to Alec. With exquisite gentleness, he treated the newborn's navel with what looked to Alec like iodine, and then placed the lamb beside the ewe's head.

Finally, he sat back on his haunches and smiled. Steam rose from the warm lamb in the cooling air. The ewe made soft bleating sounds and licked the blood off its newborn.

"We'll wait a few minutes, now," he said, "and see if she can deliver the next one on her own. Depends upon what position it's in and how tired she is."

Alec sat next to him, leaning against the wall, and looked at all the wobbly wet lambs around him. "How long have you been doing this?"

"Long as I can remember; since I was ten, I reckon, on my da's farm."

"I meant today."

"Oh." He laughed. "Since about three thirty this morning."

"My God, you must be exhausted."

"Comes with the job this time of year. We're about half through. First peak of lambing was a bit more than a week ago; this is the second one. Most ewes lamb early in the morning; some, like this one, late afternoon. No way of telling."

"You're Owen, aren't you?"

"That I am; how'd you know? You're from away."

"I'm staying at the farm; Fiona mentioned you were helping David. I'm Alec."

"Glad you happened along, Alec. Haven't seen much of David today. You've been out walking then?"

"Yeah, up on Cadair."

Owen looked up at the mountain, invisible in its cloak of cloud. "Not much of a day for it."

"So I discovered."

"A bit thick, was it?"

"Thick as milk and just as wet. I got lost."

"Ah," Owen said, nodding, "that would be Brenin Llwyd, out to bewitch you."

"Who?"

"Brenin Llwyd, 'the Lord of the Mists,' also called 'the Grey King' for obvious reasons. People hereabouts believe he rises from the mountain to claim the unwary."

Alec lifted an eyebrow.

"Yes, well, that's what they say, anyways. Me, I don't know. Not very superstitious, I suppose. But as you've seen, even when it's nice here, that mountain can breed its own weather, wrap itself in cloud. Nasty it can get up there, all of a sudden like."

Alec thought about his disorientation in the clouds, and about his mounting fear. He thought about the voice—in his head, he was sure—telling him to descend. He thought, too, about the Grey King and how, with age, he had begun to accept that much of the experience of being seems to exist just beyond the reach of the rational. Maybe that's what had been so unsettling; he'd been beyond the realm of the rational, beyond his safe zone.

Owen rose. "She's too exhausted to deliver; we'll have to help her with the other one, too."

Alec snapped into the present.

"What do we do this time?" Alec asked.

"Same as before, only easier this time. Want to give it a try yourself?"

Alec looked at him and thought about the ashes in his pack and the new life all around him.

"Yes," he said finally. "Yes, I think I do."

Owen nodded toward the disinfectant and Alec cleaned his hands and arms. He kneeled by the ewe, then hesitated.

"Go on then," Owen said.

He made a pyramid his fingers, just as Owen had, and slipped his hand into the ewe, amazed at the smoothness and breadth of the passage. He felt around it carefully, finally finding the second lamb's head.

"Got it."

"Good. Now follow down the neck to the forelegs and be sure they're facing to the rear like the head."

"Okay, yeah, that's where they are."

"Right, then. Put your thumb alongside the lamb's right cheekbone, your little finger by the left and the middle three fingers along the top of the neck, behind the ears. Then begin pulling, gently."

"Don't I need the rope?"

"Only if the legs don't come first."

Alec released the head momentarily and checked the legs.

"One's in front, the other seems to be tucking under."

"Use the rope. Slip it over the head like I did, straighten the tucked leg, then pull both legs and the rope."

"Won't the noose strangle the lamb?"

"There's a stop-knot in it; it can't close down tight. It's more like a snare."

"I can't tell if the lamb's alive," Alec said.

"Soon find out."

One last tug and out the lamb came: smaller than the first, Alec thought. Owen passed Alec the cloth and he wiped the lamb's nose. But the lamb wasn't breathing. Owen rose, leaned over the stone wall, and yanked a frond from a clump of bracken fern on the other side, stripping off the leaves. Then, gently, he pushed the tip of the frond into the newborn's nose. The lamb twitched, then sneezed mightily, and its tiny chest heaved in great gulps of air. In moments, it was struggling to its feet, like its sibling.

Alec doused the second lamb's navel with iodine and placed it beside the ewe.

"Make a good shepherd, you would," the young man said, smiling.

Alec stood up, wincing from the pain in his ribs. "Too old for it, I suspect."

Owen laughed and eased the lambs down to the ewe's udder, placing a teat near each little mouth and encouraging them to suckle.

"Besides disease," he said, "the way we lose them is exposure. They need to get as much colostrum from the ewe's milk as they can in the first few hours. It's thick as cream and loaded with antibodies. The high fat content gives them the energy they need to stay warm and dry out. Without the colostrum they'll die within twenty-four hours. Sometimes, if the ewe won't nurse, we milk her and pump it into the lamb through a tube."

Alec watched, mesmerized, at the interplay of instincts as the ewe and its lambs bonded—the nursing, the licking, the learning of one another's scent.

Alec looked at the exhausted ewe. "What about the placenta?"

"She'll expel it in an hour or so. Most ewes will eat it immediately. It's instinctive. There are hormones in it that will help the uterus shrink back to normal size. And if they don't, we collect them and bury them to keep away the predators."

"Predators?"

"Foxes. Plenty of them. They can smell the placenta and come after the newborns. They like lamb as much as we do."

Alec nodded. "What now?"

"Nothing. We're done here for the time being. Probably be a few more ewes to lamb in the other lower pasture later on, but for now I need a bite to eat."

"That makes two of us."

They cleaned up in a water bucket. The sun had nearly set and the sky over the Irish Sea looked aflame.

"Red sky in the morning, shepherds take warning," Owen said, "red sky at night, shepherds' delight." Then he turned to Alec, laughing. "Of course, around here you never know!"

Alec gathered the equipment while Owen made a final check of the lambs and ewes. Then the two of them strode downhill through the rich spring grass.

six

With only one of her three guest rooms occupied, Fiona had spent the day catching up on baking. It was a point of pride that she baked her own pastries for her guests' afternoon tea—currant scones, saffron buns with sultanas, lardy bread, and Welsh cakes, a kind of minipancake fragrant with allspice and studded with currants that she learned to make when she moved to Wales.

But though mixing the ingredients was almost second nature to her by now, she was struggling to concentrate. Her mind kept drifting off to the American. Ever since he'd arrived she'd felt as if the ground beneath her was shifting. The certainties of her life, the patterns and routines that had given it dimension and definition, had subtly altered. There was a thrumming, a kind of background harmonic, that hadn't been there before. It was in the air around her. She could sense it the same way animals could sense earthquakes before they happen.

When Alec had tea in her kitchen last night, when she'd seen him in the guests' sitting room this morning, he seemed as appropriate to those places as the furniture itself. Except, she admitted to herself guiltily, furniture isn't exciting. There was no denying it: he excited her.

He wasn't like other Americans she'd met: loud, demanding, and overfamiliar, telling you their entire life stories over breakfast. No, Alec was more reserved. Careful. She didn't think he was hiding anything; he was simply controlled. What, she wondered, needed controlling? Not others, certainly; he seemed very easygoing. Something in himself? Was it anger? No, there was only gentleness in those brilliant blue eyes. His smile, though shy, was genuinely warm and held a hint of mischief, also restrained. At the same time, he had an odd way of being very much with you one moment and gone the next. She'd noticed that last night when she asked how he'd come to be here. Something he'd promised to do on Cadair, he'd said. And then it was as if he'd vanished; his body was right there in his chair, but his essence was elsewhere. It was like a lightbulb turning off: the bulb was still there but the illumination was gone. You noticed instantly, because the light had been so intense. Yes, maybe that was what he was controlling, that intensity. If he were an artist rather than a writer, she could see him painting great swirling landscapes, like Turner's, light and dark and color wheeling around a still center. That's it, she decided; that's what he's bundling up—it's the same imaginative flame that led him to suggest the preposterous "tent-and-breakfast." She chuckled again at the memory of him standing in her doorway with his proposal. Anyone else would have accepted that she had no vacancies and moved on. But the intensity, the certainty had brought him back, and now, as then, she was happy it had. But why did he keep himself so bundled up?

She realized she hadn't a clue how old he was. He could be her age. Probably not younger, but possibly older, maybe much older—it was impossible to tell. If older, though, he neither looked nor acted like it.

And as to the way he looked, well, that was easy: lithe, taut, handsome, powerful in a contained sort of way. There was something about him that made her feel like a sea being pulled by the gravity of the moon; it was tidal. She took a baking sheet full of golden scones from the oven and began stacking them on a cooling rack by the sink. She saw her reflection in the window above the sink and wondered whether she truly recognized it.

Sometime around three o'clock, Fiona went out to her garden to cut fresh flowers for the house. It was something she always did for her guests, but she was aware of taking special care this time. The garden basked in the afternoon sun and smelled fertile and earthy, as if it were breathing. Small bouquet in hand, she turned back toward the house, glanced up at the mountain, and stopped in her tracks. The top five hundred feet were encased in cloud so dark it was nearly charcoal. Worry rose like a bird in her throat, but she willed it down again: at this hour Alec would already be descending. He'd be on the lower slopes, well beneath the cloud. Nearly home.

Home. Why not just "back"? Why did she think of him, this near stranger, as belonging here? Home to the farm? Home to her?

By five, she'd finished the baking and he still hadn't returned. She knew how long it took to climb Cadair Idris: up and down in four hours; five, tops. And he was no amateur. It had already been six hours. Where was he? She drifted around the house aimlessly for a while and finally did what many people do in a crisis: she cooked. Alec would be exhausted when he returned, she reasoned, and in no shape to go to town for supper. She'd make a meal for them both. She'd never done this for a guest before, but somehow it felt perfectly natural to do it for Alec. And it calmed her. She dusted two lamb shanks with flour, browned them in butter, laid them in an earthenware casserole, added stock, herbs, chopped leeks, and sliced carrots and parsnips, and put them in the oven to braise. It was the kind of thing that would only get better the longer it cooked.

At six thirty, after the BBC Radio Four news, she took David his dinner. On her way back, she saw Owen in the darkening farmyard walking toward his Land Rover.

"Owen! One of my guests has gone missing; have you seen anyone on the mountain?"

"I haven't, Mrs. Edwards, but if it's that Alec fellow you're looking for, I reckon he'll be in the house. Been helping me birth twin lambs, he has."

Fiona wanted to hug Owen. Instead, she blurted, "Do you mean to tell me it didn't occur to either one of you to come and tell me you were working together?!"

"No, ma'am, I guess it didn't. It was a tricky birth and he asked if he could help. I was glad to have him. We'd have lost the lambs and the ewe if he hadn't shown up."

She looked at him for a moment, shook her head in disbelief, then turned toward the house.

"Good with the animals, he is," Owen called after her.

Back in the kitchen she could hear the tub filling upstairs in Alec's room. She resolved to say nothing to him when he came down. What could she say? That she'd been terrified he'd been hurt? That she feared he might disappear from her life as abruptly as he'd appeared?

She was adding red wine to the roasting shanks a half hour later when he came down, knocked on the kitchen doorjamb, and stuck his head in.

"Hi," he said.

She straightened and faced him. She couldn't stop herself: "Three hours late and all you have to say for yourself is 'hi'?"

Alec stepped into the kitchen and blinked a couple of times. "Um . . ."

"Oh, don't mind me," she said, waving her hands dismissively. "It's just my nature to worry when my guests disappear into thin air."

"You were worried?"

"Worried?! I was about to call out the Mountain Rescue!"

"I'm sorry, Fiona; I got . . . delayed." He didn't want to tell her he'd been in trouble. It embarrassed him. And he wasn't used to having someone worry about him; that was his job, worrying about people. It was a little unnerving.

She was about to unload on him when she noticed he had his jacket on.

"And where do you think you're off to this time of night?"

"I thought I'd walk down to that pub we passed this morning, just along the road, and have dinner. The one by the lake."

"The Griffin? You must be daft! Good cask-conditioned ale, mind you, but the food's unspeakable. Can't even do a proper pickled egg."

Alec tried to comprehend a pickled egg, proper or otherwise.

"I've braised some lamb shanks for supper," she continued. "Unless lambing with Owen's put you off."

Alec laughed. "I'm so hungry after that climb I'd eat damn near anything. But no, Fiona, I won't impose upon you and David."

"No imposition at all; David's already eaten."

Once again, the invisible David.

"But I'm going to make you work for your supper. When these potatoes are just barely tender," she said, pointing to a pot bubbling on the cooker, "drain them, toss them in this flour, then put them in this roasting pan with some butter, and pop them in the oven. I'm off to take a bath myself. Think you can handle that?"

"Yes, ma'am; I think I can," Alec said, smiling.

"And don't let the shanks dry out, either; use this red wine," she said as she poured herself a glass.

Then she was gone. He wasn't used to being directed about but, as with telling him where to pitch his tent the night before, he found he felt perfectly happy having Fiona tell him what to do. It was somehow deeply comforting. He turned toward the cooker wearing an idiot's grin.

Fiona ran water in the claw-foot tub and stepped out of her clothes. She stood before the tiny window set deep into the bathroom's thick outer wall and looked absently across the darkening meadows toward the mountain, sipping her wine. Three hours late, then there he was, calm as could be. She added some bath oil and swirled it around with her hands. Then she slipped into the hot, silky water and closed her eyes. She lay there for some time, letting the heat seep into her bones. Had it really only been a day since he walked up the lane with that bloody great pack on his back? She smiled. He'd been sweaty and unshaven, but her heart had leaped just the same.

Did she believe in love at first sight? She didn't know. How could you know? Maybe it was like great art: you knew it when you saw it. All she knew was that she felt exhilarated when he was around, and slightly out of control, like when she drove too fast: scary, but thrilling.

It certainly hadn't been that way with David. She'd been a scrawny twenty-two-year-old at university in Liverpool when David appeared in her life, a friend of a friend. He was handsome in a rugged sort of way, quiet, and polite. No one else had shown much interest in her in those days. But David would drive his battered old Land Rover the sixty or so miles across Wales to England to visit her, then turn around and drive back the same night. One day he told her he loved her. No man had ever said that to her before. She decided she must be in love with him, too. Then one weekend he took her back to Dolgellau, to see Tan y Gadair. She had been awed by its raw beauty. That very weekend David asked her to marry him, and she accepted.

"And here we are," she said to herself aloud, sitting up in the tub and reaching for the wine. She drained the glass and felt the alcohol warming her belly. Or perhaps it was the thought that Alec had been in this tub just last night that made her warm. Soaping herself, she imagined that the soap was Alec's hands slipping smoothly across her skin and breasts. She wondered what sort of lover he was. Attentive, she guessed. Did he ever let that reserve down? It occurred to her that she should be shocked at having such thoughts, but she persuaded herself that it was only curiosity. Harmless really.

She rose and toweled herself down, enjoying the slight roughness of the linen-cotton blend towel that was her favorite. It made her skin feel alive. She padded into the bedroom and stood for a moment before the long oval standing mirror near the window.

"Not so scrawny anymore, are we, Fiona?" she said to her reflection. She'd put on some weight over the years. Not a great deal—what with running the bed-and-breakfast and helping out on the farm, she got plenty of exercise—but it was still more than she liked. On the other hand, despite nursing Meaghan some twenty years ago, her breasts, broad and shapely if not especially full, were still firm and had so far resisted the pull of gravity. But her belly and hips had lost some definition. There was the faintest hint of dimpling on the back of her thighs, but for the most part her legs had kept their shape. She thought about the other farm wives in the valley and decided she was doing pretty well. And, much as she disliked it, she had to admit David's vegetarian diet was helping.

The problem now was what to wear. She opened the wardrobe in her bedroom and surveyed the contents with dismay: the clothes of a farmer's wife. She thought she should wear something nice . . . but not too nice. Not suggestive, either. She laughed—as if she owned such things! She took hangers out and rejected outfits one by one: too formal, too frumpy, wrong season.

In the end, she just pulled on her jeans and slipped on a black merino wool V-necked pullover with just enough angora to look

feminine, pushing the sleeves halfway up her forearms. Then she slid
her feet into simple black flats. She added black onyx stud earrings.
Back in the bathroom, she brushed out her hair so that it framed her
face and put on the slightest hint of pale pink lipstick. Her skin was too
fair for anything bolder. As she turned to leave she stopped and put a
tiny dab of Rain perfume behind each ear.

    Ready, she said to herself, hearing a little voice inside that asked,
For what?

Alec stood in the kitchen fascinated by the enormous stove that domi-
nated the room. Ever since he and Gwynne had divorced, cooking had
become a passion—sometimes, he thought, the only passion left to him.
The massive Aga—Fiona called it the "cooker"—was unlike anything
he'd ever seen before. It was a good five feet wide, made of what looked
like cast iron, and finished in shiny ivory enamel. There were four oven
doors in the stove's face and the top had a large iron warming surface
and two round cooking elements with heavy hinged stainless-steel covers, presumably to hold in the heat. The rest of the room was equally
impressive. The kitchen cabinets and counters looked handmade and
were painted ivory like the stove. The countertops were a mix of charcoal gray slate and oak butcher's block. The walls were painted the
color of Dijon mustard. The ceiling was open to the oak beams and
cross members supporting the slanting shed roof. They were stained a
dark brown and matched a large antique oak sideboard with shelves to
display decorative platters. Above the Aga, a cast-iron rack held a collection of well-used copper and stainless-steel pots and pans. It was the
kitchen of a serious cook. It was also toasty warm, and Alec realized the
heat was coming from the Aga, which seemed designed to act like a radiant heater for the entire room. He was bent over trying to figure out
the mechanics of the thing when he heard Fiona enter the kitchen.

He stood up and turned.

"Wow!" he blurted. It was involuntary, and utterly inappropriate. Then, remembering her own words the night before, he added quickly, "You certainly do clean up nicely!"

"That's my line. And 'wow,' though much appreciated, suggests that you, sir, have been walking alone through the countryside too long."

"Perhaps you're right."

"You needn't have agreed so quickly," she said, smiling. "Hungry?"

He paused as the ambiguity hung in the air between them, then said, "Famished. What can I do to help?"

"Set the table?"

"Sure. In the dining room or here in the kitchen?"

She looked around the room.

"Here, I think. It's my favorite place in the house."

While Alec set out silverware, Fiona pulled the lamb and vegetables and the roast potatoes from the ovens and turned them out onto platters. They had no sooner sat down when she popped back up again.

"This isn't right." She dashed out of the room and returned a few moments later with a candlestick in each hand, purloined from one of the guest rooms. Fishing a box of matches from a drawer, she lit the tapers and flicked off the overhead light.

"There, that's better."

The kitchen was suddenly transformed into an intimate dining room.

Alec caught a scent in the air.

"Is that the Rain?"

Fiona glanced at the kitchen window. "Yes, I guess it's started again."

"I was referring to the perfume."

"Oh! Yes, it is; I didn't think you'd notice," she lied.

They sat motionless for a moment, saying nothing, their eyes exchanging messages: amusement, affection, trust, nervousness, desire. Fiona smiled. Alec reached for his wineglass. They began to eat. The wine was velvety and dense with dark fruit. The lamb was perfect, pink and falling off the bone. The roast potatoes were golden and crusty on the outside and fluffy inside; the braised carrots and parsnips, earthy and sweet.

Alec made appreciative noises and said, "You should have a restaurant."

Fiona laughed. "Nonsense! Far too much work for a woman my age."

Alec looked at her, smiled, and shook his head. "'Your age'? Now *that's* nonsense."

He changed the subject. "You said you were English, not Welsh. Where from?"

She paused. It might have been an intrusive question from someone else, but Americans were like that: naively direct. And, anyway, with Alec she felt at ease.

She'd been born and raised in a village called Nantwich, in Cheshire, she said between bites, just southeast of the old Roman fortified town of Chester. Her mother's family was from there and her father, a sailor, decided it was as good a place as any to settle. Arthur Armstrong had joined the Royal Navy during the war, as an engineer, and had somehow survived despite being assigned to ships protecting the Atlantic shipping lanes, which crawled with German U-boats. After the war he'd signed on with one of the major freighter companies sailing out of Liverpool and had traveled the world.

"He stayed on with the shipping company even after he married Mum and I was born. He'd throw his duffel bag over his shoulder, get on the train at Nantwich Station, and head for the port. We wouldn't see him for months.

"I was pretty much raised by my mother—Dorothy Potter was her maiden name—and her family. My grandfather Potter was the rector at St. Mary's, an ancient Anglican church in the village with a remarkable vaulted stone roof rich with carvings."

She paused and looked away for a moment. "That's odd," she said more to herself than to him. "The church I go to here in Dolgellau—not often, I confess—is also called St. Mary's; I never thought about that before . . ."

But by the sixties, she continued, jobs in the cargo ship industry declined as freighters gave way to container ships twice as large but with half the crew. When her father finally found himself without a ship, he returned to Nantwich and got a job as a lockkeeper on the Llangollen Canal, which ran through the village and across the Welsh border all the way to the market town of Llangollen, some forty miles away.

"It was all rather magical for me. Daddy was home at last and we lived in this pretty little ivy-covered brick cottage beside the canal, next to a flight of locks at Grindley Brook. The cottage came with the job. My father handled the maintenance of the locks and helped barges though them, raising the water if they were going uphill and emptying the locks if they were going down.

"He was still messing about with boats, you see, and dealing with the machinery, so he was happy. Mum was, too. She and I planted elaborate flower gardens around the cottage and the locks and we often won awards for them from the Waterway Authority.

"My father married late," Fiona explained. "So did Mum, come to that, and they were both getting on in years—especially Dad. One day, after he'd filled the Grindley top lock to lift a barge and had heaved the lock door open, he just collapsed and fell in. We never did know whether he died from a heart attack or drowned. Like many sailors in those days, he couldn't swim. The bargeman dove for him immediately, but canal water is muddy and dark and Dad had sunk like a rock."

Alec interrupted, "I didn't mean to bring up something so painful . . . I . . ."

"No, it's all right. The funny thing was, Mum died within the year. There was nothing wrong with her so far as anyone could tell. It was as if she'd just decided to stop living. She and my father had been apart for so much of their marriage that when he finally came home and we moved into that lockkeeper's cottage, it was like a second honeymoon for them. Then he went away again, for good. I guess she couldn't tolerate the final loss."

Alec refilled their wineglasses.

"I was at school in Liverpool when Mum died," Fiona continued. "Studying interior design . . ."

"That explains how this house came to be so lovely."

She smiled at him. "David showed up at school one day, visiting a friend of mine. He was a sweet man, in his quiet way. He pursued me and we married. End of story."

There was a distant look in her eyes. "Maybe I was filling the gap my dad left, I don't know."

"I have a friend who claims men always marry women who are like their mother, at least the first time; maybe women marry versions of their father?"

"Perhaps," Fiona said, looking off across the kitchen as if to some distant country in her mind. Then she returned.

"Anyway, David and I worked hard together for a couple of years to improve the farm and the flock, and then Meaghan arrived. Bit of a surprise she was, too, but by that time David could run the farm on his own so I played mum for several years. It was when she started going to nursery school that I began offering bed-and-breakfast. It was partly for my own sanity; it's pretty remote out here and this way I had people to talk to and care for a good part of the year."

"And you had just the one child?"

Fiona sighed. "Much to my husband's regret, yes. And a girl at that." She paused again for a moment, considering whether to continue, then plunged ahead. "We'd planned on having more children, but a few years after Meaghan was born I got fibroids . . . know what they are?"

"Uterine tumors, benign."

"Clever you!"

"My little sister's a gynecologist. She got the brains in the family."

Fiona hesitated, tilting her head and smiling. *And you got the looks,* she thought to herself, *and more.*

"Anyway, in those days the treatment for fibroids was a hysterectomy, so that was the end of childbearing. Sometimes I think David believes I got them on purpose, to thwart his dream of having a son to pass the farm on to. The fact that most sons these days are like his brother, Thomas, and want nothing to do with the family farm is something he chooses to ignore."

"How do you feel about all that now?"

"You mean about not having more children?"

Alec nodded.

"If I'm honest, I have to say I don't think I'm the most maternal woman on earth. Having Meaghan was magical, but it was also hard work, especially once the B and B got going. She's become a wonderful young woman and I'm very proud of her. David is, too, come to that. Maybe one was enough."

Or maybe, Alec thought, *you shifted your caregiving to your guests.*

They had finished eating. Alec stood and began gathering the dishes.

"No! I won't have it!" she scolded. "I'll take care of that later. How about if I whip up a sweet?"

"I couldn't possibly eat another thing," Alec replied. The truth was, between the climb, the lambing, and the wine he was weary. "Besides, I think it's bedtime for me," he said.

Fiona planted her hands on her hips and managed to fuse a scowl with a smile.

"A fine dinner guest you turned out to be!"

Alec walked over to where she was standing, took her hand in both of his, as he'd done the day before, and said softly, "There's nothing I'd like better than to sit up all night and talk with you, Fi, but I'm beat and I need to give the mountain another try tomorrow. I didn't finish what I set out to do."

"Which was?"

"That's a long story . . . for another day."

Fiona could almost hear the door to his heart slam shut.

He inclined his head toward her slightly. "Thank you so much for dinner. I'm not used to being taken care of like this."

"Time you were, I should think," she murmured.

"Yes. Perhaps it is," he said, his eyes far away again. Then he left the kitchen.

She had wanted more from him, much more. She'd almost taken it, almost pulled him toward her, almost wrapped her arms around him. It was more than just wanting to comfort whatever it was in him that hurt. There was a yearning in her belly. It was as if a cave had opened within her, an ever-widening chasm of longing.

Alec felt it, too. He lay in bed thinking as much about the easy companionship of his evening with Fiona as about the desire that was growing within him. It had been years since he felt this way.

april 12, 1999

seven

Somewhere a phone was ringing. Then Alec heard a voice, muffled; a woman's voice. He opened his eyes and got his bearings. Daylight, but not much of it. Beyond the French doors in his room, Cadair Idris was cloaked in cloud and rain clattered on the roof as if the gods were slinging gravel. He turned toward the clock on the bedside table and winced. He'd stiffened overnight, especially his bruised ribs. That was the problem with getting older: you could do the same things as before, like climb a mountain, but the price you paid for it in pain got higher with each passing year.

It was after eight o'clock. He pulled on the clothes he'd worn the night before, yawned, and headed for the stairs. No time to shower before breakfast. He didn't want to inconvenience Fiona by being late again.

There was a light on by the phone in the front hall, but the dining room was as dim as the day outside. He padded toward the brightly lit kitchen but found it empty. On the table was a pot of tea and two mugs, along with sugar and a small pitcher of milk. He poured himself a cup and then rummaged through the cupboards until he found a bowl. He went back to the dining room, where there were several clear-plastic storage containers with cereal selections, and filled the bowl with a chunky granola. He had just finished the cereal and poured himself a second cup of tea when the back door burst open and Fiona bounced into the room.

"Good morning, Mr. Hudson; it's a fine Welsh day!"

Water streamed off her jacket and pooled on the floor.

She tossed her wet jacket over a chair and glanced at the clock on the wall.

"Ah, just in time." She switched on a slender radio that was screwed into the underside of one of the cabinets. Alec hadn't noticed it before.

"The shipping forecast issued by the Met office, at 8:25 GMT, on behalf of the Maritime and Coast Guard Agency," the announcer intoned. *"There are warnings of gales in Rockall, Malin, Hebrides, Bailey, Faeroes, Fair Isle, and southeast Iceland.*

"The area forecasts for the next twenty-four hours: southeast Iceland, southwest 7 to gale 8, becoming cyclonic 6 to 7, rain, moderate to good. Fair Isle, Faeroes, southwest 6 to gale 8, occasionally severe gale 9, rain or show-ers, moderate. Hebrides, Bailey, Rockall, Malin, south 7 to severe 9, becom-ing cyclonic for a time, rain, heavy or moderate . . ."

Fiona switched off the radio.

"What's that all mean?" Alec asked, fascinated by the obscure language.

"It means you won't be climbing Cadair Idris today, for one thing," Fiona replied. *And you'll be here for at least another day,* her heart said.

"The numbers and descriptions are for wind speed, precipitation, and visibility," she explained. "The names are those given to different quadrants of the sea off our coast. Because my father was in the merchant marine, I got used to listening to the marine forecast. Around here, it's the best way to know what's funneling into the Irish Sea from the Atlantic."

Alec watched the rain sheeting down beyond the kitchen window. "Pretty obvious from here."

Fiona looked at him: "Okay, Mr. Smarty-pants, what's the window tell you about tomorrow?"

"Um, nothing."

"Exactly. Whereas I know from that report that tomorrow may be nearly as bad: a big low-pressure area is shoving aside yesterday afternoon's high-pressure front."

"*May* be as bad?"

"Well, this is Wales," she confessed. "You can never be too sure."

"Aha."

"Aha what?! See if you get a nice cooked breakfast!"

"Actually, the cereal's all I need. Doesn't look like I'm going to get much exercise today, anyway."

"Then again," she said, "maybe you're like those Ramblers . . ."

"Ramblers?"

"A national association of walking enthusiasts. They do very good work keeping public footpaths open and so forth. The footpaths, after all, were there long before any of us were—long before there were even roads, in some cases. But I don't know; the Ramblers who've come here seem all to be of a type."

"What type is that?"

"Oh, you know: hearty, earnest; so very intent on completing whatever walk they've chosen, rain or shine. A day like this wouldn't faze them; they'd just plod off though the downpour with their sturdy boots and their dun-colored anoraks and their clear plastic rainproof map holders hung around their necks. Where's the joy in that? Bunch of masochists is what I sometimes think. Plus, they're missing the point."

"And the point would be . . . ?"

"It's not about the peak, it's about the *place*," Fiona said with a passion that surprised him. "It's about the magic of this particular spot, this particular mountain, about how different it is from any other, about its antiquity, its drama—its danger, even. Sometimes they remind me of the bird-watchers you see down at the Mawddach estuary, ticking off bird sightings on a list, as if that were the sole reason for being there. I think some of them come just to tick Cadair Idris off their list."

Alec smiled. "That was quite a rant."

Fiona laughed. "Yes, I suppose it was. Anyway, we've got two of them coming tonight—Ramblers, that is. A couple from Cardiff, the Llewellyns. Also another couple, from Birmingham, so we'll have a full house tonight. Not bad for a Monday. Any tea left in that pot or have you hogged it?"

"There's plenty. Thanks for leaving it."

Fiona sat at the table opposite him and marveled at what was happening to her. Somehow this oddly withdrawn man, this very private gentleman who sometimes seemed like he was peeking out of a foxhole to see if it was safe to emerge, had released a playfulness in her she'd long forgotten. When she'd met and married David, she had folded herself into her husband's quiet. But before David, she'd always been the quick-witted one in her group of friends, full of sharp quips and easy laughter. It was one of her girlfriends at school who pointed out that being smart and snappy with clever remarks only scared off the boys. Now, though, it was as if all that bottled-up antic energy had been released. Was she imagining it or was the very self-contained Alec also uncurling?

"Look," she said after a few moments, "I have to go into town in a bit to do some marketing before the other guests arrive. You're welcome to stay here and write or whatever, or you could come into town if you wish." She glanced at the window and the rain. "Lovely day for sightseeing."

"I'll come. I have some things I need to do in town, too. When will you leave?"

"I need to do some tidying for the new guests; an hour?"

"Sure."

"Right. I'll give you a shout."

Alec went to his room, got his notebook, and went downstairs again to the guests' sitting room. Most of the poems Alec had written over the years were reflective, a way of coming to terms with things that had happened long ago. It was as if there was a lag between events and his emotional response to them. But here, in the shadow of the hulking mountain, that seemed to be changing. Words tumbled from him like water in a swollen stream.

He was deep into "the tunnel"—the quiet place within himself that he went to when he was writing—when he heard a car horn. It startled him. He looked at the window. Fiona was waving to him from her car. He dashed out through the kitchen, grabbed his jacket from its hook in the boot room, and jogged to the waiting car.

"Jeez, I'm sorry; I'm kind of in another world when I'm working."

"You were so still I was beginning to think I'd have to resuscitate you," Fiona teased.

"Maybe I shouldn't have moved so quickly," Alec shot back.

Fiona laughed and they were off.

Once they were on the main road Alec finally asked the question that had been plaguing him—but he did it indirectly.

"Is David very busy this time of year?"

Fiona turned to look at Alec, then returned her gaze to the road. She took a deep breath.

"David is not busy; David is ill."

For a moment, Alec was speechless.

Then he said, "Look, I didn't mean to pry. It's just that you talk about him so often but he's nowhere to be seen."

Fiona's shoulders relaxed and she kept her eyes on the road. "It's all right, Alec. It's just that I never talk about it.

"It's the sheep dip," she said.

"Sorry?"

"It's the sheep dip; it's poisoned him."

Alec hadn't a clue what she was talking about, and said so. To his surprise, Fiona started laughing.

"Of course you don't; how stupid of me! Right, then: 'sheep dip' is a pesticide. Sheep in Britain get infested with something called sheep scab mite. It's a skin disease, a mange, and it can race through a flock. It makes the sheep weak and sickly and their wool falls off in hunks. Back in 1976, the government obliged all sheep farmers to bring their sheep down from the hills every September and run them through a deep trough filled with water and chemicals—organophosphates, they're called. There are lots of different brands, but farmers just call it sheep dip. The main ingredient is something called diazinon. Undiluted, it is very nasty stuff, but in the troughs it's supposed to be safe. If you don't use sheep dip, the government fines are huge. Are you following me?"

"I'm with you."

"Right. So every fall, not long after sheep dipping, a lot of farmers get sick. They call it 'shepherds' flu'—headache, achy joints, upset stomach—that sort of thing. It goes away pretty quickly and no one's ever paid much attention to it. David got it all the time. I also noticed he seemed to tire easily, and the queer thing was that he became forgetful."

"Well, none of us is getting any younger."

"No, it wasn't that. I'd tell him something—or he'd tell me something—and then he'd have no memory of it, sometimes only an hour later. It was very strange. Then, three years ago, about a week after the sheep dipping, David had a heart attack. He was only forty-five. He'd never had any sign of heart disease. He wasn't overweight; he didn't smoke. The doctor was mystified. David and I just accepted it, even though we didn't understand it. Say what you will about the National Health, David's doctor didn't give up. He kept trying to make sense of the whole thing and, in the end, he started to find a pattern of symptoms among hill farmers. In some cases they got dizzy or listless. Some men had racing hearts. Some became temporarily paralyzed. It always happened between four days and a week after the dipping. Most people got better. Some didn't. David was one of those who got better, or so we thought."

They had arrived in Dolgellau and Fiona pulled into a parking space in the small central square. She turned off the engine but kept talking.

"The next year it happened again. Another heart attack. Six days after the dipping. He collapsed in the farmyard on his way to the kitchen for supper. I found him there, in the rain."

Fiona was staring ahead, as if watching a movie on the windscreen. Her hand still held the gearshift. Alec placed his atop hers. She didn't pull away.

"How awful for you, Fi. For you both."

She looked at their hands, then at Alec. "And that's just the beginning!" she said with an artificial brightness. "But there are errands to be run. I don't suppose you're interested in playing butler and following me around with a sack. What do you want to do?"

"I need to send a letter and get some money from the bank. Look, here's an idea: that cereal is going to wear off in a little bit. Is there a café or something where we can meet?"

Fiona thought for a moment and said, "I have a friend who has a tea shop just a few steps away. She's a terrific baker. Shall we meet there? Say an hour? It's called the Cozy."

"I'll be there," Alec said as he climbed out of the car, marveling at her change in mood.

He stood watching as she dashed beneath the arcaded front of one of the old stone buildings on the square. Then he crossed the square to a door over which hung a small, oval red sign that said, simply, POST. It was a sort of stationery and greeting card shop with a window at the back behind which a matronly woman presided over the Postal Service part of the business. Alec browsed a rack and picked out a picture post-card of the town with the mountain at its back. Then he stood aside to compose a note to Gwynne's older sister, Jane, who had taken to calling herself "Spirit" for reasons that escaped him. "Dear Jane," he wrote, feeling just a bit perverse, "I've made it to the mountain. Weather per-mitting, will take Gwynne's ashes up to the summit tomorrow. All's well here; hope you are, too." He paid for the card and the stamp and left it with the postmistress. Then he walked across the square to the Lloyd's Bank and cashed a traveler's check so he could pay Fiona for his room. At the teller's window a small sign displayed the date and he blinked in surprise; somehow, it had become April 12, his birthday.

He'd lost track of the passing days as he walked across Britain to this little town in northwest Wales. That was the beauty of walking with no fixed itinerary and no deadline for being somewhere: every day was fresh and new, every moment was the present. Alec had never un-derstood it when self-help books talked about the importance of "living in the present." For him, the present had always seemed the merest fraction of a second between grief about the past and anxiety about the future. It probably started in childhood, he guessed; the present was often a frightening place in his family, financially precarious and per-petually at risk of exploding from his father's volcanic anger. Even as a boy, Alec was constantly testing the emotional atmosphere in his turbu-lent family, anticipating what might happen next, and preparing for it. When he joined the Boy Scouts at thirteen, mostly so he could get out of the city and into the mountains on camping trips, he'd laughed to himself when he heard the Scout motto: "Be prepared." No problem there, he thought.

He'd been standing under an awning outside the bank, staring at the rain pounding the cobbles in the middle of the square, when he realized it was time to find the café. He asked directions from an elderly man in a flat tweed cap and a waxed, olive-green Barbour jacket who had sauntered across the square to the bank as if the teeming rain were just a minor inconvenience.

"You're from away, then, are you?" the man said when he heard Alec's accent. It was less a question than an accusation. "One of them tourists with their big cars clogging the streets."

"I am from away, but I walked here," Alec replied.

"A walker, then! Ah well, that's different. Come to climb old Cadair, have you?"

"I have indeed," Alec answered, warming to the man.

"Well," the old fellow said, squinting at the leaden sky, "fine day for it!"

Alec couldn't tell whether the fellow was pulling his leg or dead serious. He suspected the latter. He was a tough old bird.

Alec arrived at the Cozy just as Fiona was taking her seat. It was a charming, chintz-trimmed shop, steamy and warm and fragrant with baked goods. He joined her and was telling her about the old man when the plump proprietress arrived to take their order.

"Well, Fiona Edwards," she said brightly. "We haven't seen you in ages!"

"I know, Brandith; it's just I'm so busy."

Brandith stood and waited.

"Oh!" Fiona said at last. "Where are my manners? Brandith, this is one of my guests, Alec Hudson. Alec, Brandith Evans."

Alec stood. "Good afternoon, Mrs. Evans; a pleasure to meet you. Lovely shop."

"That'll be *Miss* Evans, thank you very much," the woman said, extending her hand and blushing, "but Brandith will do just fine. From America then, are you?"

"I am indeed," he said, releasing her hand after a moment and sitting again. "Now what do you suggest for a foul afternoon like this . . . Brandith?"

"Well, you can choose what you like from the tea cakes on the trolley just there," she said, pointing to a heavily laden pastry table on wheels by the wall, "but I've just pulled some currant scones from the oven and I have some lovely clotted cream I'm sure you'd like."

"Sounds great," Alec said, flashing her a broad smile. "And a coffee for me, please."

Fiona watched this exchange and smiled; Brandith was clearly charmed.

"And what about you, Fiona," the woman said. "The same?"

"Oh no, Brandith; just tea for me, thanks; Earl Grey, I think."

"Fiona Edwards," the owner scolded, "look at you! You eat like a bird!"

Then she softened and inclined her head toward Fiona, lowering her voice, "How's our David then, Fi?"

"About the same, I'm afraid."

"Still holed up in that hay barn, is he?"

"Yes."

Brandith sighed. "Terrible thing, that is. Terrible." She gave Fiona's shoulder a sisterly pat. "I'll just get that tea then."

Alec looked at Fiona. "Hay barn?"

"I thought you only drank tea," Fiona said.

"Sometimes I break my own rules."

"Do you indeed?" she teased.

"You're evading the question."

Fiona nodded. "In addition to weakening his heart, the poisoning's made him sensitive to practically every chemical in the environment—

anything with a fragrance, many things without, many foods, especially meat; the list is very long." She sighed.

"Anyway, living in the house became impossible for him, even though I switched to perfume-free cleaning products and changed our diet. Plus, there are the fragrances that come in with our guests. He was sick all the time."

Alec thought about the unopened bottle of Amarige in Fiona's bathroom. Of course. And now the absence of any of David's things made sense.

"But a hay barn?"

Fiona smiled. "It's probably the most expensive former hay barn in Britain. It's a stone building away off in a corner of the farm, near the mountain. Used to store hay when David's father had a cow. We had it completely renovated. Used nothing but chemical-free materials— untreated wood floors, milk-based paint, unbleached cotton fabrics. Sitting room with fire, bedroom, bath, and a small kitchen done entirely in stainless steel that I can just wipe down with simple soap and hot water."

"Does he never come out?"

"Oh, he can still do work on the farm; being outside is good for him. He can't go into the working barns, but he's out most days fixing fences and walls, moving sheep from one pasture to another, looking after pregnant ewes, culling lambs, and so forth. Even though it's lambing season now he can only work a few hours a day; he's weak and tires easily. The doctor says it's partly because his heart isn't sending enough blood through his body. The rest is just the long-term effects of the poisoning. Owen does most of the farmwork these days and, of course, the annual dipping. Doesn't seem to bother him. At least not yet."

"My God, I think I'd go mad if I were David."

"I think he is," Fiona said, shaking her head. "But it's not just being cooped up that's making him crazy. The poison's affected his nervous system. He isn't just forgetful, he has trouble thinking, sorting what needs doing and getting it done. It's as if there are fissures in his brain he can't bridge.

"He never was much of a reader, but now he just sits and watches the telly. He's depressed and angry. He was always a quiet man, but he's pulled deep inside himself. And he drinks too much; he makes Owen bring him whisky. He can become violent."

She looked up, her face bleak, her eyes not quite focused on him. "I hardly recognize David anymore; he's become someone else."

Alec didn't know what to say, but his heart hurt for her. A few moments later, Brandith arrived with the tea and coffee and scones, setting before him a pot of strawberry jam and a small bowl of thick yellow clotted cream.

"Sure you won't have anything to eat, Fi?" she asked.

Fiona rallied. "No thanks, luv; I'm not hungry. The tea will do me fine."

"Right then; if you need anything, just give us a shout."

Fiona was staring at the fogged-over shop windows as if she could see beyond them, far into the past.

He had a fleeting sense that perhaps a distance had opened between Fiona and her husband long before his illness. He'd expected sadness, even anguish, but instead Fiona seemed resigned, exhausted. He looked at the scone and jam and thick cream and found he'd lost his appetite.

"It's been very hard on Meaghan, of course; they're very close," Fiona continued. "Fathers and daughters often are. It would have been hard enough for her to leave for university even under normal circumstances, but now . . ."

He reached over and poured her another cup of tea from her pot. She looked up sharply, as if suddenly awakened.

"Listen to me rattle on! Let's change the subject, shall we? Last night you said you didn't finish something you set out to do on the mountain. Would you like to tell me what it is, or am I being rude?"

Alec looked at the woman across the table. He had planned to carry out his task quietly, privately. Now he realized he wanted to share it with someone he'd known for only two days. It was something about the softness in her eyes; he thought she might understand. It was something, too, about the way she had opened to him, telling him about David. It also occurred to him—and this came as a surprise—that he might need her support to do what he needed to do.

"You said it was a long story," she added. "I promise not to fall asleep."

And so Alec told Fiona about his life with Gwynne, about being with her through the last months of her life, about her final request, about how it had taken him a full year to bring himself to fulfill it, and about why he'd decided he had to walk to the mountain.

Fiona said nothing as he spoke. She understood now the sadness that clung to him. She wondered whether that was part of what drew her to him so powerfully. Fiona understood tragedy; it was something they had in common. Yes, it helped to explain the bond she felt with the handsome American, but it did nothing to explain the excitement she felt when she was with him. She decided that part didn't need an explanation.

When he finished they were both quiet for a few moments.

"You must have loved her very much," she said.

"Yes, I did. I guess I always did."

"And you love her still."

"No, I don't think that's true. I think what's true is that I miss her being here, on this earth—living, breathing, creating, making her magic. I miss that terribly. Is that love? A form of it, I suppose, but not the whole package. We always joked about how we were better as friends than as husband and wife. I think that's it: I've lost my best friend."

Alec looked down at his plate. Sometime during his story, the scone had vanished.

"Now that you've finished off my scone and clotted cream," he said, "shall we head home so I can have something to eat, too?"

"I just didn't want to let it go to waste," Fiona said.

"Right."

eight

They were dashing through the rain toward the car when Alec steered Fiona under the shelter of the awning over the window of the butcher's shop.

"I have something momentous to announce," Alec said.

"Do you, then!" Fiona lifted an eyebrow.

"I discovered something at the bank."

"You're overdrawn and going to skip town before paying me?"

He pretended not to hear. "I learned that today is the twelfth of April. I'll bet you can't guess the significance of that date."

Fiona looked at him, baffled. "Nelson's victory at Trafalgar?"

"Nearly as significant, but wrong."

"What then?"

"I was born on this day!"

"You're serious? This really is your birthday?"

"Afraid it is," Alec confessed. "Born exactly half a century ago."

"You're joking; you couldn't possibly be fifty."

Alec puffed himself up. "Why, thank you for that compliment, madam."

"You don't look a day over sixty," she added.

"How very kind of you to say so. Look here, I have a modest pro-posal. As we're standing here in front of 'John Lewis and Sons: Family Butchers'—how do they get away with that, by the way?"

"Get away with what?"

"Butchering families! Anyway, as we're standing here in front of the butcher's, I have an idea: how about I cook dinner for you tonight?"

"You're joking. You cook?"

"Does the pope pray?"

"Haven't a clue; I'm Anglican. I think we killed off all the papists back in Elizabeth the First's time. But if it's your birthday, shouldn't I be cooking something for you?"

"You did that last night. Tonight you're very generously going to give me the chance to cook on that hulking great beast of a stove in your kitchen."

"Cooker," Fiona corrected. She gave him that cocked-head look. "First the tent in my garden, now taking over my kitchen. Okay, you're on."

Alec was already tugging her into the shop. The balding man in the bloodstained apron behind the counter looked up from trimming the membrane from a long pork tenderloin.

"Good afternoon to you, Fiona," the butcher said, peering over his half-glasses. "Though what's good about it I don't know. Rain's relentless."

"I know, John," Fiona replied, "and the temperature is dropping. I'm a bit worried about the lambing if it gets much colder."

"Don't you go worrying your pretty head about that, Fi," he said, his meaty hands splayed on the white marble counter. "Those sheep of David's are tough stock. Now, what can I get for you today?"

She looked over to Alec, who had been prowling the premises as if on a hunt.

"Up to him, actually. Alec, meet John; John, Alec. Guest of mine who claims he can cook."

Alec smiled at the dig. "I wonder if I might have half of that tenderloin you're working on?"

"Good choice. Local pork, that is, from just up the valley."

He set to work trimming.

"How's young Owen working out, then?" the butcher asked without looking up.

"Splendidly, John; he's a good boy and a hard worker. Smart, too."

"Told you he was, didn't I?"

Owen, it turned out, was his nephew and John had recommended him when David had gotten too ill to manage the farm on his own.

"And David? How's he faring?"

"Same, John, just the same . . ." Fiona replied, her voice trailing off.

"Bloody shame, that is, pardon my language. He's not the David I knew at school, poor devil."

"No, John, he's not," Fiona agreed. Alec watched the cloud cross Fiona's face.

"Right then," John said, turning to Alec, "anything else for you, sir?"

"No thanks, that'll do it."

"Two pounds seventy pence, then, please," John said, handing him the parcel.

Alec paid and they were out the door. "Greengrocer?"

"Just opposite the car," Fiona said. "What do you need?"

"Garlic, lemon, maybe some spinach."

"I have some things wintering over in my garden: carrots, leeks, parsnips, chard, if that's any help."

"Do you have any cornmeal at the house?"

"Yes; I use it for baking."

"Excellent!" Alec said before plunging through the door of a shop called the Wine Rack.

Fiona followed him and watched as he quickly scanned the shelves, then strode to one corner of the shop and pulled down two long, thin bottles.

"Pinot Blanc, from Alsace, fragrant but dry."

He didn't ask her whether she liked the wine, but Fiona found she was delighted by this. It was wonderful being taken care of for a change, and he clearly knew what he was doing. David didn't care for wine. Felinfoel ale was his drink. That and, lately, the whisky.

Alec paid the girl at the counter. Fiona didn't know her and was relieved, then annoyed. Why should it matter? She wasn't doing anything wrong, for goodness' sake. Still, she liked the way Alec opened doors for her and ushered her through, the palm of his hand brushing against the small of her back ever so lightly. He was just being a gentleman, she knew, and she, in turn, was beginning to feel like a lady. She felt feminine; she couldn't remember the last time she'd felt that way.

"Look, Alec, you go ahead to the greengrocer's," she said as they stepped outside again. "I have one more errand to run. Won't be long."

"How will you find me?" Alec asked, watching the throngs crisscrossing the crowded market square.

Fiona looked at him towering over her and laughed. "Easy! I'll just look up!" And then she was off.

Alec crossed the square and ducked into the grocer's, marveling at the selection. When he'd first come to England, back in the sixties, he'd been surprised at how limited the vegetable and fruit choices had been. It was as if the British still lived in a state of wartime privation. But the Common Market, now the European Union, had changed all that. Alec took a clear plastic bag from a dispenser, picked out a firm head of garlic and a bunch of fresh spinach, then asked the elderly woman in the green apron if she had any lemons.

"Aren't you a lucky fellow," she said. "I've just had in a fresh shipment in from Spain. Lovely fat lemons. How many would you like?"

"Just one, thanks," he answered, fishing coins from his pocket.

When he reached the car, he saw Fiona coming out of a bookstore in the arcade. She reached the car, smiled, and unlocked the doors, and they were off again.

A couple of twists and turns and they were back on the Cadair Road, speeding west toward the farm.

"Whatever are you planning on making?"

"Top secret; but I don't think you'll be disappointed."

"Meat two nights in one week!" she said as she turned into the farm lane and they began to climb the hill. "I make these vegetarian things for David—fresh greens, beans, root vegetables, all organic and most of it from the vegetable garden at the back. It's all he seems to be able to tolerate, you see, and that's pretty much what I eat as well, especially now Meaghan's gone off to school. This is such a treat it's beginning to seem like my birthday, not yours!"

"The treat's all mine, Fi," Alec replied. "So when's your birthday?"

"Not till December. The eighteenth."

"Ah, now it all makes sense."

"What does?"

"Sagittarius. You know: troublesome, argumentative . . ."

Fiona shot out her left fist and punched him playfully in the shoulder. "And how about you, Mr. Aries the ram: stubborn, impulsive, headstrong? Refusing to take no for an answer, pitching a tent in my garden . . . shall I go on?"

Alec laughed. "Okay, okay; I plead guilty."

She parked the car in the barn and they dashed across the farmyard through the rain. Jack greeted them at the back door with manic barking and tail waving.

"Oh shush, you silly dog. All you want is food and it's too early," Fiona scolded. She glanced at the kitchen clock. "No, it's not after all; goodness, we've used up the entire afternoon! Mr. Hudson, you're turning me into a lady of leisure!"

Alec ignored her and began unpacking their parcels. A few moments later he heard a car pull into the forecourt.

"Rambler alert," he called out, but Fiona was already on her way to the front door. A few moments later, he could hear snatches of conversation—". . . awful weather . . . long drive . . . lovely house . . . tea?"—and then footsteps as Fiona led her guests upstairs to their room. A few minutes later she was back.

"And how are the Llewellyns?" Alec asked.

"Classics of the type, though a bit older than I'd expected. You'll love them."

Alec suspected she was being arch.

"They're worn out from the drive and are going to rest awhile before going into town for dinner," she said, turning on the electric kettle. "I'm going to take them up a pot of tea and some goodies. Message on the answering machine from the Birmingham people; they've canceled because of the weather."

She'd just put together a selection of tea cakes and poured the boiling water into the pot when there was a knock at the back door.

Fiona went out through the boot room and he heard her say, "Hello, Owen, how are things?"

"May I have a word, Mrs. Edwards?"

"Certainly, come in!"

"Too muddy for that, ma'am."

"Right, just a tick."

She stuck her head into the kitchen and said, "Alec, would you mind terribly taking that tray up to the Llewellyns?"

"Not at all," he answered, but she had already stepped outside and closed the door behind her.

When he returned, she was slicing vegetables. "I need to get a bit of supper together for David. He had to leave the lambing fields midafternoon and apparently he's in a black mood. Shouted at Owen."

"It must be hard for David, this busy time of year."

"Yes, I'm sure it is, but there's no reason to take it out on poor Owen; he's a good man."

"Anything I can do to help?"

She smiled. "No, it's fine. Take it easy for a bit; I'm afraid this will slow down your preparations some."

"No problem," Alec replied. "I think I'll go upstairs, clean up, then come down and get to work on supper. See you later."

He turned to leave.

"Alec?"

"Yes?"

"I had a lovely time this afternoon. Thank you."

Alec grinned, nodded, and left.

Fiona pulled down a pan from the rack above the cooker. She dropped butter into the pan and added sliced carrots and onions. In a separate pan she steamed kale and baby beet greens from the garden, then added them to the sauté pan. Finally, she stirred in a small tin of canellini beans and a bit of tomato sauce.

Letting the mixture simmer, she walked over to the sink, leaned on the edge, and stared out the window to the darkening valley below. She heard Alec moving around in his room above the dining room.

Twenty-two years, she thought to herself. *How did that happen?* Meaghan had been a sort of measuring stick for her; she traced the history of her family by her daughter's growth, by the pencil marks that crept higher on the doorjamb between the kitchen and the boot room where they recorded her height at each birthday. They were like tree rings marking the passing years. Now Meaghan was grown and gone. Fiona had looked forward to this time, the time when she and David could be just the two of them again. It had been a foolish dream from the start; David had never possessed a romantic soul. Now, with the illness, the dream had gone from foolish to impossible. She'd become resigned to the life they had now. "For better or for worse . . . in sickness and in health," she had pledged, "so help me God." But she hadn't anticipated "worse." She hadn't expected "sickness." Now here they both were.

She brought David breakfast and a bag lunch early each morning, before she started cooking for her guests. They'd talk then, mostly about the farmwork, or the news from Meaghan. She cleaned for him at midday most days, while he was out in the fields. She brought him supper. They no longer spent the evening together; David was tired by then, and often moody. Now, when she took him supper, she put her hand on the latch of the door to the old hay barn, took a deep breath, and entered with a cheery "Evening, David; look what I've brought." Sometimes he'd rise to meet her. Lately, he just sat in his chair with his back to her, staring at the telly. Often the volume wasn't even on. "David," she'd ask, "are you all right?" "What do you think, woman?" he'd bark, not even turning to address her. She'd stand there silently for a moment or two, then set down the supper, slip quietly out the door, and drive slowly back down the rough track to the farmhouse.

It wasn't his fault, of course. He hadn't brought this on himself. He'd done what a good farmer was supposed to do, what the government required him to do. But some good farmers got sick. Some even died. She didn't want that to happen to David, but she wished desperately that his bitterness and anger would die. At least, she thought, she ought to be able to nurse him, but he wouldn't even let her do that. It was as if he thought his fury could burn through the illness and make him well. But it wasn't; it was making him sicker, at least emotionally. It was making him crazy.

She spooned David's supper into a casserole dish. In the beginning, she took it to him on a covered plate, sometimes with a vase of flowers from the garden. Nowadays, he sometimes didn't touch what she'd made until late at night. She'd bought him a little microwave oven so he could warm up his supper, and she delivered the meal in a casserole dish that was microwave-safe. But she suspected he ate it cold anyway.

Now she put the lid on the dish, took her coat off the hook in the boot room, walked through the rain to the barn, and drove the car up the track toward the mountain and the hay barn.

"What do you want?!" David growled from his chair when she entered.

"What do you mean, luv? I've brought your supper," she said.

"Take it away; I don't want it."

"Don't be silly, David; you need to eat."

"What do I need to eat for?!" he roared, struggling to his feet. He came toward her and staggered, grasping the back of his chair for stability. She could smell the whisky. "I've got ewes out there lambing this very minute and I'm not there for them. How do you think that makes me feel, woman?! Bloody useless, that's how! And no son to carry on for me!"

That stung, and she knew he knew it. "You have Owen, David."

"Bloody Owen! What in hell does he know, with all his book learning?!"

"That's enough! Owen Lewis is a good man and he's working hard for us. He respects you. He looks up to you. He's as good as a son to you."

David reached her and stood very close. "He's *not a son,* damn you!" David bellowed, spittle spraying from his mouth. Fiona wanted to step back but she felt glued to the spot. As if from outside herself she watched as her husband drew his right arm backward over his left shoulder and then swung it swiftly forward again, smacking the right side of her face, hard, with the back of his hand.

She'd braced for it unconsciously, but still the blow knocked Fiona one step to her left. Even so, she was too stunned to move. David had been angry, even threatening before, but never had he struck her. Never. Finally, after what seemed forever but was probably only a few seconds, she began to back away from him toward the door.

"I'm not finished with you, woman!" he spat, advancing upon her. But his foot caught the leg of one of the chairs at his little dining table, and he stumbled and fell.

Fiona reached the door but suddenly her shock turned to strength. She straightened her back and stepped up to the place where he'd landed on his hands and knees.

"If you ever do that to me again, David Edwards," she said in a perfectly calm voice that belied her fear, "it's over and you can fend for yourself."

Then she turned and walked out the door, closing it firmly behind her.

"Fiona!" she heard him cry through the heavy door as she turned on the ignition. She ignored him. They could talk about it tomorrow. Maybe. She turned the car around and raced down the track toward home. Her face felt aflame.

It wasn't until she parked the car in the barn and turned off the lights that the tears came. They were tears of shock, not pain. She was crying, she realized, because she no longer recognized her own husband, because she felt helpless, because she didn't know what to do next. He did not seem to be getting better with time, and his emotional condition was deteriorating. He refused go to the doctor anymore, and the truth was there wasn't much the doctor could do. And what could she do? What should she do? He was growing more unpredictable and more violent as time passed.

She sat in the car, collecting herself, then walked across the farmyard toward the house. The rain was easing a bit. She looked up at the sky. The deep darkness of the countryside at night was a great comfort to her. The incomprehensible millions of the stars did not make her feel alone in the universe; they made her feel a part of it. But there would be no stars tonight.

When she walked through the boot room and into the kitchen she found Alec already there. He was slicing the pork tenderloin length-wise, butterflying it. He turned toward her.

"Hello, you . . . ," he began. Then he saw the red welt on her cheek. And the red-rimmed eyes.

"Jesus, Fi! What happened?"

"It's fine Alec, really. It's nothing. Sometimes David . . . sometimes he . . . it's just so hard for him . . . he just . . . he was drinking . . . he's just overwhelmed and angry . . . he's . . ."

Alec wiped his hands and walked across the kitchen, stopping just in front of her. He held Fiona's shoulders but remained a step away. That was all it took. She fell into his chest, sobbing. He put his arms around her. He stood there a bit stiffly, wanting to be a comfort but try-ing not to be more. After a few moments, he felt her take a deep breath, put her hands on his chest, and push away. She managed a wan smile.

"I'm sorry, Alec, so sorry you had to see this."

"Fiona," he said, leading her to one of the kitchen chairs, "I have no business interfering in your life. But here we are, in your kitchen, right now. What can I do to help?"

She looked at this man, feeling his kindness, sensing his affection, knowing it was genuine. For a moment she thought she would begin crying again, but instead she smiled. "A glass of that wine might be nice."

He hesitated for a moment. Then he whirled into action, pulling a Swiss army knife out of his pocket, flipping out its corkscrew attach-ment, snatching one of the wine bottles from the refrigerator, slicing off the foil cover, and neatly pulling the cork. He looked around the kitchen.

"Glasses, glasses . . ."

Fiona laughed at last.

"To the right of the sink. No, wait. Let's use the good ones." She disappeared into the dining room and returned with two delicate long-stemmed wineglasses with gold rims.

"They were Mother's; I never use them. Perhaps it's time I did."

He gestured for her to sit again, tossed a kitchen towel over his forearm, in the manner of a sommelier in a fine restaurant, poured a taste into her glass, stood back at attention, and awaited the verdict.

She sipped the wine. "Umm, this is lovely. When's dinner?"

He filled her glass. "It'll take forty-five minutes or so, maybe an hour."

She looked at the hand holding her glass and realized it was still shaking. "I think I'll go upstairs, have a bath, and try to make myself presentable for your birthday dinner. An hour?"

"Your wish is my command."

She smiled. If he only knew.

"See you then."

Alec stood for a moment wondering what had happened across the farm in that hay barn. He was thinking about how she felt in his arms. He was thinking about the strength she had and how it contrasted with the delicacy of her body. He was thinking about how beautiful she was—or could be if she had someone who cared.

He went to the boot room, shrugged on his rain jacket, took a bulky flashlight off a hook by the door, and went out to the vegetable garden behind the barn, glad to discover there were gravel paths between the wet beds. He found the wintered-over leeks. There was an old spading fork leaning up against the side of the barn and he plunged it into the earth. Despite the day's downpour, the soil was loose, rich, and easy to work. He forked up two thick leeks, returned the spade to the wall, and found a rain barrel under a downspout where he rinsed off the dirt clinging to the roots. Along the garden's border he found herbs. He pinched off the stems of some new parsley and snapped off a woody branch of rosemary. As he walked back toward the house he heard a car start and move away; the Llewellyns on their way to Dolgellau for supper, he guessed.

Back in the kitchen, Alec chopped the parsley together with a clove of garlic and some mint that grew in a pot by the window and spread the mixture across the butterflied pork loin, adding salt, pepper, and olive oil. Then he rolled the pork and tied it together. Next, he julienned the white parts of the leeks and softened them in a buttered pan over low heat. He put another sauté pan on the hottest burner and swirled olive oil into it. When the oil began to smoke he added the rolled tenderloin, quickly browning the sides. After a few minutes, he put the meat pan into one of the Aga's ovens to roast.

Fiona stood in her bathroom, leaning on the pedestal sink and staring at her reflection in the mirror. The bath had helped; the welt on her face had stopped stinging. Her eyes were no longer red.

In retrospect, she didn't feel anger about what David had done. What she felt was pity. What had happened to him—what was still happening—must be terrifying. The only life he'd ever known was in jeopardy. The farm was how he defined himself; its success was how he measured his worth. She knew his fury had nothing to do with her not bearing him a son, though perhaps lambing season brought the issue back to the surface for him. And she knew he was fond of Owen, as Owen was of him. He was simply afraid. Afraid of losing the farm; afraid of losing himself.

But now she was afraid, too.

She walked into the bedroom. It was Alec's birthday. He was cooking for her. She would dress up a bit and push the fear aside. She pulled a box that held some of Meaghan's castoffs from the back of her closet and picked through them. Eventually, she found a narrow, ankle-length, black gabardine skirt. In the mirror, it made her look taller. She chose a simple white broadcloth blouse and, instead of tucking it in, cinched it with a belt. She had a Victorian black velvet choker with a cameo that had been her mother's and she put it on, the knot at the nape of her neck hidden by her hair.

She went back into the bathroom. In the mirror she knew immediately the velvet choker was wrong. *You look like a present waiting to be unwrapped,* she said to herself. *And you're not.* She untied the choker and set it aside. "Better," she said aloud. Though she almost never used makeup, she smoothed on foundation to hide the fading red welt on her cheek. She added just a touch of lipstick. She reached for the Rain, then hesitated, picking up the unopened bottle of Amarige instead. She broke the seal and sniffed: dark spices, woodiness, a touch of vanilla. Exotic. She decided she liked her daughter's taste in fragrances. She sprayed a tiny bit of the perfume behind her ears. Finally, she slipped her feet into a pair of shoes with a tiny heel—"kitten heels" Meaghan had called them when they bought them together— and left her rooms.

When she reached the kitchen it was fragrant with the roasting pork, and Alec was swirling cornmeal around in a gently bubbling pot.

"What's that?" she asked.

"What it's going to be is polenta with rosemary," he said as he turned. She seemed even more beautiful than the night before, but this time he held his tongue. His eyes said it all.

"Are you sure this is your birthday and not mine?" she asked, smiling.

"I'm having a good time doing this, Fiona, truly. Besides, it's been a long time since I had the pleasure of cooking for a lovely lady."

"I don't believe that for a minute," Fiona teased.

Alec was about to respond with a wisecrack, but found himself turning serious. "Look, Fi, I'm not sure what sort of life you think I lead. Yes, I'm single, but I make a lousy Lothario. First of all, I'm fifty; there are not a lot of women interested in a man my age. Second, I'm terrible at dating. I don't know how to be 'casual' in relationships. I'm meant for marriage. I suppose that makes me old-fashioned, but there you are."

Fiona sat at the table, poured herself a glass of wine, and then said, "I have three things to say: first, I apologize for teasing you; second, you underestimate yourself terribly; third, that pot is about to boil over."

Alec spun around, turned the heat down on the polenta, and added a bit more hot water, along with salt, pepper, olive oil, and chopped rosemary.

"Thank you," he mumbled.

Fiona wasn't sure whether it was for the apology, the compliment, or the warning.

"I need a hand here," he said. "Could you stir the polenta while I work on the spinach?"

"I suppose I might manage that," Fiona said, rising and walking toward the stove. Alec wondered whether there was anything more quintessentially feminine than the sharp click of a woman's heels on a hard floor.

He tossed washed spinach leaves into the pan with the softened leeks and added butter, turning the leaves quickly as they wilted. Then he removed the tenderloin from the oven, set the meat on a plate, and made a sauce from the juice and browned bits in the pan by adding a little white wine and butter. He shooed Fiona back to the table, put a large spoonful of the soft polenta on each of their plates, arranged thin slices of the pork on top, and drizzled the sauce across the meat, finally adding the spinach and leeks on one side.

When he turned around again, Fiona had lit the candles they'd used the night before. She poured wine into his glass as he set the plates down and they sat. She lifted her glass.

"To the astonishingly old Alec Hudson on his birthday."

"How very kind you are," Alec laughed, clinking her glass. "Now, if you're finished insulting me, may I suggest we eat?"

Fiona took a bite, and slumped in a mock swoon. "Oh my *God, what is* this?!"

"I suppose there's an Italian name for it, but it's just herb-stuffed pork tenderloin with rosemary polenta. I learned it from a chef in New York. A real chef."

"Yum!" she replied, fluttering her hands and bouncing in her chair like a child. For once she wasn't teasing.

Alec grinned. "That's the nicest birthday present you could give me."

"Mmm," she mumbled, filling her mouth again. "My pleasure, I'm sure. If this is any example, he must have been a very successful chef."

"He was a she, actually, and yes, she was."

"Sounds like there's a story there . . ."

Alec made a face.

"Oops, there I go creating a romantic life for you again. Sorry."

Alec smiled. In very short order they moved on to the second bottle of wine. They talked about the farm, about lambing season, about the enigmatic mountain, about Owen and what a help he was, about the new guests. They talked, in short, about everything but what had happened at the converted hay barn. Alec didn't ask; he figured that if and when Fiona wanted to talk about David, she would.

As they ate and talked, Fiona was struck by the ease with which the conversation ebbed and flowed, sometimes playful, sometimes serious. She thought, too, about how comfortable their silences were. Why didn't she and David do this? Why had they never been like this?

When Meaghan was still at home, there would be talk about school and her friends, but David seldom joined in. It was as if he had nothing to say, as if supper were nothing more to him than a refueling stop. If he said anything at all, it was something to do with the farm. He had no life besides the farm, she now understood, either outside in the world or inside himself. It was all he knew and, apparently, all he cared to know. Fiona realized she was hungry for mature conversation. She was ravenous for it. She wondered whether she didn't miss this form of intimacy with a mate even more than lovemaking. She could hardly remember either.

The Llewellyns returned from town just as she and Alec were finishing dinner and Fiona hurried out to the hall to see to them. He could hear her inquiring about the restaurant they'd chosen. They chatted for a while and then she bid them goodnight, drifting back into the kitchen after a few minutes to find him filling the sink with soapy water.

"Leave that there, you. The chef does not do the washing up. Besides, I've started a fire in my sitting room and there's a lemon tart waiting for you there."

"If there's a tart waiting for me somewhere," he said, drying his hands, "I'll definitely follow."

"You are a cad."

"I only wish." Alec followed her across the house, watching the graceful sway of her hips.

There was Celtic fiddle music playing softly on a small radio set into Fiona's bookshelf. "Is that music all right?"

"It's lovely; this kind of music always makes me happy," Alec said. "A remnant of the Celtic part of me, I suspect."

"Hudson doesn't sound Celtic."

"It's not. It's phony."

"What?"

"It's a made-up name. The name of a river, actually. In New York."

"You made up your surname?"

"Not me, my grandparents. My father's parents, Gustav and Marie Brinkmann, moved to Brooklyn from Germany right after the turn of the century. When World War One broke out, they changed their name. A lot of Germans did; they were worried about reprisals. The story goes that they were taking a steamship excursion up the Hudson River one summer Sunday. When the boat got to the narrow, twisting part of the river up near Bear Mountain, the tour guide who was pointing out the sights along the way told them that the Hudson was known as 'the American Rhine.' Apparently, my grandfather turned to his wife and announced, 'Hudson: that will be our new name.' My grandmother knew better than to question her Prussian husband and that was that. The Brinkmann line in America became extinct."

"Well, Hudson suits you better than Brinkmann, I think."

"Thank you. Not that I had much to say about it."

"But that doesn't explain the Celtic bit."

"My mother was from Brittany."

"That's why you can cook; you're part French!"

Alec laughed. "It's a good thing my mother isn't here; she'd argue—passionately—that she was Breton, not French. It is a point of pride. Brittany was as Celtic as Ireland or Wales long ago."

"Don't tell me you have 'Onion Johnnies' in your background?!"

"Onion *who's*?"

"Johnnies! Frenchmen—excuse me, *Bretons*—who used to come across the Channel every year and travel around on bicycles strung with long braids of onions. When we had the money for a holiday, which wasn't often, my father took us to Cornwall—so he could be close to the sea, I suppose—and we'd see them there, selling onions door-to-door. I can't imagine how they made a living, but they'd been doing it since the 1800s. David told me they were here in Wales, too, when he was a boy, just after the war. Rumored to be rogues with the ladies."

"You're making that part up."

"I was hoping you wouldn't notice."

"Hmm. Is that what you were hoping, or were you hoping for a hint of that roguishness in my DNA somewhere?"

She laughed and quickly changed the subject. "Tell me what you think of the tart."

"Which one?"

"That was so rude!"

Alec was instantly serious. "You're right, Fi; it was. I'm sorry."

"Don't be silly; I'm teasing. I think I'd know it if you were insulting me. Besides, it's been a very long time since anyone's suggested I was a tart; forever, in fact. Nice at my age, actually. And anyway, I don't think you have rudeness in you; you're too well-bred."

Alec burst out laughing. "Well-bred; that's a good one." He took a bite of the tart. "Umm. Tangy. Sweet. "

"You're not?"

"Hardly."

"Well, you certainly had me fooled. Who are you, Alec Hudson?"

He noticed a decanter of sherry on a table in the corner by the fire. "Mind if I answer that over a glass of sherry?"

"Of course not. Make it a large one; I want to hear all the details."

It was a bone-dry amontillado, perfect with the lemon tart.

Alec sat down and stared at the fire for a few moments. Then he began. He told her about his troubled father; his long-suffering mother; the kid sister he adored; the tiny one-bedroom apartment, like an emotional hothouse, in which they'd all lived; the neighborhood that got rougher as the years passed and now was largely demolished. He told her about being lucky enough to receive a scholarship to go to a state college and wondering how the arc of his life might have changed had he been smart enough or rich enough to attend a better school. He told her about falling in love with writing and about working for Jimmy Carter.

Fiona did not interrupt. When he seemed to have run out of steam, she said, "I've been meaning to ask, what exactly is it that you write?"

"Boring stuff, mostly. Books on economics, welfare policy, education reform, environmental issues. That sort of thing."

"But if it's boring, which I doubt, why do people buy the books?"

"Regular people don't, but politicians and people who care about those things do. It's not the books that support me, anyway; it's the consulting work I get after they're published."

"I guess I don't understand," Fiona said, frowning.

"You're not alone. My mother doesn't, either. Okay, here's what I do: I try to figure out what major public issue is peeking its ugly head over the horizon, research it, then write a book suggesting ways that issue might best be addressed. Now, let's say you're the governor of one of our states—or, here in Britain, the government minister responsible for dealing with such things. You tell your staff to find out what is available on the subject and they come up with my book, mostly because it's the only one out on the subject yet. You read it and then call me in for a meeting. Pretty soon I have a nice short-term contract to serve as your adviser."

"It sounds pretty abstract to me."

"That's my little party trick: it isn't—that is, the books aren't. I worked at a university once and hated it. It's as if professors try to make their writing as difficult to understand as possible so they can sound important. The people I write for don't have the time for that sort of thing, and academics never publish their work fast enough for it to be useful. My books are short and easy to understand. It's been a pretty successful formula, except . . ."

He hesitated.

"What?"

"Except the only part of me that's engaged in it," he answered, holding one hand below his chin and the other above his head, "is this. My heart isn't in it; it's all intellectual. I used to persuade myself that I was helping the world a little, making life better for people who are disadvantaged. But I'm not even sure about that anymore. It's built my reputation and given me a good income . . ."

"But it doesn't make you happy."

"Something like that, yes. When Gwynne died so suddenly a year ago, it made me think about how wasted all these years of writing have been."

"Why don't you write something else?"

"I do. I write poetry from time to time. Some of it's been published. But you can't make a living as a poet. Most poets have nice, safe, tenured positions at some university. I don't fit in that world; I haven't the patience for it."

"What will you do?"

"I don't know, honestly. I need to think about it some more."

She laughed. "Isn't that the problem?"

"What?"

"Seems to me you're trying to think your way through this instead of feel. Hasn't that been the root of the problem all along?"

Alec stared at her.

"Oh dear, I'm being presumptuous."

"Not at all," he said, "it's just that I'd never thought about it that way before."

"There you go again!" she said, and now they both laughed.

Fiona rose, walked across the room, retrieved a small wrapped package from her bookshelf, and handed it to Alec as she sat again.

"Happy birthday."

Alec was speechless. Carefully, he removed the wrapping and found inside a pocket-sized Welsh-English dictionary.

He looked up. "It's a wonderful gift, and completely unnecessary."

"Oh it's silly, really; it was just a whim. You'll probably never be back again to need it. . . ." It was a something she'd said off the top of her head, but suddenly the thought was like a vise squeezing her heart.

The thought of returning to America hadn't been in Alec's mind either, and he pushed it aside. He looked at the woman sitting across from him in the firelight.

"Now," she said, "do you suppose I might have some of that sherry, too?"

Alec leaped up. "That *was* rude," he apologized. "I'll leave the decanter right here beside you."

"Are you plying me with my own liquor?" she teased.

Alec put the decanter down on the table next to her. He hesitated before her for a fraction of a second, then turned away, kneeling to add coal to the fire.

"I don't know what I'm doing, Fiona," he confessed to the flames.

Fiona said nothing for a few moments. Then she stood up and put a hand on his shoulder.

"You are a dear, sweet man."

Alec stood, took her face in his warm hands, hesitated, then placed a light kiss on her forehead.

"Thank you."

"You're very welcome," she whispered.

"I think it would be wise for me to take myself off to bed."

She understood what he was saying and smiled. "Good night, then."

"Good night, Fi, and thank you for sharing my birthday."

"My pleasure entirely."

He nodded and ducked out the door.

Fiona got her breathing under control, heard Sooty scratching at the door and let him out, then banked the fire and set up the screen to keep embers from popping out onto the rug. Finally, she went through to her bedroom. She stepped out of her clothes and took her long flannel sleeping shift off the hook on the back of the bathroom door. Then she paused, put the shift back on its hook, climbed up onto her big old bed, burrowing under the duvet and relishing the cool cotton on her bare skin. She let a delicious desire sweep over her and began to pleasure herself, imagining Alec's hands where hers were, feeling his long body spooned behind her, his left arm curved under her neck and left hand cradling one of her breasts, the warmth of his belly against the small of her back, his hardness pressed against her rump as the fingers of his right hand made slow magic.

There was a crash in the farmyard. Fiona shot bolt upright in the dark, the sweet fantasy gone in an instant. There were never sounds in the farmyard at night. They had no cows or horses in the old stone barns. There were no late arrivals tonight. The farm was remote.

David!

She slid down off the bed and crept to the window facing the farmyard. Pulling the curtain back slightly, she peered out into the gloom. The weather had broken. Low clouds sped across a sky pin-pricked with stars. There was enough moonlight that the chips of silica and quartz in the granite walls of the barn opposite glittered. She strained to see the source of the crash. Instead, the inky shadows acted like a movie screen upon which were projected the image of David brooding volcanically in his chair in front of the mute television; David struggling out of the chair and lurching toward her, his eyes aflame with fury; David advancing on her, his mouth twisted with malice; her own feet unresponsive to the urge to flee; spit like poison spewing from David's mouth as he roared; that thickly muscled arm swinging back, back, then rocketing forward, the back of his hand connecting with her jaw. Was he out there now? Had he come after her?

Fiona stood by the window, barely breathing, but nothing in the farmyard moved. The silence throbbed in her ears. Then it was broken by another sound, a mewing at the kitchen door, and her shoulders relaxed. She walked to the door of her bedroom, slipped on the flannel shift, went through her rooms and out to the kitchen. When she opened the back door, Sooty waltzed in.

"I think we've just found the source of the crash, haven't we?"

The cat, of course, ignored her.

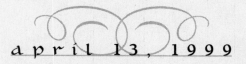

april 13, 1999

nine

Fiona awoke at dawn, feeling oddly disoriented. It had been a night of haunting dreams: her father falling into black water at the bottom of the canal lock; the bargeman plunging into the dark water, pulling the body to the surface and dragging it out, turning it over only to reveal that it was not her father, after all, but David.

She lay in bed for a few minutes and watched a wan light gather beyond her window, the window at which she'd stood, terrified, only hours earlier. What if it had been David? What would she have done? What *could* she have done? The kitchen door was always unlocked. There was no lock on the door to her rooms. Should she install one? No, that was ridiculous; David hadn't been out there. Her fears were getting ahead of reality.

But what was real? David had hit her; did that make him dangerous? Alec had kissed her forehead; did that mean he loved her? Did she love him? She needed time to think but didn't have it. It was time to get the day going; time to get David's breakfast and lunch made and delivered, time to attend to her guests. There was never time for her. As she slipped out of bed and dressed, she wondered if she'd know what to do with it if there were.

In the kitchen, Jack was waiting for her, sitting on his haunches, tongue lolling.

"Jackie my boy, what are we to do?" she said to the collie, setting his tail a-wag. "There's a strange man in the house, and I'm afraid I'm rather fond of him. Really, Jack, it's not at all right."

Jack yawned, stood, and sidled up to her.

"Oh, you're no help; you're just hungry! There's a surprise . . ."

She walked out into the boot room and put dry food in Jack's bowl. Jack made a soft "woofing" sound by way of thanks, and she ruffled the top of his head with her fingers. Then she knelt down, put her arms around the dog's neck, and gave him a hug. Jack ignored her, and it didn't matter; she knew the hug was for her, not him. She knew she was clinging to something certain, because uncertainty surrounded her.

She stood up and returned to the kitchen. Opening the refrigerator, she took out a sealed pint carton of milk and two hard-boiled eggs. She put the eggs into a small paper bag, adding a thick, buttered slice of crusty granary bread, a pared carrot, and fruit. She set the bag into a large wicker basket that sat on the end of the counter and added the milk, a box of organic muesli, a banana, and an apple. Breakfast and lunch for David. Not much to keep a farmer going, but all he seemed to want anymore.

She pulled a coat off a hook in the boot room, shrugged it on over her flannel shift, and pulled on her green wellies. Taking the basket from the counter, she took a deep breath and headed for the car.

It was a dreary morning, and cold. The clear night sky had yielded to a blanket of dense, icy mist, the kind that keeps you constantly damp but doesn't soak you through. "Pneumonia weather," her mother used to call it.

When she reached the hay barn she sat in the car for a few moments to gather her courage. Finally, she got out and knocked at the door. There was no reply. David was often off early, tending to the sheep, but when she tried the door she found it locked. She puzzled a moment, then left the basket on the doorstep. Clearly, he wanted to be left alone. After last night, she was happy to oblige.

Back in her kitchen, she filled the electric kettle and flicked on its switch. She put a scoop of tea leaves in her teapot. The kettle clicked off as the water came to a boil and she went to fetch it. When she turned around, Alec was standing in the doorway.

"Hello, you," he said.

"Hi."

They stood looking at each other, smiling shyly. Fiona broke the silence.

"You will have noted," she needled, "that my interpretation of the marine weather forecast yesterday was correct."

"I did, yes. Not a great day to give the mountain another try."

"I shouldn't think so, given your last attempt."

Alec was about to protest, but there was a knock at the back door. Fiona went to open it.

"Oh hello, Owen; come in and have a cuppa."

Owen followed her into the kitchen. "Morning, Alec," he said.

Fiona poured a cup of tea and gestured for Owen to sit.

"What do you need, Owen?"

Owen hesitated, as if searching for the right words.

"David's already gone back to his cottage. Looked done in when he arrived this morning and left after a couple of hours. A right mood he was in, too, I can tell you; angry at everything, he was. The thing is, the last rush of lambing is upon us and I'm a bit stretched to keep up with 'em."

Fiona knew from experience that this was an understatement.

Before he'd taken ill, it had been all she and David together could do to handle the surge of births at this stage in the season.

"I was hoping my assistant here might be willing to lend a hand," Owen said, nodding toward Alec.

Alec laughed. "Well, if you're willing to engage a galloping incompetent to help out, then I'm your man. But you'll have to guide me."

Fiona looked at Alec. She was beginning to expect his un-expectedness.

Owen's hunched shoulders eased and he grinned. "After yesterday, I'd say you were a natural."

"Why don't I make you both a decent breakfast before the others come down," Fiona said. "Then you two can go and play in the fields together."

"That would be right welcome, Mrs. Edwards."

Fiona went to work and Owen filled Alec in on the state of things. The good news was that the last of the lambing ewes were in the near meadow; the bad news was that the lambs were coming thick and fast. A few minutes later, Fiona had plates of fried eggs and bacon before them, along with thick slices of toasted brown bread. The two men ate quickly. Fiona had barely enough time to wipe her hands, pour herself a cup of tea, and take a seat before the two men stood, thanked her, and headed for the door. Alec pulled on his boots, then ducked his head back into the kitchen.

"By the way, miss, what're my wages?"

She laughed. "Only food, lodging, and all the comforts, I'm afraid."

"Works for me," he said, then hurried after Owen.

"There are a couple of things worrying me," Owen said as they walked through the farmyard. "We've got a fair number of young ewes about to give birth and they're always more trouble than the seasoned ones. The births are more difficult, and they often need to be trained to care for their lambs properly. The other thing's the weather. It's cold, and according to the local report, it's going to get colder throughout the day and tonight."

"You're worried about losing lambs?" Alec asked.

Owen nodded. "David's an old-fashioned hill farmer. Lambing's done in the fields and the little devils survive or they don't is his theory. That's not how I was taught."

"What would you do?"

"In normal weather that theory would be fine, but look what we've got: steady mist and deepening cold. More like winter than spring. I think we stand a chance of losing a lot of the lambs tonight, unless we shelter them. See, most farms these days, lambing's done in sheds, out of the weather. David's got the space, but doesn't believe in it."

"David's not here."

Owen looked at him. "You'd support me?"

"For what it's worth, which isn't much, sure. Seems to me the objective is to keep the lambs alive, whatever that takes. What does it take, by the way?"

They were just passing the barn when Owen stopped. "How are you with a hammer and a saw?"

"I've renovated a few houses over the years and, to the best of my knowledge, they're still standing."

"Good enough; follow me." In the barn he gestured at the largely empty space. "Ideally, I'd like a couple dozen pens, roughly four by four. No time to build permanent ones, but there's wood behind the barn and tools in the office. If you could just build a few sets of portable hurdles . . ."

"Hurdles?"

"Like in track-and-field races, like portable fence sections. We can rearrange them as needed. Ideally, I'd like a central aisle with pens on either side, bedded with that dry straw over there."

"I can do that. I'll get the wood; you get the tools and move the Land Rover and the tractor."

"Right. And Alec?" Owen said. "Thanks."

Alec waved and headed for the rear of the barn. The wood was in good shape, stacked and relatively dry. In a few trips, he'd dragged most of it into the barn. Owen headed to the lambing field.

Within a few minutes, Alec created a prototype of what he would build: two uprights braced to a footing board, three four-foot horizontal boards nailed to the uprights, and one diagonal to give the hurdle strength and stability. Then he used the pieces as templates and cut multiples of each. After that it was simply a matter of nailing the pieces together to form each hurdle unit.

At midmorning, Fiona arrived with thermoses of hot tea. She slipped into the barn and watched Alec work. He knelt on the concrete floor of the barn piecing together the sections of wood. He had stripped to one of his sleeveless T-shirts and despite the cold weather there was a dark stain of sweat between his shoulder blades. His bare, attenuated arms were sinewy and clearly strong. He didn't look his fifty years, and he didn't work like a man that age, either. He worked like a machine: no wasted movements, each nail driven straight and true in three swift, smooth hammer swings. She hadn't expected a writer to have such practical skills. There was another thing she hadn't expected, but standing there quietly watching him work, she embraced it: she was in love with him.

It had grown swiftly, this love. It had begun at her doorstep, when he first arrived, then had spread throughout the world as she knew it over the course of the next three days, like shock waves after a detonation. She thought about what a bundle of contradictions this man was: thoughtful but mischievous, quick-witted but kind, reserved but open-hearted and generous, educated but informal, controlled but caring. *I feel like I've known him forever,* she said to herself, and then suddenly she knew why. He was the kind of man she dreamed of marrying when she was a little girl: he was a gentleman.

"Tea?" she said.

Alec looked up, startled. He'd had no idea she was there. He leaned back on his haunches.

"Perfect," he said, twisting this way and that to loosen his shoulders. "How's Owen doing with the lambs?"

"Don't know. I'm on my way there now."

He reached for the thermos, ignored the cup that formed its lid, and drank the hot, milky tea straight from the lip of the container. He thanked her, dragged the back of his hand across his mouth, then picked up the hammer again. "Let me know how he is, will you?"

Then he went back to work. She smiled at his single-mindedness. She didn't feel ignored or insulted; he was focused, a man on a mission.

"Alec?"

He looked up.

"Why are you doing this for us?"

He sat back on his heels again. "Because it needed doing. I suppose it's just how I was brought up. My father called it the 'barn-raising tradition.'"

"The what?"

"Barn raising. His father's brothers farmed in central Pennsylvania and he spent summers with them. When a farmer needed to build a new barn, everyone in the community would gather to help and it would be framed and sided in a couple of days. They were German immigrants, mostly, and they had a phrase that translated roughly as 'many hands make the work light.' So when there's something that needs doing, I just pitch in. Like I said: it's how I was brought up."

Fiona looked at him and doubted that was the whole story.

"Well then, I guess I'll leave you to it. But thank you."

Alec nodded. She found two pails, filled them with water at the spigot outside the barn, then headed for the lambing meadow, a bucket in each hand and the second thermos tucked under an arm. A few minutes later she was back in the barn.

"How's Owen doing?" Alec asked her.

"So far, so good. Mostly normal births, a few ewes being stupid about caring for their lambs. He wants to know how you're coming."

Alec had by this time set up two pens, tying hurdle sections together with orange hay-baling twine. With the precut wood, he figured he could build a pen every forty-five minutes.

"We're ready for some lambs," he said, hardly looking up from his hammering. She bent over him and kissed the back of his neck.

"Be right back," she said.

Alec didn't move. The kiss was electric; it was as if someone had stuck his finger in a wall socket. The emotional jolt was stunning, galvanic. He was vibrating from the shock of it, from its tenderness. He felt simultaneously suffused with happiness and confusion.

He didn't have a lot of time to deal with these conflicting emotions; Fiona was back in just a few minutes. She had the forelegs of two lambs gripped in each hand. The mother followed behind, bleating in protest. She led the lambs and the ewe into one of the pens, knelt down in the straw beside the ewe, and, holding each lamb in turn by the shoulders, squirted milk from their mother's teats toward their mouths. It took a couple of tries, but eventually the lambs got the idea and were suckling the ewe. Their little bellies were round in no time and the ewe seemed more than happy to have the pressure in her udder relieved. Fiona brought the ewe a scoopful of food pellets and a bucket of water.

Thus it went, pen by pen, ewe by ewe. By early afternoon, five pens were filled with bleating lambs and ewes.

"How about something to eat?" Fiona asked at one point.

"Protein and water," he replied, not looking up.

"Ham sandwiches?"

"Just the ham, please, no bread; slows down the brain."

She returned a few minutes later with the ham, some cheese, and a plastic bottle of water, then took Owen his lunch.

A few minutes later she was back. "Owen needs you."

Alec headed up to the meadow at a run and found Owen much as he had the day before, trying to still a straining ewe. Owen's hair was matted flat from the continuous mist and his face was covered with dirt.

"And a handsome devil you are, I must say, young Owen," Alec cracked.

Owen looked up and laughed. "Seen yourself lately?"

"What've we got?"

"Twins, both reverse presentation—that is, hind legs first. Not what we want, but it can be managed. What you want to do is ease the top one out first, while keeping the lower one inside, so as not to crowd the cervix."

"What *I* want to do?"

"Yeah. I got another one just like her over there on the other side of the meadow, and she's in more distress."

"I'm a big fan of learning by doing, Owen, but how about a tip or two?"

"I was coming to that. I've made you a double-ended leg rope. You slip a loop over the hoof of each of the top lamb's hind legs, careful so the knot straightens the hoof rather than bending it. Pull each leg gently to the opening. Then lift the ewe's hindquarters like we did yesterday so the lower lamb settles back down in the uterus. Finally, pull both legs out evenly; the first lamb will follow. Lambs born backward can have fluid in their throat, so you'll have to grab the lamb by the

hind legs and swing it—gently, mind—in a low arc to get it out. The
rest you already know. Then do the same with the other lamb. Oh, and
use plenty of lubrication on both your arm and the birth canal; I've left
you a bucketful, plus some disposable latex gloves."

With that he dashed across the field.

Alec pulled on the gloves, lubricated his right hand and arm,
picked up the rope, and kneeled behind the ewe. But as soon as he tried
to insert his hand, the ewe stepped away. He stood up and straddled the
ewe, facing backward. With his knees holding her in place, he tried
again. It was somehow different approaching upside down; it made vi-
sualizing what was happening inside more difficult. Still, he easily located the uppermost lamb and slipped the loops over its tiny hooves. He
followed Owen's instructions and soon the hooves were at the opening.
He lifted the ewe's hind section about a foot and gave it a bit of a shake,
then began to pull the leg ropes. Sure enough, in no time the lamb appeared and slipped out onto the grass. Alec gave it a gentle swing,
cleared its nose, soaked its umbilical in iodine, and set the fragile little
creature by its mother's head. The ewe made soft bleating sounds and
began cleaning her trembling firstborn. Alec turned to the task of pulling out the second.

This time, occupied as she was, the ewe gave no trouble. He
slipped his hand into the birth canal, located the second lamb's legs, and
repeated the procedure. But as he pulled, this lamb seemed to get
jammed at the cervix. He reached in, feeling for the problem, and
found that the lamb's hooves had bent at the ankles; he'd slipped the
rope loops on wrong. He corrected the error, straightened the little legs,
and tried again. This time the lamb came into the world smoothly. He
cleared its nose and set it beside its sibling. The ewe looked at him with
what seemed to Alec like gratitude. Then she moved instinctively to
the task of licking off the birth fluids and nudging the babies toward
her udder. This ewe's maternal instincts were strong. The lambs would
survive.

Owen bounded over to him, having seen to the other ewe. "How'd it go?" he asked.

"Amazingly, just fine," Alec said with a look of bemusement at what was happening before him. "I never thought I'd ever be in training for ovine obstetrics."

Owen laughed. "Looks like you're ready for your diploma. By the way, how are things in the barn?"

"I've got ten pens made up. I could have another half dozen or so before the afternoon is out."

"Well, get to it, man; we'll have no lollygagging here in the fields!"

Alec rose, groaning as he stood. "I swear I'm too old for this."

"Nonsense," Owen chided. "You just need getting used to it. But remember, I only need the pens for the ones who seem weak to me. Whatever you can build, I'll take."

"I'm on it."

"Alec," Owen said.

Alec turned again.

"Couldn't do it without you, mate."

Alec smiled and bowed formally. "I'm at your service."

They both laughed and Alec returned to building pens. Every hour or so, Fiona would arrive with one or two newborns and their mother. At one point she showed up with two lambs but no ewe. She put them in a fresh stall, then headed back to the field with a large plastic jug, returning a few minutes later with the jug filled with ewe's milk. Alec heard her murmuring to the lambs and went over to the pen.

"What's wrong?" he asked her over the railing.

"Orphans. Sometimes a ewe dies giving birth but the lambs survive. In this case, though, the ewe's fine but she's refusing to nurse, so I've got to feed them with colostrum I've milked from the mother."

As Alec looked on, Fiona loaded a large syringe with some of the collected milk and then attached a slender rubber tube. She laid one of the lambs over her lap, lifted its head so the neck was straight, and slid the tube down the lamb's throat all the way to its stomach. Then, gently, she pushed in the plunger and emptied the syringe. She refilled and emptied the syringe a couple of times, then repeated the process with the other lamb. Alec was amazed at how quickly the lambs' little bellies filled out.

As the afternoon wore on, Owen called on Alec three times for help with difficult births. But by the time the light began to fail, Alec had managed to cobble together nearly twenty pens. Fiona had returned to the house hours earlier to attend to her guests, but Owen kept bringing lambs and ewes. In the cavernous stone barn, the noise of their bleating was deafening.

At last, Owen returned from the field empty-handed. He stood quietly for a moment behind Alec, who was still hammering hurdles together.

He rested a hand on Alec's shoulder. "Enough, my friend; this will do us for a while."

Alec put his hammer down and rose stiffly.

"You sure?"

"For now, certainly. Not many ewes left to lamb. We'll cycle these lambs out to the field in a day or so, assuming it warms up, and use the pens for any others that need special handling."

The two of them walked from pen to pen. Owen checked the water buckets, tossed a scoop of food pellets into each stall, then examined the lambs. The orphan stall now had three lambs, and here he gave each a bottle equipped with a rubber teat and taught them to nurse. He gave one bottle to Alec and brought him a lamb. It took awhile, but eventually, Alec's lamb grasped the concept and was attacking the teat vigorously, emptying the bottle in no time and bleating for more.

Tired as he was, it felt wonderful to do something so tangible and real—and so unlike writing. And then there were all these pitifully tiny, newly living things all around him, each one a minor miracle. Maybe this is a little like having a child, he mused, and suddenly the fact that he and Gwynne had never had children opened like a wound. What kind of father would he have made? Probably more a teacher than a playmate; he'd never had the knack for playing games. His natural response to children was to stand back and watch them with awe, amazed at their energetic, spongelike brains, their miniature limbs, their fragility, their promise.

Fiona was waiting for them at the back door when they reached the house. It was nearly eight o'clock, and she had changed into a skirt and blouse. She had a pint glass of foamy brown ale in each hand.

"As sweatshops go, I guess this ain't half bad," Alec cracked.

Without skipping a beat, Fiona extended one glass to Owen, then took a sip from the other and held on to it.

"Okay, okay," Alec said, his hands in the air in surrender, "you win."

She winked at Owen. "It's so hard to get good help these days, isn't it?" Then she gave Alec the glass.

"While you two have been larking about," she continued, "I've made supper—shepherd's pie. Owen, will you stay?"

"Thank you kindly, Mrs. Edwards, but I need to look in on my mam."

Fiona's faced turned serious in an instant. "How is she, then?"

"New hip's mending well, ma'am; she'll be her usual troublemaking self in no time."

"Owen Lewis! That's a fine thing to be saying about your mother . . . even if she is a bit, well, feisty," Fiona said with a wink.

Owen smiled. "People in town have been good to her since Da died; made her feel at home. Lots of new friends to look in on her."

"Owen, if your mam's recovering well, it'll be your doing. A good son you are to her. Go on then, and give her my best."

Owen seemed genuinely embarrassed by the compliment. "Thanks, Mrs. Edwards, I'll do that. And by the way, this new farm-hand we've got," he said, nodding toward Alec. "Reckon he'll do."

He extended his hand and Alec took it.

"My pleasure," Alec said, grinning.

"Best be off now," Owen said, draining his glass. "'Night, Mrs. Edwards; 'night, Alec."

Alec was staring after Owen. Fiona patted the small of his back gently.

"How you doing?"

Alec turned to her and smiled. "Pretty good, for an older guy. Tired in the body, but invigorated in the brain. Also very hungry and wondering what a shepherd's pie is and how many shepherds you had to grind up to make it."

She gave him a playful slap. "Minced lamb and onions and gravy and other good things with a mashed potato crust and it'll soon be ready to come out of the oven, so I suggest you go clean yourself up. You'll not be dining with me in the condition you're in!"

The evening was a quiet one, the two of them eating slowly, pouring more of the amber ale, talking easily, laughing often, revisiting the little epiphanies of the day. As they were cleaning up, together this time, Fiona washing, Alec drying, he asked about the one thing they hadn't discussed.

"How was David this evening?"

Fiona stopped washing and stared out the window.

"I haven't spoken to him. He didn't answer the door when I brought him his supper."

"Is he okay?"

"I suppose so; I peeked in the kitchen window and saw him in his chair, staring at the telly. I left the food outside. I expect he's angry and upset with himself about what happened last night."

"How do you feel about what happened last night?"

Fiona thought for a moment.

"Cold. Distant. Cut off, in fact. That's the thing: he seems to be wallowing in his illness. He won't see the doctor about his moods and the whisky only makes them worse."

"I'm so sorry, Fi."

She turned to him, placed her hands on his chest, and looked up.

"Don't be. It's not your responsibility. It's not even mine. I've done everything I can. Sooner or later he has to take charge of himself."

She smiled thinly and changed the subject.

"Now, I have some of that tart left over; how about it?"

"Love some. But I'd like to check the lambs in the barn first."

Fiona started to tell him they'd be fine, but held back. He had a proprietary interest in them now, it was clear, and his worry about them was sweet.

"You do that. But take a coat; it's getting colder. I'll be in my sitting room."

When he returned, she was in her chair, her legs tucked under her, a book in her hand. Sooty was curled up on his bit of carpet, basking in the heat of the fire. Alec sat in the chair opposite and she put the book down.

"They're quite miraculous, those little balls of fluff," he said, referring to the lambs.

She looked at the bemused smile on his face as he stared at the glowing coal in the grate.

"I think you would have made a very good father; I can see you raising a good and caring son."

Alec thought about this for a moment, then said, "I'm not at all sure that's true; I'm not the ball-tossing type."

She shook her head and smiled.

"Do you really think that matters? Don't you think that any son of yours—any daughter, for that matter—would have absorbed your kindness, your passion, your spirit? Men," she continued, teasing him now. "They're so dim!"

"Women," Alec countered. "They're so mysterious."

Fiona lifted an eyebrow.

"I always thought," she said softly, "we women wore our passions on our sleeves."

Alec rose and added more coal to the fire. He stood there for a few moments, hands shoved in his pockets, listening to the damp coal hiss, watching the fire glow.

"You kissed me this afternoon," he whispered. "I can still feel it. It's as if one of these coals still smoldered on the nape of my neck."

He turned to where she sat, then looked back at the fire. A moment later, very quietly, almost as if he were talking to himself, he said, "I am afraid I am very much in love with you . . . and I don't know what to do about it."

He heard a rustling and then felt her arms around his waist, her body pressed against his back.

"Me, too," she said, "and I don't know, either. Isn't it wonderful?"

He turned to face her. She looked up at his eyes and was surprised to see they were glistening. She'd never known a man whose feelings were so close to the surface and who struggled so mightily to hide them. She stretched up on tiptoes and kissed him hard, pulled back, then kissed him again, repeatedly, gripping her hands behind his neck, pulling him closer. His lips parted and her tongue searched for his.

They separated and caught their breath, never once looking away from each other's eyes—his clear blue, hers gray-green with the strange sliver of brown.

She took his hand. "Come," she said, tugging him gently toward her bedroom.

"Wait," he said, turning to the fire and setting up the screen to protect against sparks.

"Are you always so careful?"

"Yes."

"Don't be."

Fiona switched on the light by the tall antique four-poster and began unbuttoning her blouse.

"No," he said, and she stopped, confused.

He smiled. "Please, not so quickly."

He approached and placed his warm hands, hands that felt like he'd brought the fire from the sitting room with him, on her shoulders, then slid them ever so gently down her arms to her waist, coming back up again along the sides of her torso, inside her blouse, then curving slowly around to her shoulder blades. He unhooked her bra, then traced his fingers down the length of her spine, lightly, pausing briefly at each vertebra, as if to send the warmth through his fingers and deep into her. At the base of her spine the hands spread out, his palms slipping over the waistband of her skirt, then parting to caress each cheek of her rear. She arched toward him, involuntarily, making a low, hungry sound in her throat.

He slid his hands along the smooth wool challis of the fitted skirt, following the curve of the back of her thighs, then her calves, slowly kneeling before her in the process. Then he ran them up again beneath the skirt along the outside of her legs. He looked up at her, but Fiona's eyes were closed, her teeth clenched. He reached up to unzip the skirt and slowly let it fall to her feet. His warm hands again cupped her rear and he pulled her gently toward him. Still kneeling, he brought his face toward her belly and kissed it, running the tip of his tongue around and into her belly button.

Fiona had lost touch with the room. Her skin felt electrified; the air around her vibrated. Eyes wide open now, she stared off to another world, a foreign territory, a land of exquisite desire. Her breathing was shallow and rapid. Her fingers dug into Alec's long hair, pressing his face harder against her abdomen.

Then he was lifting her high, placing her on the edge of her bed. He ran his hands up along her sides and slipped her blouse and bra above her head in one fluid motion. She expected to feel his hands on her breasts, ached for the warmth and pressure of his hands on her breasts, but instead he pressed a kiss between and slightly above them, in the shallow hollow of her breastbone. It made her shiver. He put one hand behind her neck and with the other gently pressed her down onto the coverlet. She floated on the mattress as if upon a cloud, her legs still dangling over the edge.

He slipped off her panties and, moments later, lightning flashed: his tongue traced a line of electricity along the inside of her left thigh to the place where the fine hair curled. Her hips rose to meet him but the tongue skipped away and slipped down again, burning a path all the way down the inside of the other thigh, this time continuing to her foot, pausing there to caress each toe. His tongue was like a slender, wet finger, curling into every line and crease, then rising again, slowly— achingly slowly, maddeningly slowly—until it reached the dark arch between her legs. His tongue explored the landscape there, following the contours, savoring her earthiness.

"Oh . . . oh God," Fiona whispered to the sky that seemed to arch above her. She did not know what he was doing but she never wanted it to end. Gently, gently she rose up into that sky, higher and higher, opening to it, reaching for it, until she convulsed and the world as she knew it burst into shards of light, into shudders of joy.

Not long after, as if from a long distance, she heard him take off his clothes and pull down the coverlet. Then she felt herself being lifted again, so very gently, until she was stretched out on her bed, a pillow slipped beneath her head.

"Alec?"

"I'm here, Fi."

"Oh, sweetheart . . . that was . . . that was . . ."

"Shhh."

"No, please; I want more. I want you . . ."

She felt him slide into bed next to her, felt his long arms encircle her and hold her close.

"In time, Fi, in time."

"No, now. Now."

She felt him move. She opened her eyes and saw his lanky frame suspended above her, his sweet face searching hers.

"Are you sure?" she heard him ask.

"Yes, darling man, please!" she whispered, amazed at her certainty.

Alec rose up on his arms.

"But gently, sweetheart; it's been a very long time."

"I'll be careful," his sweet voice soothed.

And he was. He entered her wetness slowly, teasing her with his tip. Slowly, she opened to him, in a way she had not thought possible. He hovered there, moving gently, until she cried out for him. Then he slid into her, deep, so deep. Her eyes flew open and she gasped.

"Oh . . . my . . . sweet . . . man."

She wrapped her legs around him, pulling him deeper, her hips rising to meet him. They moved smoothly and rhythmically. She began to crest again. Her eyes grew wider and as he looked into them it was as if she had opened a window to her most secret place, a place of fear and vulnerability.

Then a sound rose from someplace deep inside her, a growl she did not recognize. She bucked up against him, again and again. Her hands curled into fists, and she pounded his back. On and on the pleasure flowed, wave upon wave. And then at last she felt him shudder, felt him filling her with himself, heard him groan, watched his eyes glaze over with the release and, to her astonishment, saw tears in his eyes. She pulled him down onto her breasts.

"Alec, my dear man . . ."

He tucked her head into the curve of his neck and they rolled onto their sides, with him still inside her. He hugged her with a fierceness that surprised her.

"I have been searching for you for so long . . . so very long."

She pulled him closer. "I've been waiting here all the time."

They were locked together like that when, after an interval that could have been either long or short, for time had ceased to have meaning, they fell asleep.

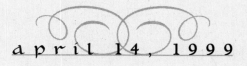

april 14, 1999

ten

*a*lec awoke to find himself alone. For the merest fraction of a second he wondered whether he'd dreamed the night before, but the covers on the other side of the bed had been folded back carefully and the slight depression on the mattress where Fiona had slept was still visible.

Sun flooded the airy bedroom. He looked at the bedside clock and sighed. What he wanted was for her to still be at his side. What he wanted was to scatter kisses across her body like confetti. What he wanted was to make love with her all morning, and all afternoon if they had it in them. But love was one thing, business another; Fiona would be downstairs getting breakfast ready for her guests. He checked the sky, decided this was the day to try the mountain again, and dressed quickly. On his way to the kitchen, he noticed the dining room table had been set for three people.

He stepped into the kitchen just as Fiona was filling a large teapot with boiling water. He slipped behind and wrapped his arms around her, burying his face in her silky hair. She turned to face him.

"Sleep well, did you?" she said in a purringly provocative voice.

"Umm. Better than I have in years."

"It's probably that expensive mattress I bought."

"Yes. No doubt that's it."

They stood awkwardly for a moment.

"I love you, Fiona. Beyond measure. But I don't know how—"

"Shh," she interrupted. "Let's not think about that now. Can't we just have this magic for a while?"

"Of course we can. For as long as you like."

Quietly, with his arms still around her, he asked, "Have you taken David his breakfast yet?"

He felt Fiona slump.

"Yes."

"How was he this morning?"

"Fine, I suppose. I don't know. I didn't see him. There was a note at the door apologizing for the night before last. I went in and left the food, but he wasn't there. Off helping Owen, I imagine. He hardly touched what I left last night. Honestly, I don't know what keeps him going. Sometimes, I think it's rage."

Alec felt suddenly helpless. He wanted to ease Fiona's anguish but knew it rose from a place, a world, a life of which he was not a part. At the same time, he confronted—not for the first time this morning—the fact that he was in love with, and had made love to, this troubled man's wife. He'd never done anything like that before; it violated the most basic standards by which he'd tried to live. And yet, at the same time that he knew it was wrong, he knew at the very foundation of his being that it was right and good. Alec realized he lived in one reality and David lived in another. Fiona was the one who moved between them, and he suddenly felt enormous sympathy for her.

Fiona changed the subject. "Will you go up the mountain again today?"

"Yes; it's clear."

"It is, for now at least, but it's very cold."

"My God, we're reduced to talking about the weather."

This, at least, brought the smile back to her face. She pushed him away playfully.

"I have guests to serve breakfast to, I'll have you know. I can't be standing here fending off your advances."

"I hadn't noticed that you'd tried."

"Be that as it may," she said, grinning.

"I noticed you set three places in the dining room; have I been banished from the kitchen?"

"Of course not; I just thought you might enjoy the Llewellyns, especially the husband. A bit of a character, he is. And, I admit, I thought I should at least pretend I'm not running a house of ill repute."

They heard footsteps descending the front stairs. She stretched up and kissed him quickly.

"Go be charming," she said, handing him a teapot.

He entered the breakfast room just as the Llewellyns did. They were an older couple—in their early seventies, he guessed. They seemed to him to have become mirror images of each other: he was compact, ruddy; she round and rosy-faced. Her hair was short and silvery; he had an equally silvery bristle-brush mustache. His own hair was so close-cropped he was nearly bald. Alec took him for ex-military. They were dressed for walking—at least the way English people of a certain age dressed for walking, which was to say that Mrs. Llewellyn had on a long floral wool skirt and sturdy shoes, topped by a sweater in a clashing pattern. Her husband wore brown twill trousers, a countryman's tattersall shirt, an olive-green tie, and a tweed jacket.

"Ah, Mr. Edwards," the husband proclaimed to the dining room and the world at large, "how very kind of you! Tea, piping hot, on the spot!"

Alec smiled. "Actually, the name's Hudson, Alec Hudson. I'm a guest here, too. But you're right about the tea. Shall I pour?"

"Goodness," the gentleman blustered, "frightfully sorry . . . just assumed . . . well, there it is . . . wrong." He grimaced and quickly sat.

"Thank you, Mr. Hudson," the man's wife said. "Tea would be very nice indeed, wouldn't it, Richard?"

"Capital," he said. "Splendid!"

Alec filled their cups and then his own and sat at his place.

There was an awkward silence. Then Alec ventured, "I understand from Mrs. Edwards that you're walkers!"

At this they came alive again. Mrs. Llewellyn said, "We are, and we hear you've had quite a walk yourself."

"Yes, well, I suppose I have," Alec answered. "From Heathrow to here. But it was just terrific; I love this country."

"You're American, I gather," Llewellyn asserted rather than asked.

"I confess I am."

"Knew a lot of them back in the Middle East."

"Now, Richard," his wife cautioned.

"Served there after the war, you know," he continued, ignoring her. "MI6. Intelligence. In the Saudi. Iraq, too. Bloody tribal barbarians is what I say. Take Iraq now: utter cock-up on our part after the first war to try to make 'em into a nation, Shias, Sunnis, Kurds. Impossible. Never happen. Didn't, actually. Not till this Hussein fellow came along and got 'em sorted."

"Well, yes, I suppose murdering your opponents is a very effective way of getting things sorted."

"Quite right. Don't agree with his methods, of course, or his allies, come to that. Still, there you are."

Alec wasn't sure where that was and was about to ask when Fiona breezed in.

"Are you two talking politics already?" she chided. She set plates down before the Llewellyns. Richard peered at his.

"What's this then?" he asked.

"Eggs Florentine, grilled mushrooms, and local sausage. Would you care for white toast or brown?"

Mrs. Llewellyn took over. "White for us both, thank you," she said, "and not too dark."

"Of course. And you, Mr. Hudson?" she asked, giving him the slightest wink.

"Brown please, Mrs. Edwards."

"Brown it is, and I'll be right in with your own breakfast."

"No hurry," he called after her as she left.

Richard Llewellyn leaned across the table toward Alec and grumbled, "Not a proper fry-up is all I can say; how's a man to keep going till lunchtime, eh?"

"Lots of vitamins in the spinach," Alec suggested.

"Spinach! That's what's in it? Humph."

Mrs. Llewellyn was studying her plate as if it were a crossword puzzle.

"Please," Alec said with a sweeping gesture, "go right ahead; don't wait for me or it will get cold." He watched with delight as the couple poked tentatively at the eggs.

Fiona swept in again with his plate and the toast.

"This looks splendid, Mrs. Edwards," he said a bit more loudly than was necessary. He could see Fiona stifling a giggle.

"Mr. Llewellyn, speaking of politics, did you know that Mr. Hudson here once worked for President Carter?" Fiona announced.

"Carter!" the man sputtered. "Bloody hash he made of it in Iran with those hostages! You weren't military, I suppose?"

"No, I wasn't," Alec answered without elaborating.

"Should have bombed Tehran is what he should have done; that'd teach them."

"I'm sure you're right, sir. To hell with the hostages," Alec replied without the slightest hint of irony.

"Damn right! Matter of principle."

They ate quietly for a while, then Alec said, "Pity you don't have any ex–prime ministers as active at trying to help the world as former president Carter."

"Don't need to," Llewellyn said through a mouth full of sausage. "Got the Queen!"

"Ah, the Queen. Forgot all about her. Sorry. Very active in international humanitarian causes she is, I'm sure."

Llewellyn didn't seem to know how to react to that and simply snorted.

Alec finished his breakfast and stood. "Well, I'm off; see you on the mountain later?"

Both Llewellyns looked up as if he were daft. "Good heavens, no," Mrs. Llewellyn piped. "We're bird-watching on the estuary!"

"Well, perhaps this evening then," Alec continued. "Think I'll take my plate in and fetch my boots. Lovely day for birding."

Llewellyn waved him off, mouth full again; his roly-poly wife smiled vacantly.

In the kitchen, Fiona was leaning up against the counter facing him, her hand over her mouth and her eyes dancing with mirth.

"When are they leaving?!" Alec hissed under his breath.

Dropping her hand, she whispered, "Not till tomorrow, I'm afraid; aren't they a pair? Might ask them to stay on just for the entertainment!"

Alec wrapped Fiona in his arms and gave her rear a lascivious squeeze. She stifled a giggle. He pulled away and gave her a quick kiss.

"I'm off, Fi. For goodness' sake don't worry about me."

"How will you go?"

"Up by way of the Fox's Path, then down the long way, on the old Pony Track. Easier on the knees that way."

"Mind that Fox's Path, now," she cautioned. "It's nothing but steep scree near the top. Hard going. Do you have a compass this time?"

"Yes, thanks. Stupid of me not to carry one the other day. I'll be more careful this time."

She went to hand him his day pack, groaning when she tried to lift it. "Lord, that's heavy!"

"It's Gwynne's ashes; she was a big girl."

"Take good care, Alec."

"I promise."

He hesitated a moment. "Brenin Llwyd didn't get me but I'm afraid Fiona Edwards has. I'm very interested in coming down again safely."

Fiona heard the emotion in his voice. Her heart swelled and she could feel her eyes brimming. She reached up and gave him a fierce kiss.

"I'll be waiting."

In the back room he laced up his boots, grabbed his walking stick, then stepped out into the yard. She was right; it was cold. The sun had cleared the summit, but frost lay on the ground in the shadow of the barn and crunched under his boots. He walked down the lane a hundred yards or so to the spot where the footpath sign pointed east, away from the farmyard, and looked back. Fiona was at the kitchen window, watching him. He waved, then went through a stock gate, closing and latching it behind him.

For reasons she couldn't pin down, Fiona felt apprehensive as Alec disappeared into the oak wood beside the lane. She knew he was an experienced climber. He knew the mountain. He was fit. But fit people died on Cadair Idris all the time. She heard the footsteps of her other guests in the front hall and turned away from the window to see them off.

Alec broke out of the wood, climbed a ladder stile built over a lichen-encrusted stone wall, and found himself in a lush green pasture filled with ewes and lambs. Owen, who was leaning against a wall on the other side drinking from a thermos, gave him a wave. To his surprise, Jack was there, too, herding sheep. The dog raced around the perimeter of the chaotically milling ewes, gradually drawing them together. From time to time he'd crouch, haunches high, muzzle on the ground, staring down the sheep. Then, in an instant, he'd adjust his place and drop again, his ever-vigilant eyes never leaving the flock. The closer the sheep bunched, the edgier they became, watching the dog's every movement with rheumy red eyes and crashing into one another. From time to time Owen whistled softly and the dog reacted in an instant, herding the skittish flock toward an open gate in the stone wall. The dog's concentration was mesmerizing, his movements low to the ground, his body rigid. Alec reached Owen just as he was closing the gate to the new pasture.

"Morning, Owen! I thought Jack was useless with the sheep."

"Useless with David," Owen said, "but fine with me. Good with the sheep and good company in the bargain."

Jack's ears perked and he barked.

"Speaking of David, I thought he'd be here with you."

"Looks like I'm working alone today. Saw him awhile back, walking toward the westward pasture. Reckon he's over there checking on the lambs. Or maybe back at his place by now. Too busy earlier to see if he'd come back down."

Owen nodded at Alec's pack. "Giving it another try?"

"Yup. Good day for it, I think."

"Maybe," Owen said, scanning the sky to the northwest, which Alec now noticed was turning milky. "Might get some weather later," Owen added. "You know you're taking the hard way up? Fox's Path is brutal near the top."

"I know," Alec said. "I thought I'd tackle it early while I have the energy, and take the easy way down."

"Good plan, I suppose. Pony Track's easy but boring if you have to walk it both ways, like the tourists do. Don't think there will be many of them up there today, though. Too cold. You're the only one I've seen this morning."

"That's fine with me; I prefer the solitude. Good luck with the lambs today."

Alec patted the young man's shoulder and headed uphill. He'd grown fond of him and thought that if he'd had a son, he'd have liked him to turn out like Owen. Kind. Thoughtful. Responsible.

The footpath through the scrubby uplands was faintly visible, but it was too early in the year for it to be well worn, so Alec paid attention as he climbed. The track rose through a moderately steep draw and then opened out along a ridge. After only perhaps a mile, he skirted the outlet of a small lake, Llyn Gafr. Beyond it the hillside steepened sharply and he settled into a slow but steady rocking gait taught him by a friend who had climbed Everest. Instead of just powering up a steep incline, this technique had you pause for just a fraction of a second on each step, briefly locking, and thereby resting, the downhill leg. Once you got the rhythm right, you could climb without stopping—slow and steady, like the tortoise in his successful race with the hare.

The landscape here was rough pasture, grass and bracken combined, broken by ledges and outcrops and spots he could tell were soggy underfoot by the reedy sedges growing there. He heard a skylark trill and saw it fifty feet or so away, hovering over what he guessed was a ground nest. Now that the sun had cleared the summit, the grassy patches sparkled with English daisies. But it wasn't a warm sun at all, and he was glad he was climbing; it kept his internal furnace burning.

After a quarter mile of steep slogging, he crested a rise and found before him Llyn y Gadair, a smooth-surfaced glacial tarn clasped in a bowl of steep, scree-scattered cliffs. Beneath the cliffs the lake looked as if it were filled with mercury, quivering silver in the weak light. This was one of Cadair Idris's often-painted beauty spots, he knew, but he found Llyn Cau, where he'd been at about this time three days earlier, far more dramatic. There was something unfriendly, almost forbidding, about this part of the mountain, he decided. The feeling was instinctive, nothing he could define.

He put the pack down, pulled out his water bottle, took a deep gulp, and scanned the ascent route. Like Llyn Cau, the path up to the summit plateau from Llyn y Gadair curved up along a viciously steep shoulder of the mountain to the left of the lake. Unlike Llyn Cau, this one was composed of loose rock and gravel, not hard ledges with firm footing. He looked at it and knew it was going to be far harder than the previous ascent. He slugged back more water, put the bottle away, and hoisted the pack back onto his shoulders.

It was every bit as bad as he'd thought it would be. The higher he climbed, the steeper the trail became, and the worse the footing. He figured the slope was at least thirty degrees. When a slope gets that steep, he knew, your natural tendency is to lean into it. But on a loose surface like this one, that's not only unwise but potentially deadly. Gravity wants to push you down. If you lean into the slope it pushes you down the slope. But if you stay as upright as possible, as if perpendicular to an imagined flat line, gravity pushes you *into* the slope and reduces the risk of slipping. It's counterintuitive, but crucial. Even climbing upright, though, progress was slow; it was two steps forward, one step slipping back, and it was wearing him out. He felt as if he were a ship plowing through heavy seas trailing a wake of scattering stones. The route ahead was even steeper. The English, he knew, charmingly called this a "scramble." *Scrambling is fine for younger folk,* he thought to himself, *but hell on older guys.* He stopped and caught his breath. There was only one thing to do, he decided: charge the slope. He grabbed his stick by the shank and ran, trying to move his feet faster uphill than they could slip downhill. It was working. He was churning up the slope like a machine, arms and legs pumping, head down to watch his footing. After what seemed forever but was probably no more than another ten minutes, he crested the rim at last and flopped down on a block of granite the size of a bed. His chest heaved and his heart pounded. His thighs were on fire, his knees wobbly with exhaustion. Once again he wondered whether he was getting too old for this sort of thing. He thought about the Llewelyns and their bird-watching, laughed, and shouted "No way!" to the sky.

That was when he noticed that the sky to the west had changed from milky to dark. He could see an angry squall line moving in fast off the Irish Sea. In what seemed like a matter of seconds, the sea, and then the coastline, vanished behind a curtain of what he assumed was heavy rain.

"Miss Davis," he said to himself as much as to the ashes in his pack, "time to move."

The good news was that he could see the short, white concrete trig pillar that marked Pen y Gadair, the summit of Cadair Idris. He struck off toward it as fast as the boulder-strewn ground would permit. The squall line reached it before he did, and the marker disappeared. He stopped to fish his rain parka out of the pack and heard a strange hissing sound off in the distance. The air around him went from dead calm to a gale in moments, and the temperature dropped. He yanked up the zipper, pulled up the hood, slung on the pack, and looked up. It wasn't a rain squall, he suddenly realized. The hissing, the invisibility: it was a hailstorm. A mean one.

Alec knew where the trig point had been moments ago. He had a pretty good idea how far away it was. The visibility was, thankfully, a little better than it had been on his previous ascent. He headed roughly west, directly into the wind. The size of the hailstones varied from moment to moment; they started small, suddenly grew large as marbles, then became pea-sized. They were blowing almost horizontally, directly at him; he pulled the hood of his jacket close around his eyes to protect his face. After perhaps ten minutes of clambering and slipping over the icy rock field, he found the pillar. His geographical memory was working just fine. He put the pillar at his back and the wind on his left shoulder and stumbled north over the rocky plateau toward the primitive stone shelter he knew was in that direction.

He found it almost immediately and ducked beneath its rusted corrugated metal roof. It was only a low stone lean-to, but he was out of the elements. Despite the chill of the day, he'd been climbing in the sleeveless shirt he preferred. That had been more than enough protection as he sweated his way up the steep north face of the mountain. The shirt was made of a fabric that wicked moisture away from his body and dried quickly. He took off his parka so the heat of his body could speed the evaporation. He'd feel cold for a few minutes, but not long enough to get chilled through. When the shirt dried, he pulled his expedition shirt out of the pack, put it on over the sleeveless one, then slipped into the parka again. He hunched down to conserve body heat and waited for the storm to pass. He realized he was hungry and ate part of the sandwich Fiona had made: sharp cheddar cheese with Indian chutney on granary bread. It was perfect, and the hot spice of the chutney was welcome.

Beyond the lean-to opening, the conditions kept changing. The hail lessened, replaced for a while by wet snow. Then the hail began again. While he waited, he packed up his lunch and removed the heavy gray plastic box that held Gwynne's remains.

Remains. It had never occurred to him until this moment how wrong that word was. The rubble in the box was not what remained of Gwynne. What remained of Gwynne was the sheer joy she had brought to his life and to the lives of everyone she touched, the incandescence of her smile, the unexpectedly throaty laugh, the childlike enthusiasm, the creative genius.

But something else, something more important, something everlasting: before their troubles had begun, she'd taught him to love. She made expressing love safe. She also made it acceptable for him to play. She had found and mined a deep seam of silliness in him that brought laughter to everything they did together, no matter how mundane or tedious. None of these things—loving, playing, laughing—had ever come easily to him. What came easily, what was second nature to him, was caretaking, planning ahead, vigilance, protecting and, above all, being responsible. What had driven him away from her in the end was his anger with what he saw as her irresponsibility, her inability to anticipate the consequences of her actions or her inaction, her refusal to take care of herself, and the ever-increasing weight of being all those things for her. It was, he'd come to realize, a very old anger, one from childhood. It had only partly to do with her.

He sat on the floor of the hut, unsealed the box with his Swiss army knife, and looked inside. The material was gray and grainy. It was the ruins of Gwynne, not her remains. It was nothing more than the ground-up bits of a superstructure, a skeleton that could have been anyone's—it had nothing to do with Gwynne. His own ashes would look exactly the same. He jostled the box and the contents shifted and rattled against the sides, a chaos of chalky pumice, nothing more.

Chaos. It was precisely this he had fought against and feared all his life: the collapse of order, the triumph of confusion, the havoc caused by irresponsibility. The aspects of himself that he had long believed were noble—his vigilance, his caretaking, his thoughtfulness—were not so much meant to benefit those he loved, he realized suddenly, as they were to reduce the thing he feared most: chaos. It put him suddenly in mind of Jack herding the sheep—the watchfulness, the intensity, the split-second response.

And he realized that what had attracted him to Gwynne in the beginning—her playfulness, her abandon—was what had repelled him in the end. She was his opposite. She was chaos to his order, carelessness to his vigilance, impulse to his rationality. And when they separated, he became, once again, half a human: competent, conscientious, caring—and safe. Vigilance elbowed aside joy; protectiveness squeezed out love.

If the pulverized particles in the box were not, in any meaningful way, his Gwynne, then scattering them on this bleak, weathershattered summit was not abandoning her after all. She was still out there. Her remains were what resided in the hearts of those she loved. Perhaps this strange request of hers was really meant to say, "Leave these stony shards of me among the rocks from which my family rose, long ago. Then take the rest of me, the things I was, the things I tried to teach you, wherever you go from here."

He was crying now, for the first time since her death. Crying at the stupidity of their separation and divorce. At the years they had both spent alone. At the waste of Gwynne's death. And perhaps at the enormity of the task before him: taking Gwynne's lessons to heart. Living them.

Alec had no idea how long he'd sat there holding the box, but in the meantime the weather had begun to clear. The clouds had shredded and the sky was milky blue above them. It was time. He rose and carried the box a hundred yards or so across the icy boulder field to the concrete pillar and slowly circumnavigated the summit, tipping out a thin stream of the brittle dust as he went.

He told her again how much he loved her, about how he'd never stopped believing in her, about her courage at the end, about the beauty she had brought to the world, about the joy she found in it, and about how desperately he missed her. When he'd completed the circle he returned to the pillar. He put the lid on the now-empty box, slipped it under his arm, and called out across the summit, *"Croeso!"* It was the Welsh word for welcome. He'd found it in the dictionary Fiona had given him. He wanted to welcome Gwynne's bones home.

He looked up and saw a peregrine falcon hovering high above

him. The raptor hung motionless on the updraft rising from the cliff
edge. Then it slipped gracefully off the wind, wings still motionless,
and ghosted west toward the sea. When he looked at the ground again,
he found he could no longer distinguish Gwynne's ashes from the rocks
on which he'd scattered them. It put him in mind of the first law of
thermodynamics: energy can be neither created nor destroyed, only
changed. Somewhere, Gwynne's energy still radiated.

He returned to the shelter and picked up his pack, so light now
without the ashes he felt he could almost soar like the falcon. The wind
had dropped, but it had gotten much colder. He thought about the
lambs that weren't penned in the barn and worried whether they'd
make it. Life is so inexpressibly delicate. He picked up his walking
stick and set off to the west, staying close to the northern rim of the
cliffs. Fiona would not have to worry; there was plenty of time for him
to get down this afternoon.

He had gone only a few hundred yards across the frost-shattered
granite wasteland when he caught a glint of light off to his right. In the
expanse of gray, fractured rock, it was something jarring, something
that shouldn't have been there. Alec clambered over the rocks and soon
discovered that what he'd seen was an empty whisky bottle. What he
hadn't seen before, because it was curled up on its side behind a massive
block of stone near the cliff edge, was a man's body. The body, wearing
only trousers, boots, and a shirt, was crusted with tiny hailstones. He
brushed the rime of ice off the shoulder and head and turned the body
upon its back. He knew the face immediately, although he'd never met
the man. It was the face in the photo in the breakfast room at Tan y
Gadair. It was David Edwards.

eleven

He called David's name. No response. He slapped the man's face gently to see if he could get him to open his eyes. Again, nothing.

Alec pulled up David's ice-stiffened shirtsleeve and placed a finger below the bony edge of the man's left wrist, feeling for a pulse. He couldn't find one. He pressed his fingers into the side of David's neck and, to his amazement, felt a faint, desperately slow throbbing there. He knelt for a moment beside the inert body of Fiona's husband. In another hour, maybe less, David would be dead.

Alec looked at David's fingertips and was both surprised and relieved to see only the beginnings of frostbite. But he knew he had to get the man out of his wet clothes and into something dry. He opened his knife and carefully sliced off David's wet shirt and undershirt. He took off his own expedition shirt and patiently inched it over David's stiff, unresponsive limbs, taking care not to jostle him. He buttoned the dry shirt over David's chest and then removed the man's shoes and socks. Not far from David's body was a nearly new waxed cotton Barbour coat, but it was wet, ice encrusted, and useless. He unbuckled David's belt, unzipped his wet trousers, and eased them off. Alec always kept a spare pair of socks in his pack and now he pulled them over David's feet, noting that the toes were beginning to redden. The nylon shorts Alec wore hiking had zip-on legs; he took the legs from the pack and pulled them up as high onto David's thick thighs as they would go. Not ideal, but better than being wet. Then he took out his first aid kit. In it was a small, tightly compacted parcel roughly the size of a pack of cigarettes. It was a space blanket, a thin expanse of plastic fabric covered in a film of aluminum. It had been invented for NASA's space program and had an almost magical ability to conserve heat in a human body under the most extreme and prolonged conditions of exposure. He'd resisted buying it when he was outfitting himself for his long walk, but the salesman had persisted, and now he blessed the man. Very gently, Alec pulled David's body away from the cliff face and onto the space blanket, wrapping it around his body, mummy fashion. The blanket would not warm David, but Alec hoped it would keep him from getting colder. At a minimum, getting a layer of insulation between his body and the rock ledge upon which it lay would slow the heat loss. Just for a moment, he looked over the cliff edge. Far below, deep in the valley, was Tan y Gadair. And then Alec understood. David had come here to die. He'd known, because he knew this place so well, that the weather would turn. He'd come up here by way of the Pony Track— knowing he hadn't the strength for the Fox's Path—swallowed most of a bottle of whisky and, while looking out over his beloved farm, waited for the cold to kill him.

Hypothermia is a gradual and remarkably gentle way to go. First there is the slow, insidious chilling, then the desperate, uncontrollable trembling—the body's built-in attempt to generate heat through movement. When that fails, there is a gradual slide into unconsciousness— peaceful, almost blissful. David's suicide was well thought out and competently executed. He wondered if David had a life insurance policy. If he did, this was a way of ending things that would be unlikely to be questioned: a hill farmer caught out in the elements.

Alec had no way of knowing how long David had been here or how far the shutting-down process in his body had progressed. He wondered whether David had greeted the hailstorm with gratitude, hoping it would speed him to his chosen end, or whether he'd already been unconscious by then. The best Alec could do, he knew, was try to keep David's condition from deteriorating further. He scanned the sky: scudding clouds but more blue than gray, and no immediate sign of rain. He checked the blanket, threw on the pack, grabbed his walking stick, and raced west along the summit rim, back to the Fox's Path again. Descending it was dangerous, he knew, but the easier Pony Track would take too long. He needed to reach help as quickly as possible.

Alec started down the steep scree slope, picking his way as quickly as he could, afraid more than anything else of wrenching a knee or breaking an ankle and being of no use to anyone. In some places he slid for several feet in the loose rubble, as if riding an escalator. Far below him he could see the black water of Llyn y Gadair and beyond that Llyn Gafr and the farm. He started sliding again, but this time it didn't stop and he realized with horror that the slide was taking him to the cliff face. He dropped to the ground, flipped onto his belly and, with both hands, dug the hooked horn handle of his walking stick into the scree, like a mountaineer's ice axe. A moment later the handle snagged a corner of bedrock. The scree slide clattered past him and over the edge, but Alec stopped.

He didn't move. He rested, his face and body pressed into the slope. Then, continuing to grip the stick with his right hand, he let go with his left and scraped away the rubble around the handle until he found the bit of ledge upon which it had caught. Then he pulled himself up into a kneeling position and looked around. He hadn't slid far; then again, there wasn't far to slide before you tipped over the edge and dropped to the shore of the lake far below. He pulled up his right knee and dug his foot into the hollow of the ledge. Then he rose to a standing position, stabilized himself with his walking stick, and stretched his other foot to what looked like another bit of firm rock. Slowly, in this crablike manner, he regained the path.

It was barely midafternoon, but he was thinking ahead. In a few hours the light would begin to fail. David needed to be brought down immediately and hospitalized. Even if he could get him down to the farm, there was no way to safely revive him there.

When Alec finally reached Llyn y Gadair, he started running down the steep, grassy hillside toward the farm. It was farther than he could run in one go, so he walked partway, then began running again. The grass was wet and several times he fell. When he crested the last ridge he was relieved to see Owen still in the lambing pastures below. He called out, but was too far away to be heard above the bleating of the sheep. It was Jack who saw him first and started barking. Owen looked up the hill and knew immediately something was wrong. He scrambled over the ladder stile and met Alec on the hillside, Jack at his heels.

Alec's chest was on fire; he wasn't used to running. He bent over, palms on knees to catch his breath.

"David," he heaved when Owen reached him. "Dying."

"What?!"

"Up there," Alec panted. "On the rim. Tried to kill himself. Whisky and exposure." As he caught his breath, Alec described how he'd found David and what he'd done. "I left him wrapped up, but he's unconscious and I don't know how long he'll live. Don't know how we'll get him down, either."

Owen looked up at the mountain. "Good Lord."

"Here's what we need to do," Alec said, getting his breath back now. "You go down to the farm and tell Fiona to raise the rescue people. I'll go back up and try to keep him alive. You join me there. All right?"

"Alec, look at you; you're knackered."

It was true; he was exhausted, dirty, and bleeding.

"No," he lied, "I'm fine. I walked here from London, remember?" Owen hesitated.

"Look," Alec said, "I know how to take care of someone with hypothermia, at least until help comes. I need you to tell Fiona and to get me that help. Besides, with those young legs of yours, you'll probably catch up with me before I reach him again. We have to get him down, Owen, very soon. Before dark."

"I can get the Land Rover up as far as Llyn y Gadair. Where is he?"

"Just west of the summit, near the northern rim. You'll see me, I'm sure. And Owen? Be careful on the scree slope, okay?"

"Right. Come on, Jackie!"

Owen sprinted across the fields toward the farm with Jack at his heels, the dog barking as if he knew what was happening. Alec turned toward the mountain, heaved a sigh, and started back up again. At Llyn y Gadair, he stopped and ate the rest of the sandwich. He'd need it.

Fiona was upstairs tidying the Llewellyns' room when she heard Jack barking and then someone pounding on the back door. When she got to the kitchen, Owen had already let himself in.

"Owen?"

"Something's happened."

"Alec!"

"No, ma'am, it's David; Alec found him on the mountain." Owen hesitated. Did she need to know David had tried to kill himself? He wasn't sure. "Injured, I guess; then he got too cold and couldn't come down. He's unconscious, but alive. Or he was when Alec left him."

"Where's Alec?"

"Gone back up."

"Jesus."

"We need to call the Mountain Rescue."

Fiona ran to the front hall phone and punched in 999.

"Mountain Rescue, please," she said to the operator who routed calls for emergency services. As she waited to be connected her head swirled with images—David two nights ago, assaulting her; yesterday's untouched food; the note he'd left by the door this morning: *Fiona, I am so very sorry, David*.

A man's voice came on the line.

"This is Fiona Edwards at Tan y Gadair farm, Dolgellau," she said. "There's been an accident on Cadair . . ."

When she was done, she turned to Owen. "They're sending a team from Outward Bound Wales and contacting the RAF to see if a helicopter is available. They've asked me to stay by the phone in case they need further instructions. You follow Alec and do what you can to help. Take the torch in the boot room to signal in case it gets dark before they get there. And be careful, both of you."

"Yes, ma'am. Will you be all right, Mrs. Edwards?"

"I'll be fine; be off now."

She followed Owen to the door and watched him race across the farmyard. He leaped into his old Land Rover and roared off toward the upland pastures.

Fiona returned to the kitchen and sat heavily on a chair at the table, the table at which she had been so happy these last three nights, the table that had become a candlelit circumference of comfort that encompassed just her and Alec, a world of deep happiness. Now everything was changing again. Jack sat beside her and put his head in her lap. She stroked his fur and stared at the kitchen window, the window where she'd seen that first flash of blue from Alec's backpack, blue as his eyes.

She wasn't at all sure she'd be fine. For the second time in a week, her world had been turned upside down. She had found the great love of her life, or rather he'd found her. They'd recognized each other instantly. She had never known it was possible to love anyone so quickly or so completely.

Now David was on the mountain and Alec was climbing up again to save him. She did not believe for a minute that there had been an accident. There was no reason for David to be up there, none at all. There were no sheep there; ancient stone walls, newer wire fences, and iron gates kept them from the upper reaches of the mountain. David had gone up there deliberately to end his life, up to the mountain that was so much a part of him.

She knew that depression was a common effect of the poisoning. The doctor had warned her. It wasn't clear, according to the studies, whether it was a direct result of the chemicals or an indirect result, brought on by the sudden loss of function—the weakness, the loss of memory—and the imposed isolation from much of normal life. Some of the farmers who'd been affected by the poison had committed suicide. Not many, but it happened. But the changes in David's mood had been so gradual. It had already been three years since the sickness began. He'd been moody and distant ever since—morose, as if the spirit had been drained from him. She should have seen this coming.

Alec had just begun ascending the scree slope of the Fox's Path when he heard Owen's Land Rover grinding up through the steep pastures in low gear. It was slow going as Owen detoured around ledges and outcrops and avoided boggy areas. Once he got above the lower pastures where the sheep were penned for lambing, though, he could leave the gates in the walls open and continue without stopping to close them again.

For the second time, Alec churned his unwilling legs up the last of the scree slope, finally reaching the summit plateau, more exhausted than he could ever recall. Owen was close on his heels. Alec rested until the young man flopped down next to him.

"Bloody scary, that route," Owen gasped. "Can't believe people do it for fun. Where is he?"

"Follow me, but watch your footing."

They picked their way westward over the rocks, past the little stone shelter, then headed toward the northern rim.

David lay as Alec had left him: swaddled in the foil blanket, head to toe. He looked like someone in a body bag. Alec lifted the blanket from David's face. The skin was a mottled blue-gray.

"Jesus! Surely he's dead, Alec."

Alec placed a finger against David's carotid artery; the pulse was still there, though very slow and faint. He lifted both eyelids and saw that David's pupils were dilated.

"Almost, Owen, but not quite. Not yet anyway. There's a phrase you learn when you take first aid training for hypothermia: 'the victim isn't dead until he's warm and dead.' David's in a sort of deep freeze. His body has automatically shut down anything that isn't critical. He's breathing, but only barely; it's all he needs because so much of him is shut down. Part of the problem here is that I can't tell whether he's unconscious because of the hypothermia or the alcohol . . . or both."

"That's my fault."

"What is?"

"The whisky. He's been having me get it for him in town for weeks. I didn't want to but he got really nasty about it and I did it."

"Owen," Alec said, putting his hand on the boy's shoulder, "you didn't cause this. None of it is your fault. This was his choice. He didn't even need the liquor to do this."

"What do we do?"

"Sadly, almost nothing."

"But surely we should try to warm him up?"

"That's the one thing we surely *don't* want to do. Let's say we start rubbing his arms or legs. That will eventually warm the peripheral blood vessels in his skin and limbs and get the blood there moving again. When that cold blood gets to David's heart, the temperature of the heart will drop suddenly and it may well stop. We'd kill him."

"Shall we try to carry him down to the farm?" Owen asked, desperate to do something.

"No, moving him around would do the same thing, only quicker."

"So we just sit here?"

"We just sit here, yes. And we keep him wrapped up to conserve what heat he's got and check his pulse every few minutes. If it stops, we try CPR, though that's not likely to help. You'd think breathing warm air from our lungs into his would help, but the difference we'd make would be negligible. The good news is that it's getting warmer. That helps a lot. What did Mountain Rescue say?"

"They're sending the Outward Bound Search and Rescue Team from Aberdovey, and they'll try to call in a Royal Air Force rescue helicopter. Aberdovey's close, less than twenty miles away, depending on what route they decide to take. There's an old farm track that comes up from Llanfihangle, just southwest of here. They'll be able to get at least halfway up the mountain before they have to get out and walk. What with the call-out and the climb, I reckon it'll be an hour or more. Helicopter will come from RAF-Valley, a base on the Isle of Anglesey. It's near Holyhead, where the ferry to Ireland is. It's about sixty miles. My guess is they'll coordinate so the helicopter gets here after the rescue team has David ready."

Alec thought for a moment. "We should make it as easy for the helicopter pilot as we can, since we have the time. Why don't I stay here
and keep an eye on David while you go find a spot beyond this rock
field where it might land. I know there are grassy areas to the east in
the direction of Mynydd Moel, but that's a long way to carry David. See
if there's someplace west of here that'll be closer, why don't you."

"Right. You'll be okay here?"

"Just fine. With any luck David will be, too."

Owen dashed off westward, bounding from rock to rock like a
mountain goat. Alec checked David's pulse again and found it, then
scanned the sky. Three hours of daylight left, but he knew David didn't
have that long.

Fiona drifted around the house. She realized she had no idea whether
she would be home when the Llewellyns returned. She wondered if she
shouldn't send them elsewhere. In the end, she wrote them a note:

> *Dear Mr. and Mrs. Llewellyn,*
>
> *I am afraid there has been an accident on the moun-
> tain involving my husband. You are welcome to stay to-
> night, but I regret to say I may not be here in the morning
> to prepare your breakfast. You will, of course, not be
> charged for this evening's accommodation. For breakfast
> tomorrow, may I recommend the Royal Ship Hotel just off
> the Square. Please accept my apologies for this inconve-
> nience.*
>
> *Respectfully,*
> *Fiona Edwards*

Next she phoned the Tourist Information Center and told Bronwen not to send anyone to her for the next week. Finally, she called the

guests who had already booked reservations and left them the Information Center's number. Thankfully, in most cases she got answering machines and simply left an apologetic message.

Then, because she did not know what else to do, Fiona checked the flowers in the dining room and the guests' sitting room. There she noticed Alec's notebook lying open, facedown, where he'd left it the day before. She turned it over and found he'd written a poem:

S K I N   H U N G E R

Ravenous,
I cleave to you,
you welcome me
and we two
make a three
who is raw desire
and naked need,
who is born of loss
and longing
for the simple gift
of skin on skin;
the hunger is expressed
the way the fingers drift
across a rising breast,
the way the nails rake
ripples down an arching spine,
the way a moistened tip
of tongue licks paths of fire
across a curving neck,
the way our arms clutch
closely as we crest,
the way we curl together later,

like some rare new life form
joined at groin and chest:
immortal, soaring, pressing
out against the membrane
of the known, slipping
through a crack in time
and space to find ourselves
a story just begun—
written on living skin
with trembling hands,
turning to page one . . .

She pressed the notebook to her breast and began to cry. She cried because she knew now with certainty that Alec loved her, and because only now did she realize how long she had ached for a man who was a kindred spirit. And yet, if her husband—her *husband!*—were to die in this way, under these circumstances, how could she ever put that horror behind her and love Alec freely? It was beyond her; the whole situation was beyond her.

High up on the north rim, Alec sat with his back against an outcropping and waited for Owen to return, from time to time checking the pulse in David's neck.

The man did not deserve to die; what had happened to him was brutally unfair. Alec wondered whether he would have been able to cope with such disabilities as long as David had. Alec had always thought suicide the coward's way out, but now, as he sat beside this comatose man, he could understand why David wanted to kill himself—not just to end his own misery, not just because he could no longer do the work that defined him as a man, but to free his wife and child from his anger and bitterness. Striking his wife of more than twenty years must have shocked him even more than it had Fiona. Perhaps he no longer recognized himself. Perhaps he was horrified by what he did recognize: that demon who lives in us all but who, under normal circumstances, we keep in the darkest shadows of our soul.

After perhaps half an hour, Owen returned.

"There you are; I was beginning to worry about you."

"Sorry. I found a possible landing spot not far to the west—a bit of a slope, but not bad. I decided to mark it with a wide circle of stones. That's what took so long. I thought an artificial shape up here would be something the pilot would notice."

"Good thinking."

"Any change?"

"None. Which is good, actually; I think he's stable."

Owen sat beside him. Alec saw that his hands were raw from hauling the rocks. The two of them sat quietly for a few minutes.

"Owen," Alec said finally, "last night you mentioned that your mother lived in town. I wondered what happened to your family's farm."

Owen looked out across the valley to the north.

"You see where the Mawddach comes down to the sea, away off to the west there?" he said, pointing.

"Yes?" Alec replied.

"There's a town there, just behind that rocky headland. Place called Barmouth. Name's an English corruption of the Welsh word, Abermawddach—meaning mouth of the Mawddach. Anyway, if you carry along to the north on the coast road, the farms begin again right at the edge of town. My father had one of them, and a lovely place it was. Broad pastures sloping down from the hills all the way to the cliffs above the sea. Pretty as it was, it wasn't arable. Bedrock just beneath the turf. We grew hay and had dairy cows and sheep both. Five years ago next month, my da was on the tractor, going down the main road to one of the pasture gates, when he rounded a bend and a car passing a slow-moving lorry hit him head-on. Killed him instantly. Driver walked away. The lorry driver was a local, a friend of ours. He came up to the house and told us. Shattered he was; never been the same since.

"After we buried my da we found out the farm was in bad financial shape. My mam never knew. We lost the farm, but the insurance was enough to get my mother a nice little place in Dolgellau. Never had liked Barmouth, anyway; too touristy for her. Me, too, come to that. I live with her, though she won't have me looking after her. Tough lady, my mam—Anna's her name—but nice tough, if you know what I mean."

"I think I do," Alec said, thinking of his own mother.

"I think she prefers living in town, you know; lots of people to talk to, everything in walking distance, especially now she's got this new hip."

"But you don't like it there."

"Nah. I'm not a townie; I'm meant to be on a farm." Owen nodded to the valley. "Like this one. I love it here."

"You seem to be well loved here as well."

"You reckon?"

"Fiona thinks the world of you."

Owen's head jerked up and turned away from him. "Hear that?"

"What?"

"A whistle. I heard a whistle. The kind you blow into. I think they're here already. Bloody amazing; they must have run up the mountain!"

The next time, they both heard it. Owen stood and clambered over the rocks to a high point and began calling. Alec rose stiffly, then bent over, picked up the whisky bottle, and flung it over the cliff edge.

After a minute or two Owen saw two men climb into sight, then more, all in identical red anoraks. He waved his arms and they waved back. Ten minutes later, they were close and he led the way toward the cliff edge. Alec was standing beside David's body when they all arrived. He was astonished by how many men had come—there were fully a dozen of them—and by how much gear they were carrying.

One of them, older than the others by a few years, held out his hand and Alec took it. "Brian Phillips, team leader; what've we got?"

"David Edwards," Alec said. "Sheep farmer from Tan y Gadair, just below us to the north. Severe hypothermia, comatose, faint pulse."

"How long's he been here?" the leader asked. He was drenched with sweat; they had indeed run up the mountain.

"We're not sure. There was a pretty nasty hailstorm up here just before I found him, a couple of hours ago; he was covered with ice."

"So we don't know how long he's been unconscious?"

"No."

"Where'd the space blanket come from?"

"It's mine. I was just up here for a day hike this morning; it's from my first aid kit."

"Bloody lucky for him you had it or he'd probably be dead by now. Wish more walkers were as well equipped; make our lives a lot easier."

"I wish I'd had more spare clothing," Alec said. "I stripped him and put on what dry clothes I could spare, but I didn't want the same thing to happen to me when I went for help."

"Understood," Phillips said.

While Phillips collected information, the rest of the men had gone to work. Two of them checked David's vital signs. Two more had removed sections of a lightweight stretcher from their backpacks and were assembling it, working together like a well-oiled machine. Several of the men were carrying full mountaineering gear—thick ropes, belts of carabiners and pitons, heavy nylon straps and slings; having no idea where the victim was, Alec guessed they had to be prepared for every eventuality. One fellow stood to one side, talking from time to time into a walkie-talkie. All Alec could hear was the occasional hiss of static, but he assumed the man was in contact with the helicopter. Two other rescuers were very carefully insulating the length of David's body. These were all burly young men, but Alec was amazed at their gentleness.

"Question is," the leader said to no one in particular, "what was he doing here in the first place? It's lambing season; hill farmers don't go out for a morning climb under most circumstances, but especially not in lambing season. Too busy and too tired."

Alec thought quickly. "I'm staying at the farm; I'm pretty sure I heard his wife say walkers had left some farm gates open yesterday and he'd gone off to get the pregnant ewes back down to the lower pasture. Also, I know he has a weak heart—sheep dip poisoning. Isn't that right, Owen?"

Owen had been standing to one side, dumbfounded by Alec's story, but he snapped to. "Dickey heart, yes. Two heart attacks in the last three years. Gets dizzy sometimes, too."

"Owen here works for David, helping out with the farm," Alec explained. "By the way," Alec added, changing the subject, "Owen's found a place just west of here where he thinks the 'copter can land. Marked it with a ring of stones."

"Well done," Phillips said. "Don't know whether the RAF boys will land or hover, but it's good to have a safe staging area."

"Ten minutes out, Brian," the communications man yelled.

"Okay, lads," Phillips called out, "what's our status?"

"Ready to be transported," one of the men beside David answered.

The assembled stretcher was set down next to David's swaddled body and four of the men gently shifted him onto its bed. There was a kind of basket attachment to stabilize David's head. Then the four took hold of the frame and one man called, "Ready . . . one, two . . . three," and they rose in unison.

While the rest of the team collected their gear, Phillips said to Owen, "Okay, lad, lead on."

Slowly and with great care, the stretcher bearers picked their way across the boulder field, talking to each other constantly to coordinate their movements so David would not be jostled. Alec followed with Phillips.

They heard the helicopter before they saw it, the low-frequency *whomp-whomp* of its blades hammering the air carried for miles. Finally, off to the northwest, Alec saw a bulbous yellow shape emerge from the haze of the late afternoon sun. The communications man was guiding them in, but here on the barren summit plateau Alec couldn't imagine the pilot would miss the red-jacketed rescuers.

The pilot circled the site, getting the lay of the land. The young man with the walkie-talkie yelled to Phillips: "He doesn't want to try to land; wants to hover."

"Right," Phillips yelled back. "It's his call."

The helicopter settled over the circle of stones Owen had made and the stretcher bearers moved to the center. Above them, a hatch door slid open in the side of the helicopter and a helmeted RAF winch man descended on a cable with another stretcher. The noise was incredible and Alec could tell the rescue workers, unable to hear one another, had the whole process down to a system. When he reached the ground, the RAF man unclipped himself and the stretcher. Then he gave a signal and the helicopter rose and moved away from the mountain for safety. With great care, the mountain rescue team and the RAF winch man transferred David from one stretcher to the other. Then the helicopter returned, lowered the cable again and winched the crewman and the stretcher back up into the belly of the bird. The door slid shut and the 'copter rose, reoriented itself, dipped its nose, and throbbed through the air to the south.

Alec watched the yellow shape slip into the haze and thought about Fiona. He knew she could hear the helicopter. She didn't even know David was still alive.

"Where will they take him?" he heard Owen ask Phillips.

"Aberystwyth," the leader replied. "There's a playing field near the hospital. They'll land there and an ambulance will be waiting. Normally, it would be Bangor, but their ER is at capacity."

"What do you think his chances are?" Alec asked.

Phillips paused. "Hard to say. It's amazing he's lived this long, to be honest. And with that weak heart there's no telling what will happen when they get his blood circulating again. Reviving him could just as easily kill him. No way to know."

Alec watched the team break down and stow the portable stretcher and shoulder their gear. The light was fading fast. He turned to Owen.

"I guess we're done here; which route down do you think we should take?"

"I've been thinking about that. If we take the Pony Track, which is safer, it'll be dark before we're down. We only have the one torch, and I don't know how much life is in it. Fox's Path is faster, but more dangerous, as you know. One good thing is that the Land Rover's at the bottom by the lake."

Alec wondered how many times they could tempt fate in one day. But descending the Pony Track in the dark was at least as dangerous as another descent by the Fox's Path.

Phillips said, "I'm with the boy; you gents look like fit climbers. I'd take the steep path over the darkness any day."

"Fox's Path it is, then," Alec said. "Besides, I'm getting to know it pretty well."

Alec thanked Phillips and the team and suddenly remembered David's chemical sensitivities. Brian said he'd radio the RAF team and the hospital as well so the room could be prepared. The men began moving southwest, the direction from which they'd come. Alec grabbed his pack and he and Owen set off east. Soon they were at the top of the scree slope, ready to begin the steep descent.

"Alec, I just need to ask: that story about walkers and the farm gates?"

"Insurance, Owen," Alec said. "I'm guessing David has a life insurance policy. If he dies and the report suggests it was suicide, Fiona will get nothing. I'm not proud of lying; I'm just trying to protect Fiona. I got rid of the bottle, too."

Owen looked at Alec for a moment, then said, "I only wish I'd thought of it."

They turned and started down.

twelve

*a*lec and Owen descended slowly, staying as far away from the cliff edge as they could. The fading light drained the landscape of contrast, and it was hard to discern loose rock from solid. Alec was stiff from having sat with David for so long, but his muscles and joints loosened as he and Owen descended. Several times the scree let go beneath them, but each time they were able to arrest their slide. They passed the point where Alec had nearly gone over the edge earlier in the afternoon. By the time they reached the bottom, perhaps an hour later, Alec's knees were rubbery and it was dusk. They climbed into the Land Rover by the shore of Llyn y Gadair. Owen turned the engine over and, with the headlights searching for the depressions the tires had made in the grass hours earlier, they slowly bumped and lurched downhill toward the farm. Every few hundred yards, Alec got out to close farm gates behind them.

Fiona had stood at the window of the unoccupied upstairs guest room from the moment she first heard the helicopter until the light began to fail. It was as if she were trying to will outcomes: David's survival; Alec's and Owen's safety. She found herself amazed that she could carry the hope of David's safety and the yearning for Alec in her heart simultaneously, yet she could.

The Llewellyns had come in, apparently seen the note, gone quietly to their room, and left shortly thereafter, presumably for dinner in town. She hadn't bothered to greet them.

It was nearly dark when she heard the engine of Owen's old Land Rover laboring in low gear. She watched as the twin cones of its headlights bounced down the hill. When the lights neared the farm, she went downstairs, opened the back door, and waited there in the pool of light from the boot room. Owen and Alec got out of the car and walked stiffly to where she stood.

"David?"

"Alive, Fi," Alec said.

Fiona threw her arms around them and held them tight for several moments, the two men dwarfing her. It was only partly from gratitude; the fixed constellations of her world were suddenly whirling around her and she clung to the men as if to keep from being cast into the spinning void.

"They've taken him to Aberystwyth," she heard Alec say. "Have they called?"

She shook her head, pulled away, and looked up at them.

"Thank you. Both of you. Come in and I'll put on the kettle."

They had only just reached the kitchen when the phone rang. The three of them were frozen in place for a moment, and then Fiona ran to the hall. The two men followed her.

Her hand hesitated over the handle of the telephone and then she lifted it. "Hello, Tan y Gadair Farm," she said. "Yes, this is she . . . Yes . . . I see, yes . . . He is; wonderful! Yes, I understand. It was *what?* Yes, of course it would . . . No, I'm all right, there's someone here to look after me; thank you for asking. Yes, I'll be right here by the phone . . . Yes, good . . . Thank you; thank you very much."

She put the phone back on its receiver and stared at it for a moment.

"He's alive. Barely. In a coma. They're warming him but they're also keeping him sedated; apparently that helps protect his brain somehow. They won't let me see him just yet. Meanwhile, apparently they've done a few tests."

She looked at each of them in turn.

"His blood alcohol level was very high. It was suicide, wasn't it?"

Owen looked at Alec and Alec answered, "Yes, Fi, it was. He'd thrown aside his coat, drunk maybe as much as a bottle of whisky, sat down among the rocks overlooking the farm, and waited. Perhaps we should have told you sooner. I'm sorry."

Fiona's face was blank for a moment; then her eyes refocused. She squared her shoulders and smiled.

"No need for apologies," she said, "from either of you. David's choices were his alone. Thanks to you two, he failed. What happens next is not in our hands. They've asked me to stay close to the phone and wait for further instructions."

She shook her head. "As if I might skip off to the cinema!"

Alec wondered whether she had always been this resilient and guessed she had been, perhaps as far back as the day her father drowned.

She took them both by the hand and they returned to the kitchen. The two men sat at the table and she poured water into the teapot.

"Mrs. Edwards, ma'am," Owen asked, "have you called Meaghan?"

"I did, shortly after you left. There was no reply. Just as well, I suppose; I didn't know whether David was alive or dead at that point."

They were silent again.

"Speaking of calling," Fiona said, "would you like to call your mam, Owen?"

"Good idea," he replied and went out to the hall to phone.

Alec was slumped in his chair, staring blankly. He'd climbed the mountain twice and had been running on adrenaline for hours. Now that the crisis was over, he'd hit empty.

Fiona sat beside him.

He smiled at her.

Owen returned. "Mam sends her love and prayers, Mrs. Edwards; says if there's anything you need, just call. I think I'll head home now if that's okay."

"Of course, luv," Fiona said. She gave him another quick hug. "A gem is what you are, Owen Lewis; I'm so glad you came to us."

Owen blushed. "Can't think of anywhere I'd rather be, Mrs. Edwards. Will you be calling Meaghan again, then, later?"

She looked at him, saw something she'd never seen before, and smiled.

"I will, Owen."

When the young man had left, she sat down at the table opposite Alec.

"If it hadn't been for you, David wouldn't be alive tonight. You were wonderful today and I'm beyond grateful. I have no idea what will happen next, but what you did was heroic. Insanely so, I suspect, but then I'm beginning to expect that sort of thing from you."

He looked across at her and shrugged.

"You are the most wonderful man, Alec Hudson . . . and you are very, very dirty."

Alec looked at himself for the first time. He was, indeed, filthy. In addition to the dirt, his arms and legs were a mass of bloody scratches from the rockslide.

"Guess I could use a bath, huh?"

He started to unlace his boots. Fiona rose and helped pulled them off. The tops of his socks were bloodstained. He stood up and groaned.

She took his hand.

"Come with me."

He followed her through the house to her private quarters. She sat him in the chair by the fireplace, then went into her bathroom and ran water in the big claw-foot tub. When it was nearly filled she went back to her sitting room and found him staring empty-eyed at the cold hearth. She pulled him up and took him to the bathroom.

Slowly, tenderly, she helped him out of his clothes. There was a dark purple bruise the size of a dinner plate on his side.

"What happened here?"

"Tried to fall off the mountain. Almost succeeded."

"You idiot; I told you to be careful."

She helped him into the tub. He slid into the hot water, wincing. She kneeled beside the tub and poured hot water over his head several times, then squeezed shampoo into her hand and slowly washed his hair, massaging his scalp. Alec felt as if he were floating in the water, not reclining in it. When she finished, she poured more water over his head and rinsed his long hair thoroughly.

"Soak here for a while," she said. "Do your bones good, you old relic. I'm going to put together a simple cold dinner from whatever is in the fridge. We can have it in my sitting room, by the fire."

"I promise not to run away," Alec said as his eyelids closed.

She had just returned with a tray of bread and cheese and sliced apples and a bottle of wine, when the phone rang by her bed. She leaped at it.

"Hello? This is she, yes. No, it's quite all right, what's happened? I see . . . yes, I understand . . . Yes, of course I will; I'm in Dolgellau, so it will be awhile . . . Yes, I know you can't, I understand. Thank you very much. Yes, fine; thank you for asking. No, I know where it is, thanks. Yes, bye."

She hung up. Alec was standing in the bathroom doorway, dripping wet.

"He's fibrillating, right?"

"How did you know?"

"It's what happens. I didn't want to tell you."

"I need to go to the hospital; they don't know if they can keep him alive."

"We'll both go," Alec said as he began rubbing himself down with a towel.

"No, Alec."

He looked up.

"I know it's your nature to want to be there, to help, to be supportive, but this is something I need to do myself."

She crossed the room and gave him a long hug. She heard the Llewellyns return from dinner and ignored them. They could fend for themselves.

"I need to go now. I'll call if . . . anything happens."

"Fiona?"

"Yes?"

"I hope he's okay."

"Thank you. Me, too."

A few moments later he heard her car start. The transmission whined as she reversed quickly out of the barn, there was the rattle of flying gravel, and she was gone. It was so quiet down in the valley that he could hear the pitch of the engine alter with each gear change as she raced up the main road to Dolgellau.

The clock on the dashboard said 10:15. Dolgellau's tangled streets were nearly deserted and in minutes she was flying up the A470. She didn't even pause at the Cross Foxes, she simply downshifted to third and roared up to the top of the pass. On the descent through the Bwlch Llyn Bach, she used the whole road, moving smoothly from the southbound to the northbound lanes, apexing each curve to straighten the road as it twisted down through the narrow valley. The engine whined as she upshifted and downshifted, but she never made a tire squeal. Fiona loved driving the way a chef loves his stove: the individual and the machinery became one.

She reached the valley bottom near Tal y Llyn and downshifted again for the climb up through the pass to Corris. Then the road dove steeply down into the next valley under an arching canopy of black-leafed trees, the car's headlights boring a tunnel through the darkness. The tarmac leveled suddenly and she crossed the old bridge over the river Dyfi. On the other side, as she entered Machynlleth, she stood on the brakes and brought the car down to the speed limit. There was no sense in getting a speeding ticket, assuming the police were even abroad at this hour. She passed the ancient clock tower at the western end of the town square. On the other side of town, she pushed the accelerator down again and raced south on the A487. The topography eased and the road straightened. The little red car flashed through the sleeping villages of Tal y Bont and Bow Street.

When she reached the WELCOME TO ABERYSTWYTH sign, the dashboard clock read 11:00. Forty-five minutes. Not bad for a one-hour drive.

Fiona gave her name at the hospital reception desk and was directed to the intensive care unit, where a nurse met her. She was a big woman with a sweet smile and a gentle manner. Her lapel pin read MEUDWEN.

"I'm sorry we dragged you down here at this hour," the nurse explained, "but it was touch-and-go there for a bit and we thought we might lose him. We had to use the defibrillator on him twice, but he came back both times. His temperature is nearly back up to normal now. But we have no way of knowing whether he'll come out of his coma when we reduce the sedation. Or, for that matter, what condition he'll be in if and when he does. He's got a good doctor, though: James Pryce. Young chap, and a mountaineer; he's our expert on exposure."

The nurse led the way down a dimly lit corridor. Dark rooms flickered with little red and yellow and green lights and small video screens that kept a running record of vital signs. Fiona thought about how inadequate such machinery was to the task of monitoring a human spirit. The only sound on the ward was the ticking or beeping of the life-support equipment. Finally, the nurse turned into a room and said, "Here he is then, luv. If you need anything, I'll be at the nurses' station." She checked the equipment and then left Fiona alone.

Fiona drew up a chair and sat facing her unconscious husband. Thick, clear vinyl sheeting hung from a fixture in the ceiling and surrounded the bed to isolate David from chemicals in the hospital. A thin plastic tube fed oxygen through his nose.

She'd spent half her life with this man and she did not want him to die. David had given her the life she now embraced as her own. He had brought her to his valley, and she had been happy for years, though in a quiet sort of way. The rhythms of the farm had been a source of genuine comfort to her. True, running the farm was something he seldom consulted her about. But while he resisted the bed-and-breakfast idea at first, and the implicit message that he wasn't earning enough from the farm, she sensed the success of her business had become a source of pride for him. Then, after he'd become sick and knew she was carrying the household, he'd begun to resent her. It was understandable, if painful to live with. He was losing his hold on his own life. That's what was so horrible about this situation, she thought: David was not now, nor had he ever been, a bad man. She knew women—women right in their own valley—whose husbands controlled every aspect of their lives. That was never David.

But Alec's appearance in her life had shone a spotlight on all the places in her marriage that had been in shadow, gathering dust. She and David did not have—had never had—the kind of deep intimacy she had hoped for. They had certainly never made love the way she and Alec had. They were more like business partners than "soul mates." He helped with bringing up Meaghan, especially in her fierce early teens when she seemed to listen only to him. That was the most important thing they'd shared. But as she watched him behind his clear plastic curtain, she suddenly realized that in many other respects she and David had been living utterly separate lives, even when they still shared the same household and bed. She'd felt lonely all these years for the simple reason that she was, for all intents and purposes, alone. Their separate planets did not collide, but they didn't orbit together, either. When he'd had to move out to the hay barn, she'd barely noticed the difference. She and Alec, on the other hand, were Earth and Moon, bound by their mutual gravitational pull.

She watched the pattern of David's heartbeats on the monitor beside his bed; a scrolling yellow line traced jagged peaks and valleys, the landscape of David's being, across a black screen. Up, down. Pump, rest. Life, death.

Alec sat by the fire in Fiona's sitting room and nibbled idly on the meal she'd left for him. He was still in his damp towel. He was too tired to dress, too tired even to be hungry. And too anxious. The situation in which he found himself was untenable. In a hospital room an hour away, David Edwards lay critically ill. His wife was at her husband's bedside, willing her husband to live. This was as it should be. Alec was simply Fiona's new friend, someone who'd wandered into her life, found her dying husband, and kept him alive until someone more capable could take over. That story made sense. What didn't make sense was the other story, running in parallel, in which he and Fiona were lovers, and they were at the kitchen table enjoying dinner together, and they were in bed, and they were dreaming of being together forever.

A part of him wished David had died—as David himself

apparently had wished—and he was horrified he could feel that way. He thought about Gwynne's death and the weeks he'd spent in her hospital room. He thought about his grief when she died, and the fact that divorce doesn't sweep away the history of two lives lived together. Even death doesn't do that. If anything, death intensifies the memories. Gywnne was still with him, not just a memory but a palpable presence. He was sure there had been many happy times in Fiona's and David's marriage. As he watched the fire flicker, he imagined her reliving them right now.

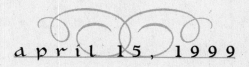

april 15, 1999

thirteen

a hand touched Fiona's shoulder and she jerked awake.

"Mrs. Edwards?" It was Meudwen, the nurse. "Dr. Pryce is here."

Fiona stood quickly. Too quickly; she had to hold on to the chair while her head cleared.

"I'm so sorry; I guess I fell asleep."

"I'm envious. If I weren't on call tonight, I'd be asleep, too. Jamie Pryce," the doctor said, extending his hand.

James Pryce was a big man—a good six feet tall and broad-shouldered. Fiona took him to be about thirty years old. The nurse had said he was a mountaineer and she had no trouble believing it. He checked his patient and then turned to her. He had a warm and calming smile.

"You'd like to know how your husband is doing, I'm sure, Mrs. Edwards, but there is not much that I can tell you with any certainty at this point. Your husband is alive. We have brought him out of his hypothermia. He has weathered two ventricular fibrillation events. To put it simply, we won't know much until he wakes up."

"What will he be like when he does?"

"I wish I could say. Between the hypothermia and the heart irregularities, the blood and oxygen flow to his brain have been compromised. He could be perfectly fine. He could have certain brain function impairments."

"What should we do next?"

"If I were you, Mrs. Edwards, I'd go home and try to get some rest. I also know that is a ludicrous thing to say to a patient's wife in this situation, but there is no way of knowing, really, how long this process will take. We'll take him off sedation gradually and see what happens."

"Is David still in danger of dying?"

"No, I don't think so. He's out of immediate danger."

Fiona took a deep breath. "Thank you, Dr. Pryce."

The doctor smiled and Meudwen followed him to the door.

"As soon as there is the slightest change in his condition, we'll call you, Mrs. Edwards," the nurse said.

Fiona stood at the foot of her husband's bed, gazed at his inert form behind the clear plastic, then turned and left the room.

It wasn't until she got outside that Fiona realized she must have been asleep for several hours. Beyond the Cambrian Mountains to the east, the sky was turning a pale primrose yellow. It would be a clear morning. There was a public phone in the lobby and she decided to try Meaghan again. Better now, before she left for classes.

The phone rang several times and finally a sleepy voice answered.

"Hello?"

"Hello, darling, it's me."

"Mother! What are you doing calling at . . ."—there was a pause as Meaghan obviously looked at her clock—". . . this hour? Is something wrong? It's Daddy, isn't it? He's had another attack!"

"Meaghan, calm down. It's not another heart attack. Your father's had an accident on the mountain and got too cold while he was up there. He's in hospital in Aberystwyth. He's unconscious, but out of danger."

Fiona heard another voice, male. Meaghan's hand covered the mouthpiece and there was some kind of muffled exchange. Then she came back on the line.

"I'm on my way; I'll be there this evening, Mum. I'll call when I know the arrival time at Barmouth. Or should I go to Aberystwyth?"

"Meaghan, you don't need to come home. There's nothing any of us can do until he regains consciousness."

"Barmouth or Aberystwyth, Mother?"

Fiona closed her eyes and sighed. "Barmouth, dear."

"Right. I'll call later with the train information," Meaghan said. Then, in what seemed to Fiona like an afterthought, she said, "Mum? Are you okay?"

"Yes, dear, I'm fine."

Fiona put the phone down. Suddenly, she ached.

She drove north. Just after she crossed the river Dyfi bridge at Machynlleth, she turned left, onto the A493 toward Aberdovey and the coast. She loved the sea and needed its vast and comforting certainty. The surface of the Dyfi estuary was smooth and silvery, reflecting the gathering morning light. There were ducks in the water and cormorants skimming the surface on long black wings.

She followed the A493 north to the seacoast town of Tywyn. The road turned inland here for a few miles to circumvent the meanders of the river Dysynni and then swung out to the coast again. At the seaside village of Fairbourne, at the mouth of the Mawddach, she found a café that was open, ordered a coffee, and took it out to the deserted beach. It was a cool morning and a slight onshore breeze fretted the ocean surface. Herring gulls wheeled and complained overhead. Just beyond the shore break, terns plunged from the sky to scoop up tiny fish swimming near the surface. Legions of plovers, probing the wet sand with their lancelike beaks, skittered away as one when she approached them. The air was tangy with salt and tingled in her nostrils. She wandered along the beach, following the line of sea wrack left by the last tide.

There were, she realized, three forces doing battle in her heart: habit, duty, and passion. She thought about David and the two decades of their marriage and realized the odds for a life with Alec were two against one. It was habit and duty against passion.

She felt trapped. Exhausted and trapped.

When she got home, the house was still in the shadow of the mountain. In the front hall, she noticed that the Llewellyns had left a check by the telephone. She went into her own rooms and found Alec asleep in the chair where she'd left him, the fire long dead. She woke him with kisses.

He blinked and looked around.

"Oops," he said.

"I can't believe you're still in this chair."

"How's David?"

"Still unconscious, but the doctor says he's out of danger."

"I'm glad, Fi."

She knew he was telling the truth.

"Come with me, you," she said, taking his hand.

In her bedroom, she began to undress.

"Fi, don't you think we need to talk about . . ."

"No." She put her slender hand over his mouth and pulled him onto the old bed. She climbed atop him, pressing her naked body against his.

"Whatever happens, know this," she whispered into his ear. "I love you with every ounce of my being."

Alec drew her closer. Fiona planted a trail of kisses, featherlight, down Alec's breastbone, through the delta of hair on his belly, to the thicker hair between his legs. She took him in her mouth, nibbling the skin on the underside, until he was fully erect. Then she lowered herself gently upon him.

That was all she did. It was all she needed: to be joined with him. Alec understood and did not move in her. She pulled him onto his side, still inside her, and held him tight. Never had she felt so complete. Alec buried his face in her hair, mumbling endearments.

They were both asleep in moments.

When the phone chirped at her bedside, Fiona lurched for it, instantly awake.

"Hello?" She heard the panicky edge in her own voice. "Oh, thank goodness, it's you; I thought it was the hospital again."

She mouthed "Meaghan" to Alec, who had sat up, propped on an elbow.

"No, nothing's changed. He's unconscious, but stable. Right. Five-fifty. Someone will meet you, sweetie. Yes. Bye."

"What time is it?" Alec asked.

"Amazingly, well after noon. She called from the station in Birmingham, where she changes trains."

Fiona dropped back onto her pillow and sighed.

"How do you feel?"

She turned to him. "Frightened."

"About David?"

"About everything. Meaghan will be here in a few hours and I don't know what to say about you. Which means I don't know what to do about us."

"I know. Neither do I." He stared at the ceiling. "We're changing, Fi. No, that's not it; we're being changed. I used to believe that if I just worked hard enough at things, stayed vigilant and thought fast enough, I could make sure everything turned out all right. I believed it fervently. It's taken me years to accept that I can't. I don't have that power; no one does. I don't believe much in either faith or fate, but I think all the two of us can do from now on is keep faith with each other and wait to see what fate delivers."

She pulled him close. "I thought you were more of a romantic."

"My heart is; this is my head talking."

"I like your heart better."

She rolled away from him and stood. He thought her the most beautiful creature on earth. He climbed out of bed and instantly wished he hadn't. Everything hurt.

"I'm either too old for running up mountains or for sleeping in chairs." He laughed. "Possibly both."

She came around and stroked his cheek.

"I'm so sorry," she said. She came up on tiptoes and kissed the tip of his nose. "I'd better get moving."

"I'm right behind you."

They were only in the kitchen a few moments before they heard Owen's Land Rover coming from one of the pastures. Automatically, Fiona filled the electric kettle and switched it on.

Owen knocked at the back door, and Fiona called, "Come in!"

The door opened and Owen came through the boot room and peeked into the kitchen.

"Sorry, Mrs. Edwards, it's just . . ."

"Yes, I know," Fiona interrupted, "it's how you were raised. Look, you've been with us for more than a year, right?"

"Yes, ma'am."

"Don't you think it's time you stopped calling me 'Mrs. Edwards'? Makes me feel like an old lady. The name's Fiona—preferably, Fi. Okay?"

"Yes, ma'am."

"And stop 'ma'am-ing' me!"

"Yes, ma'am."

Fiona burst out laughing and Owen understood that David had survived.

"How is he, then?"

"He's still with us. They'll call when he regains consciousness. Tea?"

"Tea would be lovely, Fiona . . . ma'am," Owen stumbled.

Not for the first time, Alec wondered what the English would have done if tea hadn't arrived from the Far East in the seventeenth century. It was as if this modest beverage was the lubricant that eased the passage from one event to the next in the course of a day—no matter how mundane or portentous those events might be. Tea was the constant.

Owen sat at the table and Fiona told him what little she'd learned from the doctor. He nodded, taking it all in.

She brought the tea and sat opposite him. "Owen?"

"Ma'am?"

She smiled. "You're in charge of the farm from now on. Even if David recovers, I don't know what he will be able to do or even what he will comprehend. Do you understand? I'd like you to take control. You can do it, Owen, I know you can, and I can't think of anybody I'd rather have running things around here."

Owen was momentarily speechless. Then the young man pulled himself upright in his chair.

"I'll do my best . . . Fiona," he said, still trying to get used to using her first name.

"I know you will, Owen Lewis."

She held up her teacup and they toasted each other.

"One more thing. I've called Meaghan. She'll be here on the

afternoon train. Do you think you might be able to collect her at the station at Barmouth?"

"Reckon I can."

"Good. That'll be a big help. Now, be off and make sure we don't lose too many lambs. It's on your head now, young man!"

Owen drained his cup, rose, patted Alec's shoulder companionably, and walked out the back door.

Fiona watched him go.

"I love that boy," she said, mostly to herself.

"Fiona. What sort of plan are you hatching here?"

She looked at him and smiled. "I'm sure I have no idea what you're talking about."

"Right."

They sat quietly at the kitchen table for a while. Alec scanned the room, each nook and cranny so familiar to him now.

"I love this room, Fi."

She looked up. "And I love you in it." And though she smiled, it seemed to him the smile was pained.

"Well, I guess I'd better put something together for supper. I wonder if you'd do something for me?"

"Anything, Fi."

"Would you pop into town and get a couple of bottles of wine? We're out, and I think I'm going to need it tonight."

Alec took the hint. She needed time alone.

"Sure. Red or white?"

"Red."

"I'm on it. Where are the keys?"

"In the ignition, city boy," she teased.

He drove along Cadair Road slowly. The ancient stone walls and old trees cast long shadows in the late afternoon sun. The window was down and the air was warm and fragrant. Spring was well advanced. The pale greens of early spring were deepening, and the buds on the hawthorn trees were about to burst. He turned into the square in Dolgellau and parked. He wandered through the streets, greeted John Lewis, the butcher, who was standing in the doorway of his shop, and stepped into the wine store, where he bought two bottles of Australian shiraz. Back at the car, he looked around the square. There was no reason for it, rationally, but he felt completely at home here. He never wanted to leave.

"What smells so good?" Alec asked as he entered the kitchen and set down the wine.

"Oh, it's just bits and bobs," Fiona said, smiling. "I've boiled some potatoes and green beans and browned some bacon, sausage, and onions. I topped it all with grated cheese and it's in the oven."

"Sounds and smells savory and good; I'm starving. What can I do to help?"

"Set the table? For four, I should think. I have a feeling Owen will want to stay. He's at the station, collecting Meaghan."

A few minutes later they heard Owen's Land Rover laboring up the lane. It turned into the farmyard and stopped, engine running. A door slammed and then the engine gunned as Owen put the car in the barn. The back door opened and a young woman strode into the kitchen. Her face was fine-boned and delicately sculpted, her skin pale, almost translucent. Her hair, black as a crow's wing, was pulled to one side and fell in an inky cascade nearly to her chest. Except for the hair and her bottomless brown eyes, she was the image of Fiona, slender and petite. Alec had been expecting a college student's uniform—shapeless sweater over faded jeans. Instead, Meaghan wore a charcoal two-piece suit with a fitted skirt, opaque stockings, and sober black heels.

Behind her slouched an angular young man only slightly taller

than the girl. His dark hair was short, spiky, and tipped with dyed
blond highlights. He wore a black suit with faint lavender pinstripes, a
white shirt unbuttoned at the neck, and a loosely knotted purple tie. In
the lobe of one ear was a small gold hoop, as if he were a pirate in training. From their clothes, it looked like they were prepared for the worst.

"Meaghan, love," Fiona said, taking her daughter in her arms.

"How's Daddy?"

"Stable. Still unconscious as far as we know. We haven't heard
anything more this evening."

There was an awkward silence when they separated. Fiona
waited.

"Oh! Mother, this is Gerald. Gerald Wilson."

Alec wondered whether Meaghan always called Fiona "Mother"
or whether the formality was for her friend's benefit.

The young man nodded his head in Fiona's direction, but said
nothing.

Perhaps it was the cheap, double-breasted black suit, or his pecu-
liar silence, or the situation in which they all found themselves, but
Gerald Wilson put Alec in mind of an undertaker, and for some reason
he sensed the boy was no more sincere.

Owen came through the doorway.

"Any news then, Mrs. Edwards?"

"No change, I'm afraid, Owen. You're staying for supper, I hope?"

But the young man's face answered before his voice did. Owen was
clearly disappointed by the arrival of a boyfriend. "Thanks, but no; got
to look in on my mam."

Fiona cocked her head and pursed her lips together in a sad smile,
signaling that she understood. "Give her my love then, Owen."

"Will do. 'Night, Meaghan," he said. He looked at Alec, nodded,
and withdrew. Meagan turned, but Owen was already gone.

"And you would be . . . ?" Meaghan said, turning back and

addressing Alec more sharply than he thought was strictly polite. He was standing by the kitchen window, watching the taillights of Owen's car disappear down the lane.

"Oh my goodness," Fiona said, "I'm so sorry. This is Alec, Alec Hudson. He found your father on the mountain. Alec was . . . is . . . staying here; Alec, my daughter, Meaghan."

"I'm grateful to you, Mr. Hudson," the girl said stiffly. She did not offer him her hand.

Alec inclined his head slightly. "I'm pleased to meet you, Meaghan."

"Well," Fiona said, "I'll bet you two are ravenous. Shall we eat? I'm afraid it's rather simple, something my grandmother used to make. I haven't been able to get to the market, what with everything else." Fiona wondered why she felt a need to apologize, under the circumstances.

Alec pulled out a chair for Fiona and then one for himself.

"You're eating with us?" Meaghan said to Alec.

"Meaghan!" Fiona snapped. "Alec Hudson saved your father's life; of course he's eating with us."

They took their seats. Fiona took a deep breath to calm herself while Alec poured wine. As he did, she told her daughter what had happened on the mountain and what Alec and Owen had done. When she finished, Meaghan turned to Alec.

"I'm terribly sorry, Mr. Hudson; you must think me very rude."

"I think you're upset by what's happened," he replied, giving her a warm smile, "and I think it's perfectly normal. The name is Alec, by the way."

Meaghan softened. "Thank you, Alec. You're from the States?"

"Yes, Seattle."

"Now, Gerald," Fiona interrupted as she served each of them, "tell us about yourself. Are you at the university, too?"

"Yeah. Part-time, like. Doing finance, but I already have a position at Colliers, the commercial estate agents."

Meaghan took over. "Gerald thinks the real-estate boom in London is about to leapfrog to the countryside, don't you, Gerald?"

"Yeah."

Alec looked at him. "What do you think about the land use implications of greenfield development versus, say, creative reuse of older, abandoned industrial structures?"

The boy looked at him blankly.

"I don't get into none o' that," Gerald said, and Alec wondered if Gerald was anything more than a mail boy at Colliers.

Meaghan came to her boyfriend's rescue. "And what do you do, Alec, when you're not saving people on mountaintops?"

"I'm a writer."

"Really? Should I know you?"

Alec saw her mother shoot Meaghan a look, but he was used to this question; it was one everyone asked.

"Probably not, unless you read a lot of economics and public policy."

"Alec was a speechwriter for Jimmy Carter," Fiona volunteered.

"Who?" Gerald asked.

Alec laughed. "Former U.S. president. Almost before your time."

Turning back to Meaghan, he continued: "I do a lot of ghostwriting for other folks, too, so my name often doesn't appear on the cover of the books I write."

"Gerald," Fiona interjected, "you're not eating. Aren't you hungry?"

"Um. . . ."

"Gerald's a vegetarian, Mum," Meaghan announced proudly, as if the boy had been awarded a knighthood for his gastronomic restraint. "He believes it's cruel to eat other sentient beings."

Fiona was only momentarily taken aback. "Well then," she chirped, "you just push the animal bits aside, dear, and have the vegetables. Meaghan, you have warned Gerald here that he's on a sheep farm, haven't you? Gerald, would you like some bread? How about butter; is that okay?"

"Bread and butter would be okay."

As the three of them ate and Gerald moved things around on his plate, the conversation returned to David. Meaghan wanted to see her father immediately. Fiona said it would be pointless until David was conscious. As the two of them went back and forth, Alec was struck by how similar they were. Meaghan had her mother's tendency to cock her head to one side when she was thinking. They had similar hand gestures and turns of phrase. Alec looked at Gerald, who appeared hypnotized with boredom. He wondered what Meaghan saw in the boy. A veneer of urban savvy, perhaps, that she hadn't experienced here in the valley. A certain cockiness. But Alec suspected Gerald Wilson was more style than substance.

Meaghan finished eating, pushed back her chair, and stood.

"Well, if we're not going to the hospital tonight, I think we'll change and stop down at the pub."

At this announcement, Gerald appeared to regain consciousness, and he stood as well. As Meaghan led the way, Gerald grabbed their single suitcase, and Fiona followed them out and through the house.

"Where would you like us?" Alec heard Meaghan ask.

"Alec's in the big room but the other two are both available," Fiona answered.

Now Meaghan was laughing, "Oh, *Mother,* we don't need two rooms, we're lovers!"

Alec was clearing the table, privately wondering why Meaghan hadn't volunteered to do the washing up, when Fiona returned and slumped into a chair.

"My God," she said. "She's having sex with that weasel."

Alec chuckled.

"It's not funny!"

"I know it's not, Fi. I was just thinking about what I'd do if she were my daughter. I don't think I could be shocked. Not if she were Meaghan's age. I was thinking I'd want to talk to her about being a little choosier. I mean, really, an earring."

"I think it's the style now," Fiona said gloomily. "It's just that she seems so shameless about it," she added, shaking her head.

"Should she be ashamed, Fi?"

"Well, she certainly could have been a bit more circumspect."

"Circumspect. Hmm. As in lie to you? As in tiptoe from room to room in the middle of the night?"

Fiona glared at him. "You don't understand at all."

Alec dried his hands, walked to where Fiona sat, and kissed the top of her head. She hugged one of his long legs, then slapped his rear and said, "You'd have made a terrible parent, although you make a pretty good lover."

"There's that word again," Alec said.

Suddenly, she sat upright, her hand over her mouth. "Oh my God; I just figured out what you've been hinting."

"A bit of the pot calling the kettle black, you mean?"

She nodded, then found herself giggling. "A fine one I am to talk!"

Alec hugged her shoulder. "The situation's not exactly comparable, though. They're just having sex; we're in a lot more trouble than that."

Fiona cocked her head again and seemed about to say something, but they heard Meaghan and Gerald coming through the dining room.

"Where are the car keys, Mum?" Meaghan asked as she breezed into the kitchen.

"Darling, the pub isn't even half a mile away; you never needed a car to get there before."

Meaghan made a face.

"If the hospital calls," Alec interjected, "your mother may need to move pretty quickly. Perhaps I could drop you two off down there instead, and then you could walk back under the stars?"

This only seemed to irritate Meaghan more. "Forget it," she snapped, turning on her heel. "Come, Gerald."

Gerald was looking down at what were obviously his best shoes, as if considering the prospect of manure-splattered farm lanes, but he followed her dutifully out the door.

Fiona was fuming. "That girl is so willful!"

"That woman," Alec corrected. "And I wonder if I might make an observation or two?"

Fiona looked at him.

"First, Gerald and Meaghan won't last more than a couple of months; they're too busy vying for control. Second, it would appear to me that Meaghan comes by her spirit naturally. Is she another Sagittarius?"

Fiona moved to punch Alec in the arm but he dodged her, laughing.

"Now," he said, "how about we go for a walk as well; I could use the air."

"But the phone . . ."

"You've got an answering machine. And I think it's fair to say the crisis is over."

"Which one?"

He didn't respond. He just reached out his hand and she took it. They walked through the boot room, took their jackets off the hooks there, and stepped outside. The weather had continued to moderate and the night was soft and fragrant with warming earth and fresh blossoms. The sky was ablaze with starlight; the Milky Way looked practically fluorescent. Alec had always been a city person, but looking at the night sky here, where there was no ambient urban light to obscure the

celestial show, he decided he could be very happy in the Welsh countryside, and not just because of Fiona.

They had just reached the main road and started back up the lane
when headlights turned in after them.

"That'll be Owen," Fiona said. She waved at him as he approached
and he stopped. The windows were open.

"Evening, Fiona. Alec. Just heading up to check the ewes one
last time."

"I'm sorry about how things turned out, Owen," Fiona said.

"Bloody shame it is, Mrs. Edwards; David's a good soul deep
down; just ill and troubled."

"That's not what I meant, Owen."

"Oh, that. Well, yes. Bit of a surprise, that was, but never mind.
Anyway, best be off before it gets much later. I'm behind as it is."

Fiona slapped the side of the fender. "Off you go then."

"Good man, that one," Alec said as the Land Rover roared up
the hill.

"The best. Make someone a wonderful husband, if that someone
has half a brain."

"Patience, Fi."

Fiona turned to him and gave his hand a squeeze. "Thank you."

They turned and headed back up toward the house.

"I'll just check the answering machine," Fiona said as they took off
their jackets.

He was easing himself into a kitchen chair when Fiona called from
the hall.

"Alec?"

He didn't like the quaver in her voice. He hurried to her.

A green light blinked on the answering machine. There was a
pause between each blink. One message.

He pushed the message button. It was Dr. Pryce. He was calling to say David had opened his eyes. Her husband was confused and did not understand where he was. He'd said her name. They were sedating him again slightly to ensure that he slept and that his brain recovered slowly. It was too early to say whether there was any impairment. The doctor was pleased with this development. The message ended.

Fiona sat in the chair in the hall and began crying quietly. Alec knelt in front of her and held her knees. She put her hands on his.

After a few moments, she heaved a sigh and scrubbed the tears off her face.

"I don't know why I'm crying."

Alec said nothing for a few moments. Then he said, "Maybe you're crying, Fi, because you're lost."

"You're right: I don't know what I'm doing. I don't know what to hope for."

"Let me see if I can help," he said, pulling her to her feet and wrapping her in his arms. "I love you beyond measure. I want to spend every minute of every day of the rest of my life with you. I want to be absolutely clear about that. I will move here. I will take you away from here, if you want that. Whatever is necessary."

He held her shoulders a little away from him. "Do you understand?"

She nodded, smiling. "I do."

"But the decision is yours to make. I have no right to insist. If I tried, it would poison what we have. I will stay here as long as you want. I will leave the moment you ask me to. But no matter where I am or what I'm doing, I will love you utterly."

Fiona's eyes filled with tears.

"I don't know how to decide," she said.

"You won't have to; life will decide."

Fiona clutched Alec tightly and neither of them said anything for a few moments.

"Meaghan and that boy will be home in a few minutes. It's almost closing time," she said finally.

"Well, they better not find us like this, I suppose."

"No, I don't suppose they should. But I wish I could just crawl into bed with you and hold on tight; I just never knew a love like this was possible."

"Me, either."

She stood on tiptoes and kissed him quickly. "Good night, my love; I need to leave Meaghan a note about the call."

"Good night, Fi."

He climbed the stairs, went to his room, left his clothes where they fell, and lay in bed. Moonlight pooled on the carpet by the French doors. Despite the morning nap, he felt exhausted. He couldn't tell if he was still physically tired or simply anxious. He was still staring at the ceiling when he heard Meaghan and her boyfriend stumbling up the stairs, trying to stifle laughter. They were obviously tipsy. Later still he heard a sharp cry from the room behind his, followed by a soft mewing sound. Meaghan made the same sound after lovemaking that her mother did.

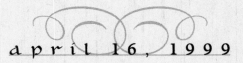

april 16, 1999

O wen Lewis arrived at Tan y Gadair before dawn, still trying to come to terms with Fiona's instructions the afternoon before. "I'd like you to take control," she had said. It wasn't that he doubted his ability to do so; by now he'd come to think of the farm as a living, breathing entity he understood. He'd mastered its rhythms, got used to its surprises. He supposed he'd just received some sort of promotion; it would still be David and Fiona's farm, but apparently he was to manage it. And yet, there had been such affection in Fiona's voice, as if she were in some fashion making the farm a gift to him. But of course that was impossible. It was a puzzle.

He headed uphill to the meadows. He was especially fond of the farm in the wee hours. The night sky began to soften and a faint light etched the rim of the summit plateau. The birds awakened and began to call to one another. The mist still clung to the grass like a wispy white angora blanket. He walked through the ground fog and watched as it swirled around his wet green rubber wellies. Apart from the bleating of the sheep and, just now, the higher-pitched cries of the newborn lambs, the sounds of the land seemed dampened, muffled, the hills almost in slumber.

A farmer's hours were long and hard, yes, but there were gifts you could not measure in time or money, gifts the land gave you every day. You got rich on a farm from those gifts, not from the money you made; hill farms seldom did more than break even. If that. When he thought about his school chums and their headlong rush to leave the valley for a "real" job in London or Cardiff, he felt like something of a throwback. But he felt sorry for them, too: as far as "riches" were concerned, he reckoned he'd come out ahead. It was all down to how you defined "rich."

Jack appeared from somewhere and loped beside him. Owen moved among the sheep, murmuring to the ewes and checking on the progress of the lambs. He could see only one lamb in danger of being ignored by its mother, one he might have to add to the orphans' pen in the barn. The rest of the lambs and ewes that had been in Alec's stalls he'd released to the lush lower pastures yesterday.

As the sky brightened, the English daisies scattered across the grass beneath his feet shone like fallen stars. His preliminary rounds done, he leaned against a stone wall, Jack curled at his feet. Owen drank some of the sweet, milky tea his mother put in a thermos for him every morning, getting up before him and then returning to bed when he left.

He thought about meeting Meaghan at the train station in Barmouth, the way his heart soared when he saw her wind-whipped black hair as she stepped down from the train to the platform, and then sank when he saw her turn to address the fellow in the suit who joined her and carried her bag. She had climbed into the front passenger seat next to him and grilled him about her father. Assured that he was recovering, she pumped Owen for news of the valley. Every once in a while she'd remember her boyfriend in the back and try to draw him in to the conversation, but he seemed uninterested.

Owen had known Meaghan for years. She was four years younger than he, and for the longest time that had seemed a vast gap. First, she was a child, he a teenager. Then she was a teenager, he a young adult going off to college. But the older they became, the less significant the years between them seemed to be. Last year, when he came to work on the farm and she was entering university, they had spent more time together—or at least in each other's presence—than ever before. What she did not know, what he would not let on, was that he was in love with her. Since she was going off to Leeds, there seemed no point in telling her.

But the longer she'd been away, the stronger his feelings for her had grown. A ruggedly handsome and well-built young man with a gentle soul, Owen had no shortage of admirers among the young women of Dolgellau. His easy smile and green-gold eyes seemed to mesmerize them. But with the women who were drawn to him, and whom he sometimes dated, there was always something missing. He didn't have to tell them; they worked it out for themselves. There was something he was holding back, something they could not reach, and eventually they let him go—not in anger, but in disappointment and, truth be told, with a lasting affection. Several young women in Dolgellau held a special place in their hearts for Owen Lewis, but there was only one who held that same place in his.

He looked downhill to the farmhouse and thought about Meaghan there with her boyfriend. He couldn't for the life of him understand the attraction. The fellow had sat stiffly on the jump seat in the rear of the Land Rover, in his fancy suit, and hadn't said a word all the way back to the farm. Owen had a sense that he feigned boredom but was busily taking everything in, as if calculating something in his head. Given her father's condition, he couldn't understand why she'd brought the boyfriend at all. It was as if she wanted to flaunt him, maybe to show her mother how worldly she'd become while away at university. Still, Owen knew Meaghan was cut from the same good cloth as her mother, and Fiona had none of the attitude Meaghan currently displayed. Fiona managed to be a perfect lady and a friend all at once, and he had enormous respect for her. He had no doubt Meaghan had the same qualities. He'd seen them; he knew who she really was. And he wondered how he might win her love.

He closed the thermos, roused Jack, and headed back to the barn. He had record keeping to do in the tiny office in the back of the barn, and his rattletrap old Land Rover needed an oil change.

Meaghan awakened early, as she always did on the farm, and dragged her unwilling beau out of bed to show him around. She dressed quickly in jeans and a sweater, told him to get a move on, and went downstairs to get them both coffee. Fiona was already in the kitchen, making tea, but she set that task aside to make her daughter the coffee she apparently required now that she was a city girl. Meaghan sat at the kitchen table and rattled on about college and about the brilliant Gerald while Fiona waited on her.

Fiona only half listened, still struggling with the image of her daughter sharing a bed with her weedy boyfriend. She wondered where Alec was, longing for his company, and decided he was giving her a chance to reconnect with Meaghan. All hope of that was quashed when the boy shuffled into the kitchen a few minutes later and sat at the table. He was dressed in the suit in which he'd arrived, as if it was all he'd brought, although this morning the tie was gone. As he sat blinking in the sunny kitchen, she wondered whether Gerald had ever been up this early in his entire life. It didn't look like it. She pushed a cup of fresh coffee across the table to him. He wrapped his hands around it and lowered his head as if the steaming cup were a religious relic over which he was about to pray.

"And what are your plans this morning?" Fiona asked Meaghan.

"I thought we were going to see Daddy."

"Not this early, dear; we need to wait till we hear from the hospital."

"Well, I think I'll show Gerald around the farm."

"I'm sure Gerald will be fascinated," Fiona said, glancing at the nearly catatonic boy. "Would either of you like something to eat first?"

Gerald looked up from his devotions.

She was sure Gerald was about to say yes, but Meaghan cut him off. "Oh no, we only ever just have coffee in the morning, don't we, Gerald?"

Meaghan stood and Gerald, as if on a wire, did the same. The two of them took their coffee cups out through the boot room to the farmyard.

"You might want to see if any of the wellies out there fit you, Gerald," Fiona called after them.

A few minutes later, the phone rang. She dashed into the front hall and met Alec as he descended the stairs.

"Tan y Gadair Farm. Yes, this is she. Oh, wonderful; that is very good news indeed." She smiled at Alec, then her face darkened. "He does? Yes, certainly we can. Ten o'clock? Yes, we'll be there. Thank you."

Fiona rang off. "That was the nurse. David's awake and we can visit him. But Dr. Pryce wants to see me first. I don't think that bodes well."

"Perhaps, Fi, but you don't know yet, do you?"

"No, you're right, I don't. I'll just get my things. There's tea in the kitchen. I'd like you to come with me this time, but if you come Meaghan will want that odious boy to come, too, and I won't stand for it. I'm sorry."

"I understand. I'll try to keep him entertained. Any suggestions?"

She laughed. "Walk him off a cliff? No, that's a bit extreme. How about having him clean out the pens you made for the newborns?"

"I'm sure he'll be delighted."

"Would you round up Meaghan for me and tell her the doctor's called and we're leaving?"

"Sure."

She turned toward her room.

"Fiona?"

She turned back again.

"Good morning, my love."

Fiona smiled, came back, and rested her forehead on his chest. He slipped his arms around her. She hugged him tight. Neither of them said anything. Finally, Alec eased her away and held her there, steadying her.

"Whatever it is, Fiona, we'll deal with it. Together. You're not alone."

"I know that; I do. I'm just anxious. I have no idea how he is, or will be."

"That's a temporary problem."

"Yes. Yes, I guess it is. Thank you, darling."

He smiled. "'Darling.' Yes, I think I like that better than 'you old relic.'"

She gave him a quick kiss and was gone.

In the kitchen, Alec poured himself a mug of tea and looked at the clock. It had just gone eight thirty; they wouldn't have to hurry. He stepped outside to a sparkling morning redolent of damp earth and new grass. He saw that Owen's Land Rover was parked in the barn and walked across the farmyard. Jack rounded a corner of the barn and bounded up to him. Not for the first time, Alec noticed that something in the shape and coloring of Jack's jaw made him look like he was always smiling. He ruffled the good-natured dog's coat and guessed that wherever Jack had come from he'd find Owen, and he was right. The young man was leaning against a sunny corner of an outbuilding, drinking from his thermos and looking off across the fields. Alec followed his eyes and saw Meaghan leading Gerald through a far meadow filled with scampering lambs. Gerald walked with exaggerated care and gave the ewes wide berth, as if the skittish animals were razor-fanged wild dogs.

Owen heard him approach and turned.

"Morning, Owen."

"Lot of opinions, that fellow has," Owen replied, tilting the thermos toward the distant couple.

"Really? I don't think I've heard him speak a complete sentence yet. I thought Meaghan did all his talking."

"Oh, yes, lots of opinions, about how the farm should be run. Like he'd know anything about running a farm . . ."

Alec put his arm around Owen's broad shoulders. "Patience, Owen. Meaghan's not stupid, just a bit full of herself, I suspect. She'll sort him out soon enough."

Owen relaxed and smiled. "Yeah, reckon she will."

"Fiona's heard from the hospital. The doctor wants to see her at ten o'clock. She's taking Meaghan, but I get to spend the morning with his nibs over there. Fiona suggests I invite him to muck out the pens."

Owen burst out laughing. "Not bloody likely!"

"No, probably not."

Alec put two fingers between his lips and let loose an earsplitting whistle. Meaghan's and Gerald's heads snapped upward, as did those of the ewes. It was almost comical. He waved the couple back, and they came quickly.

"See you a bit later, friend," Alec said.

"I'll be in the upper pastures; got a gate to mend before I let the sheep up there for the summer."

The note of proprietorship was unmistakable and Alec smiled. Yes, Owen would do very well indeed.

Fiona came out of the house and across the farmyard just as Meaghan and Gerald arrived. She told the two of them what the doctor's nurse had said.

"You boys relax; we shouldn't be more than a few hours."

Alec watched, fascinated, as the two women conducted a wordless negotiation with their eyes. Meaghan looked at Gerald and then back at her mother. Fiona gazed at her placidly. The message was clear: Alec wasn't coming, despite his role in helping save David; therefore, Gerald wasn't coming, either. Finally, Meaghan nodded and Fiona gave her the car keys.

"Why don't you drive, darling; I know you love to."

Like a man banished to an island with cannibals as his only neighbors, Gerald watched the car descend out of sight. He looked bereft.

"Right then," Alec said with exaggerated heartiness. "Why don't we do something useful while they're gone, eh?"

"Um, what?"

"Right this way." Alec led Gerald to the barn. All but one of the pens, the one holding three orphan lambs, were empty now, the lambs and ewes having been put out to the lush lower pastures.

"I tell you what, Gerald, you should have been in here a couple of days ago. Barn was filled with bleating ewes and lambs. Just the weakest ones, you see; the rest stay out in the field. And noise? My God, it was deafening. But all those lambs sure were cute. Tiny little fuzzballs. Hard work making up all these pens, but it was wonderful to see them warm and protected in here."

"You come from farming?"

"Me?" Alec laughed. "New York City born and bred. But I guess that saying is wrong: you *can* teach an old dog new tricks, at least this old dog. Anyway, what needs doing now is cleaning out the pens. We should be able to finish up before lunchtime."

Gerald looked at the manure-splattered straw with horror. Alec struggled to keep a straight face.

"Uh, I'm not exactly dressed for this sort of thing."

"Oh, I'll bet we'll be able to find something for you to wear."

"No, that's okay."

"Attaboy! I like a man who isn't afraid of a little sheep shit on his suit."

"No, I mean, I think I'll take a walk instead . . . if you don't mind."

"Mind? Hell no, that way I get to have all the fun. But you don't know what you'll be missing."

"Yeah, maybe not." He was already backing out of the barn.

"You be careful of those ewes out there, now, won't you, Gerald?"

But the boy had vanished.

Alec chuckled and went to work. By noon, he'd raked out the straw, hosed down the concrete floor, and stacked the hurdles behind the barn.

At the hospital, Fiona and Meaghan were taken immediately to Dr. Pryce's office. The doctor rose from his desk, greeted Fiona warmly, and introduced Gemma Barnes, the hospital's social worker. Fiona introduced her daughter. They gathered in a seating area in front of his desk. Fiona noticed that in addition to the usual medical diplomas and certifications, the walls of Dr. Pryce's office were decorated with photographs of climbers hanging from cliff faces. She realized they were pictures of the doctor himself.

Once they'd settled in their chairs, he began.

"Mrs. Edwards, your husband is a very lucky man. Put simply, he's come very close to dying three times in the past forty-eight hours. I'd like to walk you through your husband's last two days. There are aspects of his case you should know about for the future. Do you feel up to that?"

Fiona nodded.

"First, your husband was not on that mountain by accident or misadventure. He went up there to commit suicide."

"What?!" Meaghan blurted.

Fiona held up her hand but did not turn toward her daughter. "Please continue, Doctor."

"Mr. Edwards's blood alcohol level when he arrived here was consistent with someone who has consumed a great deal of alcohol—nearly a lethal dose in and of itself. The chap who found him"—here he checked his notes—"a Mr. Hudson, reported to the Mountain Rescue Team that there had been a storm and David had been covered with hailstones. To be honest, I don't know how your husband survived that one-two punch, but he did.

"The alcohol your husband ingested dilated his blood vessels. That helped protect him from the most severe forms of frostbite, but it also accelerated his hypothermia. Curiously, just before losing consciousness, hypothermia victims often feel too warm; that may explain why your husband's jacket was found tossed aside.

"Reviving someone with Mr. Edwards's degree of exposure is a tricky business. We do it very slowly. In this case, we began pumping warm liquids into David's stomach, warming the core organs gradually. Nonetheless, the risk of ventricular fibrillation was still very high and, as I told you last night, that happened twice as we warmed him."

Fiona interrupted. "Have you a sense of what effect these events have had on my husband?"

"Hypothermia and the brain have a curious relationship, Mrs. Edwards. Researchers have recently found, for example, that inducing a degree of hypothermia in cases of brain trauma or stroke reduces further brain damage. But between the initial hypothermia and ischemia—sorry, the interruptions in the flow of blood and oxygen—during fibrillation, your husband's brain has been challenged repeatedly and not, I am sorry to say, without effect."

Even though Fiona had expected it, the doctor's words still felt like a blow to the chest.

"Your husband is conscious and alert, Mrs. Edwards. He will, I believe, recognize you and be able to converse with you fairly normally. The principal cognitive effect of these challenges so far seems to be an impairment of what I will call, for simplicity's sake, his 'mapping ability.' What I mean by this is that he has difficulty moving correctly in the direction of his desired activity. If he wants to go to the bathroom, for example, he may walk toward the window instead and be confused to find himself there. There appears to have been some damage to the area of his brain that controls these activities. How much, we don't know yet; because of his chemical sensitivities, we haven't let him wander around much. It might be wise for you to arrange to have someone care for him full-time for a while, if that's possible. You may have to make other adjustments; there's no way to tell at this point. I'm afraid it's just wait and see from here on.

"Overall, his demeanor is cheerful, almost bemused; he seems to think he's had another heart attack and that's why he's here. He does not appear to recall what he tried to do, and, if I may, I'd like to suggest you not tell him. He could not possibly be helped by that knowledge. I should stop there and ask if you have any questions."

"Only one," Fiona said, her voice calm and strong. "When can he come home?"

"He could go home today, actually. But with your permission,

I'd like to keep him under observation for another day, so one of our neurologists can determine whether there are other impairments. Beyond that, and barring any further complications, he is free to return home."

Miss Barnes now spoke. "That's where I come in, Mrs. Edwards. My job is to make sure you and your husband have the kind of help you need at home. I've already contacted the Gwynedd County Council office in Dolgellau, and they'll be sending a care assessor to visit you sometime tomorrow. Home health care help is available and you may wish to consider it, especially for the first few weeks until we know the full extent of your husband's impairment. If you have questions about his care—or if you just need someone to talk to—call me. That's what I'm here for."

Fiona thanked her.

"Will Daddy get better?" Meaghan asked.

"I'm afraid I have no way of predicting that, Miss Edwards," the doctor said. "The brain is such a delicate instrument, but it also can be remarkably resilient. I have seen stroke victims, for example, whose brains have managed to create new neurological pathways to accomplish tasks, bypassing damaged areas, as if the brain were rewiring itself. But the simple answer, I'm afraid, is that I don't know. And, of course, your father's health had been compromised long before this latest event.

"In that regard," he went on, directing his attention again to Fiona, "David's heart is very weak; his previous attacks have taken a toll. I cannot promise he won't have more. I suspect a cardiologist would advise you to try to help him curtail strenuous activities, but I'll leave that to the cardio people."

"I understand, Dr. Pryce," Fiona said quietly. "Thank you for saving my husband."

"Don't thank me, thank this Hudson chap."

The doctor rose and they did as well.

"By the way," the doctor added, "we've moved your husband out of intensive care to a private room. Miss Barnes can take you there."

Fiona thanked the doctor again, took her daughter's hand, and said, "Let's go see Daddy, shall we?"

Alec found Gerald sprawled in a chair in the guests' sitting room, watching television.

"I could use some lunch, how about you?"

"Works for me."

In the kitchen, Alec prowled through the refrigerator.

"What *do* you eat, besides shrubbery?"

"Beans, mostly."

Alec laughed. "Better you than me, pal."

He found a large piece of sharp cheddar in the fridge. "What about cheese?"

"Yeah. Sometimes."

"Does sometimes include now?"

"Sure."

"Beer?"

"Uh-huh." Gracious, Gerald was not.

Alec found a cutting board and a loaf of crusty bread, cut a few thick slices, poured two cans of ale into dimple-glass pint mugs, and they began to eat.

"You seem like you know your way around the place," Gerald ventured. "How long you been here?"

Alec smiled, enjoying the game of Gerald trying to gather intelligence. He considered several responses and decided to go with shock value.

"Just a couple of days. I came here to scatter my late wife's ashes up on Cadair Idris."

"Whoa, no shit? Way up there?!"

Alec just smiled. "It was her last request. We climbed it years ago. I'd just taken care of it when I found David."

He'd caught Gerald completely off-guard, a state in which he suspected the wily young man seldom found himself. He wondered what sort of story Gerald had imagined to explain Alec's presence at the farm.

"With David in the hospital, I've just been helping out."

"Oh."

"So tell me," Alec said, lobbing the ball into the other court, "how long have you and Meaghan been together?"

"Few months. Took a course together. She was different from the others . . . classy, like. Older seeming than she is and all. Mind you"— Gerald winked—"I think I was her first."

Alec leaned in, conspiratorially. "Always a triumph, eh?"

"You got that right."

"Still, this hasn't exactly been a romantic weekend in the country, has it?"

"I don't know; last night wasn't bad," Gerald shrugged.

Alec despised the boy, but not because of this coarseness; he'd already figured out there was less to Gerald than met the eye. No, there was something else, something he couldn't put his finger on.

"What's your family think of Meaghan?"

"Family? Haven't got much. Mum died years ago; the smoking got her. Dad works in the Potteries, in Stoke. Paints flowers on dishes and stuff. Hasn't met her. Probably be all over her if he did, filthy bastard. No, a self-made man is what I am. Figure to be a director at Colliers in a few years."

"Very admirable," Alec said, draining his pint.

Gerald munched on the last piece of bread. "This thing about her father is really gonna fuck Meaghan up."

"Inconvenient, isn't it?"

Gerald shot him a look that evolved swiftly from smirk to suspicion. Alec could tell the boy had just realized he'd revealed too much of himself.

Fiona and Meaghan were back at the farm by midafternoon. Alec was feeding the orphan lambs when he heard them coming up the lane. Fiona was walking slowly to the house when he appeared in the barn door. She saw him and gave him a limp wave.

In the kitchen, Fiona slumped into a chair and stared at the window. Alec was just coming through the door as Meaghan put her hand on Fiona's shoulder and said softly, "You look ghastly, Mum."

"Do I? Yes, I suppose I must." She smiled at Alec as he entered the room. Gerald drifted in from somewhere else in the house.

"Have you two eaten?" she asked Alec.

"We have. Can I make you something?"

"Thank you, no; we stopped on the way home." Fiona rose. "I think I need to rest for a bit." As she passed him, she patted Alec's arm.

"Why don't I go into town and rustle up something nice for supper?" he suggested.

"That would be very kind, Alec," she said, pausing briefly to look at him. Then she slipped out of the room.

He watched the empty doorway for a moment, then turned to Gerald.

"I don't suppose you eat fish?"

"Uh-uh."

"Right. I'll see what I can scare up."

The boy just shrugged. Meaghan, he noticed, ignored the entire exchange.

"Anything special you'd like, Meaghan?" Alec asked.

"Fish is fine," she said, without enthusiasm, but at least with a smile.

Alec left the two of them in the kitchen. He longed to look in on

Fiona but could find no way to do so without drawing attention, and he suspected she needed to be alone for a while. He climbed into the red Golf and drove out of the farmyard, thinking yet again about how perfectly at home he felt in Fiona's house, in her car, in her valley.

In Dolgellau, Alec stopped in at the butcher shop. John was behind the counter.

"Mr. Lewis, if I were looking for nice fresh salmon steaks, where might I find them?"

Lewis grinned. "Salmon steaks, you say; why, I'm not sure we carry that particular cut. We have rump steak, and loin and rib eye steak, and filet steak, of course. Let me ask my brother. Harold!" Lewis called back to the freezer room. "Have we any salmon steak?"

"Never heard of it!" the invisible Harold shouted.

By now both Alec and John were laughing. John leaned across the counter and whispered to Alec.

"Now don't tell Harold I've let on, but I hear there's some of them salmon steaks at the fishmonger's, which you'll find in the alley back behind the Royal Ship Hotel, though, of course, we've never been there . . ."

Alec gave John an exaggerated wink. "I'll keep it under my hat."

As promised, the fishmonger's was right behind the hotel. The shop was brilliantly lit, a place of spotless white tile, slick marble counters, and that impossibly sweet smell of very fresh fish. The fish themselves, whole and filleted, finfish and shellfish, and including some he'd never seen or heard of, were presented like artwork on beds of crushed ice edged with fresh green parsley. They sparkled and shone like jewels. Alec settled on a large fillet of fresh Scottish salmon, rather than individual steaks, paid the rosy-cheeked woman behind the counter, and walked across the square to the greengrocer's. Here, too, the proprietress remembered him.

"How was that lemon, then?"

Alec spread his arms wide. "Splendid, madam; redolent with the tang of the Iberian Peninsula the moment the knife pierced its golden rind."

"Oh, go on, you," she replied with a blush. "What'll it be today?"

"How about some new potatoes, a fennel bulb, and . . . hmm . . . a bagful of these lovely fava beans."

"Would that be a metric bagful, or just the regular kind?" the woman countered.

"Regular will be fine." Alec loved the fact that in Britain shops still specialized: the "family butcher," the fishmonger, the greengrocer, the baker, the cheesemonger. He knew their time was probably running out, that the supermarkets would soon squeeze them out, but he was glad to support the shops to the extent he could.

He moved on to the Wine Rack and picked out three bottles of an inexpensive French white burgundy, some of which he would use to poach the fish. On his way back to the car, a pear tart in the bakery window caught his eye, and he stopped in to buy that, too.

As he started up Cadair Road toward the farm, Alec thought about how the making of food always seemed to bring peace to moments of crisis. People had to eat, no matter how unhappy they were, and the simple communal act of sharing food seemed to reestablish the pattern and balance that had been disrupted by strife or tragedy.

fifteen

O wen Lewis was under his ancient Land Rover in the barn. He had just drained the oil from the crankcase when he heard voices.

"Christ, woman, use your imagination! You're supposed to be creative."

Owen recognized the voice.

"Right, then; I'll spell it out for you," Gerald said with patronizing slowness. "From those fields you can see all the way to the Irish Sea, yeah? Plus you've got this bloody big mountain right behind. Now, in your mind, make those old stone walls on the slopes below the mountain disappear. And imagine instead a series of terraces—properly built, mind you. And on each of them, stepping down the hillside, there'd be rows of custom-made holiday caravans, or maybe wooden chalets on elevated platforms. Dozens of them. You'd be able to hire them out at least six months of the year, maybe more. Just think of the income that would generate! Plus, I'm thinking there needs to be a kiddie park, just beyond that garden in front of the house. A real attraction that would be from the parents' point of view, know what I mean? Come to think of it, lose the bloody flower garden; nothing but a maintenance cost is what that is. We could have a petting zoo there; you know, sheep and goats and whatever. Maybe a cow. And a pony. Must have a pony."

"We could never do that, Gerald. My family's been farming here for generations. I couldn't imagine these fields filled with caravans. It's just too . . . too . . ."

"What, too low class? You don't think factory workers in the Midlands deserve a nice holiday in the mountains? You think this place is too good for them? Or maybe *you're* too good for them? Look, I'm guessing the only reason your father hasn't gone belly-up is your mum's business; this farm's a relic."

"It is not; Daddy's made a profit most years!"

"Yeah, sure he has, thanks to the government subsidies. How long you think they'll last?"

"I don't know. But you'd never get planning permission from the council for something like that."

"Don't be daft, girl; a little money in the right place will buy off any county council in the country."

Meaghan was stunned by his cynicism. "Besides, Mum and Daddy would never allow it; I'm sure they wouldn't."

"That's a laugh, that is," Gerald sneered. "First of all, your old man's a goner. How long d'you think he's got?"

"How can you say that?" Meaghan shouted, but he kept on.

"And who's he going to pass the farm to, besides you? Nobody, that's who. When we get married, they'll have no choice; we can do whatever we like."

"Married? Are you asking me to marry you?" Now there was confusion in Meagan's voice, a mix of surprise and, suddenly, fear. She stared at Gerald; it was like a door had been flung open to a sinister in-

terior landscape she'd never sensed in him before. She'd talked about
the farm constantly and had thought her affection for it was part of
what he loved about her. But now a different reality was setting in.
He'd been scheming all along; she was a means to an end, a gold mine
for him. No wonder he'd offered to come home with her when her
mother called. She'd thought it sweet and caring of him; instead, he
was only surveying the territory.

"Mum would never leave," she said, struggling for a coherent
thought.

Gerald snorted. "Your mother? That's a laugh, that is. As soon
as the old man croaks, she'll be off to America with that new lover
of hers!"

"What are you *talking* about?!" There was panic in her voice now.

Owen eased himself out from under the Land Rover.

Gerald laughed at her. "You don't mean to tell me you don't see
the way she looks at him? You blind as well as dim?"

"You certainly have a way with the ladies, don't you, Gerald?" a
calm voice said from the door of the barn.

"Owen!" Meaghan cried.

Gerald spun around but Owen was already upon him. With both
hands, Owen grasped the lapels of Gerald's suit jacket, lifted him off
the ground, and slammed him against the stone wall of the barn. Quietly, but with unmistakable fury, he said, "A gentleman does not insult
his lady. A gentleman does not dishonor his lady's mother, or the reputation of another gentleman. But you wouldn't know any of that,
would you, you miserable lowlife!"

Gerald dangled like a marionette but was smart enough to keep
his mouth shut.

"Now, unless I miss my guess, I think your little visit here has
come to an end," Owen said, glancing at Meaghan for confirmation.

Meaghan nodded.

Owen dropped Gerald back to the ground but did not release him. "Let's fetch your things, shall we? I'm sure there's a train soon." He marched the boy back to the house just as Alec drove into the farmyard. Meaghan was standing beside the barn like a statue, her arms clutched across her breasts as if she were naked. Alec stopped the car in the middle of the yard, took in the scene, and went to her.

"What is it, Meaghan? What's happened?"

Meaghan said nothing. Instead, soundlessly, she pressed her face into his chest. He put his hands on her shoulders and held her a little away from himself. He looked toward the door to the house and then back at Meaghan.

"Has he hurt you?"

Meaghan shook her head, her eyes blank.

"Well then, it looks to me like a fine afternoon for a walk. Shall we?" He took her elbow and they set off for the front garden and, from there, the fields beyond. Holding open a gate for her, Alec said, "Do you want to talk about it?"

Meaghan shook her head again, but this time she smiled at Alec with what seemed to him to be the most genuine wordless "thank you" he had ever experienced.

They walked in silence for a while.

"Mr. Hudson . . ."

He stopped. Her eyes were dry but she looked shattered.

"Please, it's Alec."

"Alec. I can't thank you enough for all you've done. I am so very sorry I was rude to you yesterday. So much has changed, hasn't it?"

"Has it really, Meaghan? I wonder. Let's set Gerald to one side for a moment. Before this, your father was an invalid. Today, he's still an invalid. He may require just a little more active care than before. But my guess is he'd want you to stay on at university, do well, and make him proud—as I suspect he already is."

Meaghan stared at him. "How did you know I was thinking of quitting?"

"Because your mother has told me how devoted you are to your father. I think that's wonderful. But caring for him isn't your job, if you'll permit me to say so; it's your mother's. Your job is to keep becoming who you were meant to be. It's what your father would want."

Tears formed in the corners of her deep brown eyes and she smiled. She knew almost nothing about the man before her, except that she found it easy to trust him.

"Thank you, Alec."

When they returned to the house half an hour later the red Golf was gone. Fiona was at the door. The two women looked at each other. Fiona's eyes were soft and full of love.

"Oh, Mother, I'm so sorry . . ."

"Shush, darling; Owen told me. You have nothing to apologize for or be ashamed of. He was a mistake, that's all. We all make them. I daresay there will be more. It's called 'experience.' Some experiences are just a little harder than others."

Meaghan stood for a moment, first fighting back tears, then almost visibly gathering strength from the safety and familiarity of her surroundings.

"I'm going to go take a bath," she announced with a thin smile. Then she was gone.

"Tea?" Fiona asked Alec as they entered the house.

"The hell with the tea; what in God's name is going on?"

"She didn't tell you?"

"No."

"Well, then, let's just say the brilliant Gerald is a thing of the past and leave it there."

"Did he hurt her?"

"No, not physically."

"You're not going to tell me, are you?"

"Not now, no. Perhaps later. It's not important."

Alec knew this wasn't true, but he didn't press. He heard the car roar into the farmyard and met Owen as he was wrestling the groceries from the backseat.

"Sorry about hijacking these; I'd just drained the oil from the Rover."

"Sounds like it was for a good cause. When's the next train?"

"Not for hours," Owen said, beaming, and they both laughed.

"Will you have dinner with us tonight, Owen?"

Owen hesitated, looking toward the house. "I don't know. Depends on how Meaghan's faring, I reckon."

Alec nodded. "How about you look in later?"

"Sure. I'll be under the Land Rover for a while, then up with the sheep."

"Owen?"

The young man looked at him.

"Whatever you did this afternoon, thanks."

Owen bowed slightly and grinned. "My pleasure."

Fiona walked through the house and into her suite of rooms. She knew Meaghan loved the big claw-foot tub in her mother's bathroom and that she'd find her there. She knocked gently at the door.

"Yes?" Meaghan called, an edge to her voice.

"It's just me, darling; may I come in?"

"Of course, Mum."

Fiona found Meaghan encased in bubbles, looking much more like her little girl than the grown woman she'd become. She leaned over the tub and kissed her daughter's damp forehead, then sat on a terry-cloth-covered stool she used when she was drying off.

"I thought perhaps you'd like some company, but if you'd rather be alone . . ."

"No, Mummy, stay." Meaghan rested her head on the back of the tub. "The company helps."

"I'm sorry things turned out badly for you and Gerald."

"I just feel so stupid. He seemed so much older and smarter than the other boys. Stronger, you know? He criticized me a lot, but I thought, well, he just knew more. I didn't see the other stuff; I didn't know him at all."

"Darling, you aren't the first woman to mistake arrogance for power, or sex for passion. Unfortunately, you won't be the last, either. It's so awfully common."

"You mean *he* was so awfully common."

"No, Meaghan, I don't. And commonness is not a failing; this has nothing to do with class. There are good and kind and solid 'common' men. Your father, for one. Until he took sick, I don't think your father ever said an unkind word to me in all our years together. It's only since then he's become difficult. But I suspect abusiveness of one kind or another is a way of life for Gerald. You would have discovered that sooner or later. I'm glad it was sooner."

"Me, too."

"There will be other men and I'm sure you'll choose a bit more carefully next time. There are many charming, thoughtful, and caring men out there in the world."

"You mean like Alec."

Fiona looked at her daughter for a moment. "Yes, like Mr. Hudson."

"But Gerald said—"

Fiona cut her off. "Gerald Wilson, my love, was a nasty piece of work, despite the flashy suit. Alec Hudson is the reason I'm not wearing black today. And since your father's . . . accident, I don't know what

I would have done without him. That man, that stranger sent to us from God only knows where, has been the calm in the center of this whole terrible, tragic week. I am beyond grateful to him; I am forever in his debt. And you should be, too."

"I am, Mother, truly. I didn't mean to . . ."

"I know you didn't. Now it's my turn to apologize; that came out a bit harsher than I meant it to."

Fiona sighed. "Look, after all that's happened in the last day or two, I want you to know I love you more than ever. I suspect we're going to need each other's support in the coming weeks and months. I won't be able to give Daddy the kind of extra attention he will need now and still keep the bed-and-breakfast going. I'm going to arrange for someone to come in and look after him. I've also asked Owen to take over the farm; he's an exceptional young man and he'll do brilliantly—he practically runs the farm already. What I hope you'll do . . ."

"I know, Mum. You'd like me to go back to school. And I will. As soon as we've got Daddy sorted. But I'll be here if you need me."

Fiona smiled. "I'd better let you get on with your bath. Besides, Alec will be starting dinner soon, and I'd like to freshen up, too."

"Mum?"

"Yes, dear?"

"I love you, and I think you've been very brave."

"Thank you, sweetie. I love you, too, always."

She closed the door. *I wonder,* she thought as she walked through her bedroom, *how brave am I?*

When Alec returned with the groceries, Fiona was gone and he guessed she was with her daughter. He put the fish and wine in the refrigerator and sat for a while sipping the tea she'd left him and staring vacantly out the window. When he and Fiona were together, he was overcome by two emotions he'd always thought were polar opposites— excitement and peace. The thrill of her presence came wrapped in a cloak of comfort. It was as if the two of them had been fashioned to be perfectly interlinked parts but a careless inventor had misplaced them. Somehow, they'd been found again, and they had slipped together seamlessly—not just in lovemaking, but in the smallest of exchanges. He had never known such love, even with Gwynne. And now he did not know what to do or where to go with it. Ever since her meeting with the doctor, he had felt her slipping away. He was struggling to balance his own needs with hers, his own dreams with the awful reality of her life at this moment.

"A penny for your thoughts." Fiona's voice.

He turned toward the dining room door where she stood, but didn't answer. He didn't think he could and still keep his composure. She came to him and they held each other, breathing slowly and deeply, as if each was gathering strength from the other.

"I'll tell you what I'm thinking," she finally said. "I'm thinking it's been a long time since lunch and I'm ravenous."

He started laughing from deep in his belly, a wonderful, liberating laughter. There it was again, the excitement and the peace . . . and the fun. He straightened up.

"And I'm also thinking," she continued, "that you probably bought wine and I would dearly like to have a glass."

"And so you shall," Alec said, his heart joyous again.

He opened the fridge, took out a bottle of the Mâcon Blanc, and set about opening it.

Fiona watched him and then said, "And what, Chef Alec, have you in mind for us tonight?"

"*Le plat du jour, madame,*" he answered, adopting a patently phony French chef's accent, "is fee-lay de sal-moan poach-ed in whaht wine, wis a cream and sautéed fennel sauce, accompanied by . . . um"—and here the accent failed him—". . . something to do with fava beans."

Fiona started giggling. She had never know Alec to be at a loss for words when it came to food.

He poured her a glass of wine and they sat down facing each other at the kitchen table, the bond between them so intimate they might have been in bed.

Then Alec asked the question that had troubled him all afternoon: "What is David like now?"

Instead of looking away, as she often did when considering an answer, Fiona looked at Alec directly.

"Different."

She paused for a moment, as if trying to pinpoint the difference, then continued: "He knows who he is and who we are and where he is. He thinks he knows how he got there, but of course he doesn't. He can converse fairly normally, though sometimes he seems to struggle to find a word. As Dr. Pryce said, he seems to have lost the ability to find his way from one place to the next. He knows where he wants to go, but he goes the wrong way. It's very odd.

"And there's something else . . . ," she said, looking even more intently into Alec's eyes. "He smiles too much. Do you know what I mean? It's a sweet smile, but blank. It takes over his face the moment he's not thinking or saying or doing anything else."

"Like a child?"

"Like a child with brain damage, maybe."

Alec said nothing. He reached across the table and took Fiona's hand in his. Far away, he could hear the ewes calling their lambs.

Fiona lifted her head and smiled across the table. "On the other hand, his anger seems to have vanished. I doubt he is a danger to anyone anymore, including himself, but I suppose we'll have to wait and see about that."

For a while, silence expanded between them.

"Fi," Alec said finally, "I don't know what to say that would make what has happened better."

"Tell me you love me?"

He looked into her eyes and then grinned.

"Completely, utterly, deeply, furiously, joyously, and forever. Will that do?"

"For now," Fiona said, grinning back.

"If I can get my daughter to release my bathroom, I'm going to go wash this day off of me," she continued. "Is there anything I can do here?"

"Tell me you love me?" Alec echoed.

Fiona got up, walked around the table, and pressed Alec's face to her breasts. "More than you can imagine," she whispered.

She kissed the top of his head, burying her face in his hair for a moment, and then slipped out of the room.

Alec went to the sink to scrub the potatoes. He felt spent, but he knew the cooking would revive him; it always did. The pleasure it gave him was beyond explaining. If he'd known about it earlier, he would have had a restaurant, but he knew that was a young man's game. And he wasn't a young man anymore. What did he have left, after all? Twenty-five years, perhaps? Two-thirds of his life had already passed. With all his being, he wanted to spend what was left with Fiona.

He was rinsing the salmon when he heard heels clicking down the front stairs. A moment later, Meaghan entered the kitchen. She was transformed, her face radiant and carefully made up. She was wearing a fitted, button-front, sleeveless dress in a rust brown that comple-mented her eyes. She'd wrapped several strands of colorful peasant beads around her throat. She was, Alec noticed again, Rose Red to her mother's Snow White. Alec marveled at the way both mother and daughter bounced back from crises.

"What can I do to help?" she asked.

Alec laughed. "First of all, you're dressed far too elegantly to be my sous chef. Second, I have to confess I'm not very good at delegating in the kitchen; I'm usually having too much fun. But here's something I hope won't be too taxing. There's a nice white burgundy open in the fridge; how about you pour us both a glass and keep me company? I'd like that very much."

"Which, the wine or the company?"

Alec stopped what he was doing, looked at her, and chuckled. "You are definitely your mother's daughter. But the answer is both."

Meaghan poured the wine and brought a glass to him as he was pulling the last of the rib bones from the salmon fillet. He set the glistening fish aside, stood a fennel bulb upright on a cutting board, and sliced it lengthwise so a portion of the core remained to hold together each slice.

"What's that?"

"You're joking."

"No, really. Some kind of onion?"

"Well, I have to admit it looks like one, but smell." Alec held a slice to her nose.

She scrunched her face. "It smells like licorice."

"Right. It's fennel, also called anise, and there's a licorice-flavored liqueur called anisette that's made from its seeds. Anyway, the great thing about fennel is that when you braise it in butter and a bit of broth or salted water, the sharpness disappears and it becomes soft, golden, sweet, and fragrant, the same way a Spanish onion does when you caramelize it. It's completely transformed."

Meaghan stood by him as he worked. "How do you know all this? I mean, how did you learn how to cook like this?"

"I learned because I love to eat."

"So do I, but that doesn't mean I can cook."

"All right, sit down and I'll tell you how I got started."

Meaghan returned to the kitchen table and sipped her wine.

"Years ago, when I was about sixteen—let's see, that was back in 1843, as I recall—"

"Oh, go on!" Meaghan erupted.

"Okay, but long before you were born, I had an aunt I adored. Actually, she was my father's second cousin or something, but I had no aunts, so I sort of adopted her. She was, to put it bluntly, an original: smoked like a chimney, cursed like a trooper, drank like a fish. In short, not the sort of person my parents would have approved of, had they really known her character—which means, as an aunt, she was perfect."

Alec slid the fennel into a sauté pan with some butter and let the slices brown slowly.

"Anyway, the year I turned eighteen I got really sick and she volunteered to take care of me during part of my recuperation. I moved into her house for a few weeks and she took it upon herself to become my tutor in worldly matters. She taught me to make her martinis, for example: start with very cold gin, wave the unopened vermouth bottle over the rim of the shaker, swirl with ice, pour, add an olive. She set me up with a beautiful friend of her daughter's but I was too shy to make a move. One day, after she'd had two or three martinis, she said, 'I have decided to give you the secret to attracting women, young man. Learn this and learn it well.' Well, I can tell you, I was all ears. I'll never forget it. She was peering at me sagely over the rim of her glass, and this is what she said: 'Learn to cook a few things brilliantly, and learn to iron flawlessly.'"

Meaghan laughed outright.

Alec turned to her, grinning. "It's never failed yet."

"But wait! You've no wedding band; you're single!"

Alec turned away, reduced the heat under the fennel, added a bit of water and salt, and covered the sauté pan. "I wasn't always."

"Oh dear; I've said something wrong."

"No, no; not at all. It's just that I was on the mountain scattering my late ex-wife's ashes when I found your father. She and I . . . well, let's just say we were the best of friends."

"I had no idea."

"Well, how could you? Anyway, life goes on for the rest of us—just as yours will despite what happened today."

"Yes. Yes, I suppose it will." She paused for a moment, then recovered. "Right. So what's next after the fennel thingie?"

"When it's softened, the fennel thingie—and I note you used the technical term—will actually be minced to a fine paste and mixed with cream to form a sauce for the poached salmon. But first we need to make the *court bouillon*."

"Okay, you've got me again: '*court bouillon*'?"

Alec grabbed the fish and held it up.

"Look at this lovely piece of salmon, Scotland's finest. We wouldn't cook it in plain water, would we? Of course not," he ranted. "No, we would poach it gently in a *court bouillon!*" He slipped back into his normal voice. "Which is nothing more than a broth made with some finely chopped vegetables, herbs, and wine, but the French sounds so fancy."

Alec had already arranged the ingredients—a carrot, some onion, parsley, a stem of the fennel. His knife was a blur as he began chopping the parsley.

"That's scary-looking," Meaghan said as the knife flew.

"Actually, it's safer than any other way of handling a knife. Here, want to try?"

She rose and went to the counter where he was working.

"Your mother has some good knives. This one, with its wide blade and sharp point, is called a chef's knife. It's mainly for chopping but I use it more than any other. Take it in your hand."

Meaghan gripped it like a hammer.

"No, move your hand forward. Put your thumb on the left side of the blade's shank, and your bent forefinger on the right side. See how much more stable it feels?"

"Um, sort of."

"Okay, now take this parsley and hold it down with your left hand, but with your fingers curled inward and the first knuckle of each finger facing the upright blade, even resting against it. That'll protect your fingertips, see? Now, instead of lifting the knife off the board altogether, just rock it from tip to shank, moving it across the herbs. That's why the blade is slightly curved, so it can rock. Go ahead, try it."

Meaghan did, slowly, picking up speed as she got used to it.

"That's so cool!"

Alec smiled. "End of lesson one: 'How to Hold the Chef's Knife.'"

"Is there more to chop?" she said, brandishing the knife. It was as if she'd just been given a new toy.

Alec pushed the carrot and fennel greens toward her. "If you slice the carrot lengthwise several times first, it won't be so thick and will be easier to chop."

Meaghan went to work with the concentration of a diamond cutter. When she came to the onion he stopped her.

"How do you usually chop an onion?" he asked.

"Slice it, then dice it, then wipe away the tears."

"Okay, here's a suggestion. First, cut the onion in half lengthwise, not crosswise, right down the middle, just like the fennel bulb."

Meaghan did so.

"Now peel back the skin of one of the halves and, with the tip of the knife, make long lengthwise parallel cuts, but not as far down as the core."

She followed his advice.

"Now, turn the half onion a quarter turn and hold it just like you held the carrot sections and chop crossways. What once took many steps now takes only three. Plus, you don't tear up as much."

"I hate when the onion mist gets in my eyes!"

"Next time, hold your breath when you're chopping. The mist doesn't get in your eyes, it gets there through your nose; you breathe it in as you work. That's what makes your eyes water. End of lesson two: 'Chopping Onions.'"

He took the knife from her hand. "Now get out of my way so I can cook."

Meaghan giggled, returned to the table, and drank more of her wine. "Thank you, Alec."

"Anytime," he said over his shoulder.

"No, I mean for everything. Especially finding Daddy and protecting him."

Alec turned toward her. "Anyone would have done the same thing, Meaghan."

"But maybe not as well."

"I suppose that's one advantage of years; you learn things. Like how to chop an onion . . ." *And you lose things, too,* he thought to himself, thinking of Gwynne and praying he wouldn't lose Fiona, too.

Alec sautéed the finely chopped vegetables in a little butter, then added white wine, a bay leaf, salt, pepper, and water. The young woman and the much older man shared the space quietly and companionably, their growing friendship warming the room as if there were a fire glowing in the nonexistent hearth.

Fiona stepped out of her tub, rubbed herself down with the rough linen towel, threw her bathrobe over her shoulders, and climbed up onto her bed, her body flushed pink from the hot bath. She propped her back against the pillows, pulled up her legs, clutched her knees, and stared into nothingness. There was a soft thump on the mattress; Sooty had leaped up to join her.

In this bed, for years, she had been lonely beyond enduring, though she *had* endured. In this same bed, only three nights ago, she had been happier than she could ever have imagined. The lover, the partner she had always dreamed of, had come to her, by some miracle, at last. Tomorrow, the husband to whom she had been wed for nearly a quarter century would return home, too, more an invalid than he'd been only a few days before. It was, she thought, as if her horizons had expanded at the expense of his, as if there were a fixed quantity of happiness in the world and if yours increased, someone else's had to decrease.

She had sidestepped her daughter's question this evening—cut her off, in fact. Owen had told Fiona what Gerald had said about her and Alec; she'd wondered if Owen's face had been red from embarrassment for her or anger with Gerald, and thought again how fond she was of the young man and how confident she was about handing him control of the farm. And she realized she was confident, too, about withholding the truth about Alec from her daughter. When and if Meaghan needed to know, she would tell her. But not now. Possibly never. Between mother and daughter, not everything could or should be shared.

When Fiona entered the kitchen a little later, Meaghan was giggling, slightly tipsy from spending an hour sipping white wine.

"Well," Fiona huffed, "I can see you have plied my daughter with alcohol. Any chance you might do the same for me?"

"In the fridge. The chef is too busy to play waiter, too."

She smiled at him, gave her daughter a kiss on the cheek, and took the nearly empty bottle of wine out of the refrigerator. She looked at her daughter and noticed how carefully she had dressed for dinner. "You've drunk all this?"

"Mother! He poured half the bottle into the *court bouillon!*"

"The what?"

"You know, minced veg and herbs and wine and stuff."

Fiona walked over to where Alec was working. "Teaching my daughter racy French phrases! Sir, I hope your intentions are honorable!"

"My intentions, madam, are purely culinary," Alec replied with exaggerated formality. "We have been discussing matters of cuisine, and nothing more, I assure you."

"Well, I should certainly hope so," she said, grinning at her daughter. She hadn't seen Meaghan so happy in a long time, and she knew it wasn't the wine.

"Dinner in moments," Alec announced. "May I suggest you ladies set the table?"

Alec had hoped Owen would join them, but he'd seen the lad drive out of the farmyard and down the lane toward the main road as darkness had fallen. He was disappointed, but also impressed: Owen had a sense of timing and knew Meaghan needed breathing room. He wasn't sure whether he'd have possessed the same wisdom at Owen's age; it was too far back to remember, anyway.

Fiona bustled about the kitchen and was suffused with the sense of how right the three of them were together. Alec had confessed to her that he'd always wished he'd had a daughter, and here he and Meaghan were, getting along famously. She had to remind herself that this was not her true family. Once again, she felt guilty about her happiness, but she pushed it aside. This was about the moment: this moment, in this kitchen, on this evening, with these two other individuals, about to share a lovely meal. Be happy with what you have.

Meaghan had arranged the table settings while Fiona sorted out the serving dishes. Alec, she noticed, had drained the potatoes, put the lid back on the pot, and returned it to the hob.

"Won't they burn?"

"Not unless we forget about them. A few moments more on the hob will evaporate the moisture in the potatoes and leave them dry and fluffy."

"Fluffy?"

"That is the technical term, yes." Alec had already removed the cooked salmon and strained the poaching liquid, returning the broth to the Aga's hottest hob to boil down. At the last minute, he swirled in the nearly pureed braised fennel and a small amount of cream, stirring constantly. Next he poured the sauce over the salmon fillet, then threw salt and chopped parsley on the potatoes and scooped them into a serving dish. In a bowl, he dressed bright green boiled and shelled fava beans in olive oil and lemon, then carried the serving dishes to the table.

"For God's sake, somebody pour me a glass of wine," he said, wiping his brow with a kitchen towel.

They sat.

"Wow," Meaghan said.

Alec lifted his glass. "To David, and to his safe return to this wonderful home."

Tears welled in Meaghan's eyes. Fiona smiled at Alec. She knew he meant every word. She knew he understood their plight. She knew he would do anything for her, even if it hurt him, and she knew this was more heroic than anything he had done on the mountain.

They clinked glasses and sipped, and dinner began.

The two women were appreciative and voracious diners and Alec was delighted. They talked about the early spring, the successful lambing, Meaghan's university courses, the books Alec had written. The conversation was at once trivial and intimate. When they were done, Alec pulled the pear tart from the warming oven, but Meaghan begged off, saying she was stuffed and sleepy. Fiona walked with her as far as the stairs to make sure she was all right and returned to find that Alec had placed two thin slices of the tart on plates and managed to find the

sherry. She turned off a few of the kitchen lights and they ate quietly together, content simply to be in each other's company.

When they were done, Fiona rose. "Tea?"

"Oh, I don't think so; it'll only keep me awake."

She walked around the table, hitched up her skirt, threw a leg over
Alec, and settled on his lap. "Then how about me?"

"That would certainly keep me awake, and ensure a good night's
sleep as well." He held her shoulders and pressed a kiss into the little
depression beneath her neck where her collarbones joined, a place he
found irresistible on her. He teased the spot with the tip of his tongue
and then placed miniature, nipping kisses up along the left side of her
neck until he was nibbling on her earlobe. She turned and met his lips
with hers. They were gentle, tender kisses. After a few moments, Alec
felt her body relax into his.

"Don't ever leave me," Fiona mumbled into his shoulder. "Ever."

Alec pulled her closer, but said nothing.

After a few moments, Fiona sat up and smiled. "We can't be together tonight, but I want you to know I wish we could."

"Me, too."

"Mmm. I can tell," she breathed, feeling his hardness beneath her.

She kissed him again and rose from his lap. Together, they cleared
the table and washed the pots and pans, moving around the kitchen
easily, as if they'd had years of practice. When they were done, Fiona
turned off the lights and the two of them walked hand in hand to the
front hall. Fiona got up on tiptoes and Alec leaned down to kiss
her again.

"Good night, dear man."

"Good night, Fi."

They parted, and Alec watched Fiona pass through the low door
to her rooms before slowly climbing the stairs to his own.

• • •

Fiona lay in bed, emotionally spent but sleepless, and thought about God. Though her grandfather had been an Anglican priest, and she'd been baptized in the faith, she'd never been an especially devout member of the Church. It wasn't that she was a nonbeliever; she'd just fallen away. She'd been taught that God was her redeemer but she'd never felt that God was an active presence in her life. Now she couldn't help but wonder whether He was punishing her for having found happiness at last. She had committed adultery. What's more, she had done it joyfully. She loved Alec with all her heart and knew, at a level deeper than any memorized catechism, that they were meant to be together. Yet no sooner had she reached that certainty, when God—or fate, or something—brought about David's attempted suicide and now his even greater disability. Perhaps He was punishing them both.

april 17, 1999

s i x t e e n

*a*lec was awakened by voices in the hall. He had slept later than usual. The sky outside was overcast. There was a knock at his door and Fiona ducked her head into his room.

"Meaghan and I are going to church this morning, and then I have some papers to sign at the Gwynedd Council offices. Want to join us?"

"Come here, you," he whispered.

She looked quickly over her shoulder and slipped into his room, dashing to the bed. She was fully dressed, but he pulled her down atop him anyway, slipping his hand beneath her full print skirt and running it up along the back of her thigh.

"Stop that," she mumbled into his chest. "We'll get caught!"

He let her go.

"Wherever you are is where I want to be," he said. "Give me a moment to shave and I'll be right down."

When he reached the kitchen, both women were ready to go.

Meaghan was wearing jeans, a black T-shirt, and her suit jacket. He noticed she was wearing her mother's black flats and that, in turn, Fiona was wearing her daughter's heels. She had the car keys in her hand and a cardigan draped over her shoulders.

"Whatever happened to the 'breakfast' in bed-and-breakfast?"

"You'll live." Fiona chided.

They walked out to the barn and Fiona gave her daughter the keys. "Alec, you sit up front with Meaghan; you need the leg room."

Alec would have protested but Fiona had already slipped into the backseat. Meaghan backed the car out, put the car in first gear, and they sped out of the farmyard as if launched by a catapult. As they twisted down the curling farm lane toward the road, Alec said, "Your mother teach you to drive?"

"How'd you know?"

"Hey!" Fiona said as she leaned forward and punched him in the shoulder.

"Because you both drive like professionals, of course," he said, rubbing his arm.

St. Mary's Church proved to be a small stone-built structure with a squat, crenellated clock tower. It was tucked into a grassy courtyard close to the center of Dolgellau. After Meaghan parked, the three of them walked through a small graveyard crowded with headstones, all of which seemed ancient. Alec wondered whether parishioners had simply stopped dying several centuries ago.

They entered the church by a side door and found the sanctuary empty.

Alec leaned toward Fiona and said, "I think I'll just wait back here."

Fiona nodded and the two women walked up the central aisle of the nave and slipped into a pew near the altar.

Alec had always felt oppressed, rather than uplifted, in churches.

He considered himself a Christian, and sought to live by the tenets of the faith, but its politics left him cold. Now, though, he was struck by the airy austerity of St. Mary's. He picked up the parish newsletter from a stack on a table by the door and learned that although the current church dated from only 1716, it was built upon a twelfth-century foundation.

He sat in a rear pew and looked around. The thick walls were plastered and largely undecorated. They were punctured by deep-set, elongated stained-glass windows surmounted by sturdy, rounded arches. The nave had a barrel-vaulted timber ceiling that was supported not by stone piers but by narrow wooden pillars that seemed almost too delicate to bear the weight. He didn't know a great deal about Anglicanism; he'd always thought of it as a version of Catholicism where priests got to marry. But this simple church had none of the ornate trappings of Catholicism; it could easily have doubled as a Quaker meetinghouse.

He wondered how religious Fiona was and realized there were so many things he didn't know. At the front of the church, Meaghan sat with her head bowed, but Fiona simply leaned her elbows on the back of the pew in front of her, chin cupped in her hands, and stared fixedly at the altar. After several minutes, Meaghan looked up and touched her mother's arm. Fiona responded as if she'd been startled. She rose immediately, stepped into the aisle, took Meaghan's hand. As they walked back up the long nave to where Alec waited, he could see Fiona had been crying.

Outside the church, the weather had improved. There were patches of filmy blue sky between scudding clouds. They walked back through the graveyard to the car, got in, and headed toward the town center.

"Look," Alec said, "you two certainly don't need me at the council office and I'm dizzy with hunger. Why don't you drop me at the coffee shop. I'll meet you there when you're finished."

"Good idea," Fiona said. "I'm afraid we haven't looked after you very well this morning."

Alec smiled. "I enjoyed St. Mary's, truly. But now I'd enjoy a scone."

They paused at the Cozy, Alec jumped out, and Meaghan roared away. As before, the place was packed. Still, Brandith hurried over, ushered him to a table, and promptly sat down opposite him.

"Oh, Mr. Hudson, we've all heard about poor David's accident. Terrible, it is. But what a mercy you were on the mountain and found him before it was too late. How is he?"

Alec wondered how long it had taken for the word to spread. Minutes probably.

"He's doing well, Brandith; he should be coming home sometime today."

"Fiona must be so relieved. Now, what can I bring you this morning?"

"A pot of tea and one of your fine scones, please."

Brandith bustled off and one of the other ladies in the shop soon returned with his order. He poured a cup of tea and looked again at the parish newsletter. It was the usual mix of announcements, schedules, brief mentions of weddings and funerals, and ads placed by parishioners. Off to his left he heard someone whisper, "That's that American fellow who saved David Edwards, you know." He looked up and realized many of the people in the shop were looking at him. Suddenly, Brandith appeared again and plumped herself down in the chair across from him.

"Now you tell our Fiona," she said as he ate, "that we'll all be looking out for her. I've already arranged for some folks to bring food around later this afternoon and someone will be looking in every day."

"That's very kind, Brandith, but I'm not sure . . ."

"Not a word of it," she said, holding up a hand. "We all love Fi and

David; it's our duty to help however we can. And you, well, I suppose you'll be heading back to America now your work here is done."

"Well, I suppose . . ."

"But you'll always be welcome in this town, Mr. Hudson; we don't forget people we care about."

Brandith was fairly sparkling with neighborly affection, but Alec suddenly felt as if he were suffocating. He looked at the clock on the wall in the rear, gulped the tea in his cup, and rose quickly.

"I am so sorry, Brandith, but I've lost track of the time and I'm late. I hope you won't fault me for rushing off like this. Will this cover the bill?"

Brandith rose as well, looked at the money he'd slapped on the table, and nodded. As he rushed for the door, she called after him, "Be sure you come to see us next time you're in Wales!"

He waved as he slipped out the front door.

Alec got to the next corner, stopped, leaned against a dark slate-stone wall, and gulped air. As he recovered his composure, he realized that it wasn't the fact that everyone in this small town knew everything about everyone else that had gotten to him, or that they were massing in support of Fiona and David, their beleaguered neighbors. He found that soul nourishing and beyond anything he had ever known. No, what had sent him fleeing Brandith's shop was a sudden recognition: there was no place for him in that warm, communal embrace. People were grateful for what he had done, they wished him well, they hoped he'd return again, but now they expected him to be on his way.

It stunned him. He and Fiona fit together so easily, so naturally, and so passionately it had never occurred to him that he might not fit in her world, that he might be a source of scandal, that his presence in her life might erode the comforting certainties that gave her a sense of belonging in and to this valley—this valley she loved so deeply.

A horn startled him. He looked up and saw that Meaghan had stopped the red car at the curb directly in front of him. He hadn't even noticed. He climbed into the passenger seat. Fiona leaned forward as Meaghan pulled out into the street and asked, "Are you all right? You looked a bit like a lost tourist back there."

"I suppose I did." The image settled over him like a shroud. He asked how the meeting had gone at the council.

"The hospital social worker had briefed them on David's condition, as she said she would. They had all the paperwork ready. Of course, we've had dealings with them in the past, what with the poisoning and the chemical sensitivity. The home care staff are sending around an assessor in an hour or two to determine David's needs. People complain about the council's bureaucracy, but we saw none of it this morning, did we, Meaghan?"

Meaghan kept her eyes on the road but smiled. "Well, I don't suppose it hurt that the new head of that office is another of Daddy's distant cousins . . . Might explain why she was there on a Saturday, too."

Alec smiled, too, but inwardly winced. It was another example of the town rallying to care for one of its own . . . and of his own marginality.

When they got back to the farm, Owen was waiting for them.

"I hope you won't mind, Mrs. Edwards . . . ," he began as they got out of the car.

"Owen?!" Fiona said to him, hands on hips.

"Sorry . . . Fiona. Anyway, I took the liberty of making myself some tea and the phone rang. I thought it might be you, so I answered it."

"And . . . ?"

"Well, it was the hospital. They'd like you to come collect David. I hope I haven't overstepped . . ."

"For God's sake, Owen," Fiona teased, "I've asked you to take over the farm; I hardly think answering the phone is a transgression!"

Owen smiled, then turned. "Afternoon, Meaghan; how are you this day?"

Meaghan had been leaning against the car, watching this affectionate exchange between her mother and the young man. She had her head tilted to one side, the way her mother did when she was puzzling something out. A quiet smile formed on her lips. She realized, not in a lightning flash of recognition, but gradually, like a tide advancing slowly on a beach, that Owen Lewis was exactly the "good and kind and solid" sort of man her mother had spoken about just the night before.

"I'm well, Owen. How are the lambs?"

"I'm just off to bottle-feed a few of the orphans. Like to come?"

She glanced at her mother, saw her nod almost imperceptibly, and said, "Yes. I'd like that."

Fiona walked toward the house and Alec followed. Once inside the door, he grabbed her hair in his fist, pulled her toward him, and kissed her fiercely and deeply until they were both breathless.

Fiona thought the tears in his eyes were tears of happiness.

The phone rang in the front hall. Fiona hesitated momentarily and then broke free of him to answer it. When she returned a few minutes later, she looked distracted.

"What is it, Fi?"

"The home care assessor; she'll be here in an hour," she said, her face furrowed in thought.

"This is difficult," she said finally. "Meaghan and I need to go to Aberystwyth to fetch David. The car only seats four comfortably and, on the chance that we might need assistance from a third person, I think it should come from Owen. David knows Owen, whereas your presence might confuse him."

Again, Alec felt the world closing in on him.

Fiona saw his face darken. "Please understand, darling. I know it's unfair, but please understand."

It wasn't that Alec didn't understand, it was that he didn't want to. His calm, clear rational mind, upon which he had relied for decades, was in complete agreement. But his heart was in rebellion.

"Of course I understand."

"Plus, I need someone here when the assessor arrives. Would you be willing to take her to David's cottage, show her around, and see what she recommends?"

"Fi, I don't even know where it is."

Fiona looked at Alec and suddenly realized how much of the landscape of their respective lives was uncharted still. Passion was not enough. Only dailiness could make those landscapes known. She ached for that dailiness, for the certainty of him, for the comfort of the passage of time shared.

"Of course you don't. Come, I'll show you how to get there."

She led him past the barn and its outbuildings to a grassy lane that ran between high stone walls, explaining that the former hay barn was beyond the far ridge to the west, near the farm's western boundary. On the way back toward the house, they stopped at the barn where the orphaned lambs were penned and heard Meaghan laughing. She was holding two baby bottles, each of which had an insistently hungry lamb attached. The lambs lunged at the bottles the same rough way they nursed at the ewes. Owen was leaning against the pen, smiling. The scene should have pleased Fiona, but she was swept by a deep sadness instead: why hadn't she and Alec met when they'd been Owen's and Meaghan's ages? She thought briefly about the life they might have led, then pushed those thoughts aside.

"Owen, I wonder if I might ask you to come with Meaghan and me to fetch David?"

Owen glanced at Alec, and Fiona noticed.

"Alec has agreed to stay here to wait for the care assessor from the council."

"I'm happy to help," Owen replied.

"Thank you, Owen." Then, to no one in particular, perhaps to herself, she said quietly, "We should be going," and drifted out of the barn toward the house.

seventeen

*A*lec watched the car disappear down the lane. It would take them an hour to reach Aberystwyth and an hour to drive back. In between there would be dressing David in the fresh clothes Fiona had taken him, handling his discharge paperwork, and maneuvering him to the car. After what he'd been through and the days he'd spent in bed, David would be weak. However long all these steps took, Alec knew that in a matter of a few hours their lives would be changed. Precisely how remained to be seen. But Alec felt hollow in the pit of his stomach and he knew it wasn't hunger. It was fear. There had never been much Alec feared, whether due to confidence or foolishness he'd never quite known. Perhaps both. But ever since Gwynne had died so suddenly, there was something he was afraid of. He was afraid of loss. And he was afraid of it now.

He'd just entered the kitchen when the crunch of tires on gravel brought him out of his fear. He walked through the house and opened the front door just as a plump woman of indeterminate age with short salt-and-pepper hair was about to knock.

"Good afternoon. You'd be the home care assessor, I imagine?"

"I would be. Emma Jones," she said, thrusting out her hand. "And you would be . . . ?"

"Alec Hudson, friend of the family. They've gone to collect David—Mr. Edwards—from the hospital in Aberystwyth. Mrs. Edwards asked me to show you around."

He stepped out of the front door, and Miss Jones seemed confused.

"Oh, I guess you don't know. David doesn't live here at the house."

"Ah yes," Miss Jones said, bending over to rummage about in an overstuffed briefcase. She pulled out a thick file folder. "I seem to remember: chemical sensitivity or something, right?"

"Right. David has his own quarters. I'll show you the way."

As they bumped up the farm lane, Miss Jones nodded to herself and mumbled, "Yes, now I see the difficulty."

"Difficulty?"

"Oh, sorry. You see, we don't usually get requests for intensive home care unless the patient is quite elderly. I was confused when I saw how young Mr. Edwards is—well, not confused, you understand, but surprised. But now it's beginning to make sense. His wife couldn't possibly keep an eye on him all the time way out here, now could she?"

"I shouldn't think so," Alec agreed as they pulled up before the renovated hay barn.

It was a simple and very old stone-built, gable-roofed outbuilding, but Alec noticed that the oak windows and roofing slates were new. When he and Miss Jones stepped inside, both were surprised at how modern the interior was and how comfortable the space seemed. Miss Jones set her briefcase down on the kitchen table and surveyed the space approvingly. "Wouldn't mind living here myself," she said.

There was a stainless steel galley kitchen against the wall to the right and a pine table and two chairs just inside the door. To the left was the sitting area, with two leather easy chairs set before a new-looking stone hearth. One of the chairs was turned to face a television. At the back of the cottage, in what seemed to Alec to be a new shed addition, were David's bedroom and bathroom. The floors were bare wood, but two washable throw rugs softened the austerity. The stripped-down, almost Scandinavian simplicity of the decorating was all, of course, on account of David's chemical sensitivities. And the place was spotless.

"Before this accident," Alec explained, "David could still do some of the farmwork. Fiona brought him his meals. Now, well, I don't think we know exactly what David will be capable of doing."

"I take it there has been some brain damage," she said, looking at her file folder.

"So I gather. My understanding is that David has trouble figuring out where things are, even though he knows where he wants to go. It's also my understanding that he has become somewhat ... um ..."

"Childlike," Miss Jones said, filling in the blank. "At least that's what it says here. I suppose that means he's become unreliable, or perhaps impulsive. Combine that with the directional problems and Mrs. Edwards might well have a handful, especially with him being up here alone."

"Well, I think that's what Mrs. Edwards is trying to avoid." Alec felt strange acting as David's advocate.

"That's what home care is all about," she responded, slapping the folder closed. She pushed the file back into her briefcase, walked quickly through David's rooms, and paid particular attention to the drawers in the kitchen, opening each of them and inspecting the contents. Alec realized that the hospital record must, of course, have mentioned his suicide attempt; she was looking for things David might use to hurt himself.

At last she peered up at Alec and said, "Well, I think we're done here!"

On the way back to the house, she told Alec that she would make a written report but saw no reason why someone couldn't begin looking after David immediately.

"Of course, it will take a day to get someone assigned and it isn't round-the-clock care; the council couldn't afford that. As it is, Mrs. Edwards will be paying for what care we can provide, although the cost is based upon ability to pay. She could, of course, add private caretakers as well, and I'll leave her a list of providers. This would be so much easier if it weren't for these chemical sensitivities."

"I'm sure David would agree."

"Oh dear," she said quickly, "that sounded awful, didn't it? I'm so sorry; it's not what I meant to say, of course . . ."

Alec smiled at her. "I know that, Miss Jones. I expect it will be a while before anyone in the valley knows exactly what to say. It's a difficult situation for the entire family."

As he stepped out of her car, Miss Jones, apparently still embarrassed, said, "I promise I'll do everything I can."

Alec bent down. "I'm sure you will."

Back in the kitchen, he found an apple in the refrigerator. He was munching it when an idea occurred to him. He walked across the kitchen to the small desk Fiona used as her office and found fresh paper, tape, and a felt-tipped pen. Then he hiked back up the lane to David's cottage.

Fiona was glad she'd asked Owen to come. David had needed Owen's support as he walked uncertainly through the corridors of the hospital and out to the car. He was cheerful and happy to be going home but still confused about how he'd ended up in hospital in the first place. It was clear to Fiona that he had absolutely no memory of the events that brought him close to death on the mountain. That, she decided, was a great mercy. He was cogent enough to ask Meaghan why she wasn't at university, but had asked the question three times, as if he could not hold on to her explanation. In the same fashion, he had asked Owen several times how the lambing was going. It was as if in the chambered villa of his mind, some of the rooms had open windows and information just blew through.

When Alec was done at David's cottage, he decided to go for a walk. The sky was bright out over the Irish Sea, and the air was warm. He crossed from meadow to meadow, through a confetti of yellow buttercups and pink-edged English daisies. After passing through several rusted iron farm gates, he reached the rougher slopes of Cadair Idris and walked east along the base of its precipitous flanks, eventually reaching Llyn y Gadair, its placid waters reflecting the pewter of the sky above. He sat on a rock by the shore and thought about his first climb past the lake, carrying the physical and emotional burden of Gwynne's ashes on his back. And the second, scrambling up the treacherous slope to save David. He was not a superstitious man, but some part of him wondered whether Gwynne's mischievous spirit hadn't engineered these events to shake up his life. Well, if that was the case, she'd succeeded: his heart was in turmoil.

Eventually, he rose and began walking back toward the farm. The light was fading. It would be dark in another hour.

Fiona opened the door of David's cottage as Meaghan and Owen helped David out of the car. When the trio entered, Fiona was at the sink, her arms braced on its edge, her head tilted down. Meaghan saw her mother's back shudder and knew she was sobbing. Then she looked around the cottage and understood. There was a fire burning in the grate and taped to the walls at strategic locations there were simple block-lettered signs with directional arrows: TOILET, and KITCHEN, and BEDROOM and FRONT DOOR. Meaghan went to her mother and Owen took over.

"Well, here we are, home at last, eh, David? Bet it feels good to be back. Here's your favorite chair, right here by the fire. Why don't you rest here a moment?"

David dropped into the chair as if he were made of lead. He'd been exhausted by the journey and yet was elated to find himself in familiar surroundings. He saw the signs taped to the walls and read the messages but couldn't quite figure out why they were there. Perhaps he would later. Or tomorrow. He was so tired.

Owen walked over to Fiona, put a hand on her shoulder, bent his head toward her ear, and whispered, "It's going to be all right, Fi. We'll all do our part. He won't be a prisoner here."

But of course that wasn't it at all. What had broken through the protective wall Fiona had erected to make it possible for her to deal calmly and capably with hospital officials during the transfer of her husband was the sheer kindness inherent in these simple directional signs. That, and the fact that she recognized the handwriting, the same hand that had penned the poem she so cherished. Alec's hand.

David seemed happily mesmerized by the flames dancing in the fire grate. Meaghan said, "How about if I stay here with Daddy until dinner, Mum? We'll watch the telly. Why don't you take a break?"

"Yes. Perhaps that would be a good idea. Owen, would you be so kind as to drive?"

Owen nodded to Meaghan, put his arm around her mother's shoulders, and guided her out of the cottage. Fiona leaned into him gratefully.

"I don't know what I would do without you, Owen," Fiona said as he drove carefully back to the house down the long, grassy lane. "And

I'm not sure I can express what you mean to me, what you mean to us, without embarrassing you."

Owen turned to her, and for the first time in her memory, there was no shyness in his face. "You don't need to, Mrs. Edwards; I understand. I'll take care of you and Meaghan and this farm as long as you'll let me."

"That might be forever, Owen."

"I'm not going anywhere else, ma'am."

"Fiona."

"Fiona."

"Owen?"

"Yes, ma'am . . . Fiona?"

"Do you love Meaghan?"

"I do."

Fiona sighed and smiled.

"I thought so. Let's hope she arrives at the same conclusion."

"She's got a ways to go yet, I think."

"Perhaps she does. But don't give up, Owen. Don't ever give up on love."

Owen pulled the car into the barn next to his Land Rover. "Shall I stay with David tonight, Fiona?"

"No, dear, you go home to your mam. I'll take care of him tonight. It would be lovely, though, if you'd come by first thing in the morning."

"I'll be there—and call me if anything comes up."

"Thank you, Owen; I'm sure we'll be fine."

Fiona crossed the farmyard toward the house.

Don't ever give up on love, she'd told Owen. She wondered whether she could heed her own advice. Even more, she wondered whether that advice held any meaning for her at all. Which was the love she should not give up on? Was her comment advice about fidelity, or passion, or patience? Her fidelity lived in one part of her heart, her passion in another. Which of them required her patience? She realized she'd considered the matter of fidelity to be about David, but what about fidelity to her love for Alec? And passion? All her life she'd been taught—by her grandfather the rector, by her mother the seaman's wife—that passion was transitory, that true love was about patience and constancy in adversity, about the comforts of dailiness. Yet for all their dailiness—nearly a quarter century's worth—she had never thought of David as her companion, much less her lover. They cohabited. They were partners in an enterprise. Occasionally—very occasionally—they copulated, but that was long ago. The comforts of the relationship, such as they were, had mostly to do with routine, child rearing, and this achingly beautiful valley.

And here was her husband, now an invalid twice over—not just shackled by the effects of the poisoning, but also by a subtly scrambled brain. During their ride home, he sometimes seemed completely normal. And then she'd see a smile cross his face and freeze there, as if someone—David himself?—had pressed the "pause" button. Then, some time later, it would release and he'd be animated again.

She entered the kitchen, expecting to find Alec there. That was the vision she had of her home now: Alec in the kitchen whipping up something delicious. Her kitchen seemed his natural habitat.

But he wasn't there.

"Alec?!"

"Right here," he said from behind her, kicking mud off his boots. She flung herself at him. He felt her trembling and held her close.

"Fi? Is everything okay?"

"I was just . . . yes, everything's fine. I just . . . I just love you."

The two of them entered the kitchen, awkwardly, two bodies trying to move as one. There was a big pot on the Aga, and there were two polyethylene bags on the kitchen table. Alec went to the cooker and lifted the lid on the pot.

"Soup. Vegetable and bean; very chunky."

"Bread," Fiona said, rummaging in one of the bags, "fresh from the bakery. And a wedge of cheese.

"Also," she said, looking into the other bag, "a cake—from Brandith, unless I miss my guess."

"Yes, Brandith said she'd put the word out."

He turned to her. "These people love you, Fi, you and David. They'd do anything for you." Again, the family, the community.

"At a minimum," he continued, forcing a smile, "you won't starve."

Fiona hadn't missed the "you and David," but she didn't know how to respond. Instead, she walked across the kitchen, lifted the lid on the soup pot, leaned into Alec, and said, "Umm." It was ambiguous, she knew, but it was the best she could do.

Fiona sprinkled a few drops of water on the top of the rotund loaf of granary bread that had been left and slipped it into one of the Aga's ovens to crisp. Then she went into the dining room, opened a door in the credenza by the breakfast table, and brought out one of the bottles of sherry she normally decanted into small carafes for her guest rooms. She poured generously into two wineglasses and sat at the kitchen table. Sensing he was being summoned, Alec joined her.

"In a little while, sweetheart," she began, "I'm going to take most of that pot of soup and the other food up to David's cottage."

Alec nodded.

"Meaghan and I will have dinner there, and we'll see how David does. Then I'm going to send Meaghan back here to bed, and I will stay tonight with David. There's a fold-up bed in his closet. I don't want to, Alec, but I must. Do you understand?"

Alec nodded again.

The two of them sat quietly, sipping sherry. Alec wanted to ask her about David. He wanted to hold her hand. But he did neither.

Fiona was staring dully at her glass, her shoulders slumped forward, her hair nearly obscuring her face.

"Miss Jones, the home care assessor, said someone would be here perhaps as soon as tomorrow," Alec said. "It won't be round-the-clock, but she also left a list of private care services."

Fiona nodded. "Thank you for sorting that for me." Now she looked up at him, tears in her eyes. "And thank you for making the signs. It was such a sweet and thoughtful thing to do."

"Just thinking ahead. Bad habit I have."

"Ahead," Fiona repeated. "I don't know what's ahead. I can barely comprehend right now."

She looked at Alec with a face so bleak that it reminded him of old pictures of World War I battlefields—shattered, barren.

"Twenty-two years ago, I vowed 'to have and to hold' David 'in sickness and in health.' I may not love my husband—I don't know— but he needs me now even more than before. I have a duty to care for him. I must. I promised. Before God."

"I've known that from the moment I found him on the mountain, Fi."

"But I don't want to lose you, Alec. I don't want to lose us. We can keep that, can't we? We can protect it? Please, sweetheart, tell me we can! We'll figure something out?"

There was desperation in her voice. Now Alec took her hand and held it.

"It's what I want, too; I'm just not sure how."

She was crying now, silently, her head bowed.

Alec kneeled beside her and brushed her tears away with his fingertips, caressing her cheeks as he did.

After a while, he said, "Come on, love; I'll help you take the food to the car." She nodded, rose, and ladled some of the soup into a small pot for Alec, setting aside some of the bread and cheese as well.

Night had come, and as the two of them walked out through the darkened farmyard to the car, the sky was awash in stars. He settled the big soup pot on the floor in front of the passenger seat, then walked around to the driver's side and took Fiona in his arms, holding her tenderly, stroking her hair.

Fiona pulled him close, pressing her body against his, as if trying to merge their two envelopes of skin to become one being, complete. Finally, she pulled away and sat in the car.

"Will you be okay?" he asked.

Fiona nodded. "Yes. He's fine. Docile. Rather sweet, actually."

"Off you go then. Call if you need me."

"I always need you, Alec."

He bent to kiss her, then straightened and closed the car door.

Alec stood in the dark a long time after she left. Jack appeared from somewhere and sat beside him, panting. A sliver of moon had risen, brightening the sky further. The great bulk of Cadair Idris loomed, silent and black, to the south. He thought again of Gwynne, of love and of loss. Finally, he leaned down and patted the dog's head.

"What do you say, Jackie; let's get us something to eat."

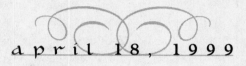

april 18, 1999

eighteen

O wen Lewis arrived at David's cottage the next morning with the sun. He brought fresh milk for tea and pastries his mother had made for Fiona the night before. He was surprised to see Meaghan asleep in her father's customary chair. Fiona was just coming out of the bathroom and was already dressed.

"How's David?" he whispered.

"Still asleep. Worn out, I shouldn't wonder."

"No need to whisper, you two," Meaghan mumbled from the other side of the room. "I'm awake."

"And stiff, too, I should think," Fiona said. "Why didn't you sleep at home?"

"I'm fine, Mother" was all Meaghan said, standing and stretching. She wore one of her father's flannel shirts as a nightgown. It wasn't quite long enough to serve as a dress, and it hid little. Owen looked at her slender legs and sleepy face and turned away.

"Perhaps it would be a good idea to put on something decent, darling," Fiona chided.

"Oh, Mother! It's just Owen, for goodness' sake!"

Owen looked at Fiona with a wry smile. Fiona patted him on the back. "Now then," she said, "what delights have you brought us?"

There was a shuffling sound in the bedroom and in a moment David appeared, in undershorts and a T-shirt. "Morning, everyone!" he said brightly, heading for the front door.

"Where are you going?" Fiona asked.

"To the bathroom, if you must know."

"It's back there, dear, next to your bedroom. See the sign?"

David looked around, slightly confused but smiling. He saw the sign. "Ah! So it is, so it is."

Fiona followed him toward the bathroom. "I'll just put out some clothes for you, shall I?"

"Thank you, dearest. Very kind of you," he said as he closed the bathroom door.

She looked at the others and shrugged.

Fiona intercepted her husband as he came out of the bathroom and began drifting back to his sitting room.

"Clothes?" she said.

"Right, right; forgot there for a moment."

When he was dressed, he and Fiona sat at the small table while Meaghan poured tea and Owen set out scones and tea cakes.

"So, Owen, my boy," David said between bites, "how's the lambing coming along?"

"Pretty much done, sir, and the mortality rate's low this season, too."

"Good, good. Orphans?"

"Just a few. I've got them penned in the barn and Meaghan and I have been bottle-feeding them. As for the ewes and the rest of the lambs, I've let them out to the spring pasture. What with the warm weather, the grass is growing thick and fast."

Fiona and her daughter looked at each other and smiled. This was going well.

David stood suddenly. "Well, let's get to it, lad; the day's a wasting!" He walked to the door, stepped outside, and started across the gravel drive.

"Ouch! Damn!" He started to turn back and found Fiona standing in the open doorway with his work boots.

"Shoes, David?"

"Good idea."

A few minutes later Owen and David went out across the fields to check the ewes. Fiona began cleaning the cottage but Meaghan intervened.

"I'll take care of that, Mum. It'll make me feel useful at least."

Fiona put her arms around her daughter. "Thank you for staying here last night, darling. I know you did it for me, and I'm grateful."

"Well, I didn't know what he might . . ."

"I know. Neither did I. It was wonderful to have you here. The good news is we'll have professional help starting tomorrow."

"What needs doing in the meantime, Mum? Have we guests arriving? Do you need me to do the marketing?"

"No, I've told the Tourist Board not to send anyone and I called those who'd made reservations. As for marketing, I have some chicken in the freezer. I'll think of something for dinner."

"You mean our resident chef will think of something."

"Alec. Yes. Well, I suppose I'd better look in on him. Shall I take the car?"

"Yes, Mum. I can walk back down when I'm done here."

Fiona picked up the empty soup pot and carried it out to the car. She could see Owen opening a gate for David in a distant pasture. She wondered how much strength David had in him.

Back at the house, she parked the car in the barn and carried the soup pot to the kitchen, expecting to find Alec there. But the kitchen was empty. She checked the clock and smiled. Nearly half eight and still in bed! She crossed the main floor and tiptoed up the stairs to Alec's room, very carefully opening his door, hoping to surprise him.

But the bed was empty, carefully made.

"Alec?" She checked his bathroom. Empty.

Fiona whirled around to the corner of the room where Alec kept his backpack. It was gone.

"Alec?! Oh Jesus, God . . . No!" she breathed, racing back down the stairs.

"Alec!"

Hoping against hope, hoping for a miracle, she burst into her rooms, wanting to find him asleep in her bed. Sooty looked up from his accustomed place, but ignored her. On her bed, instead of Alec, was an envelope with her name on it, written in his hand.

"No!" she screamed. "No, no, *no*!!"

She grabbed the envelope and ran out again. In the front hall she noticed her personal phone book was open. She looked at the page and saw the phone number for the taxi service in Dolgellau, the one she always used for her guests.

She dialed the number frantically and got the dispatcher.

"Did you collect a guest at Tan y Gadair Farm this morning?" she demanded, her voice quavering uncontrollably.

"One moment please, madam," the bored voice said.

She looked at the letter in her hand and watched it shake. It was as if someone else's hand held it, for all the control she had over it.

The voice came back on the line. "We did indeed, madam. A gentleman. At about seven o'clock this morning. Took him to Barmouth for the early train."

Fiona felt dizzy. She looked at the phone and slowly replaced the receiver.

She stumbled back to the kitchen, fell into a chair, and stared at the envelope in her hand. She tore open the flap and unfolded the letter.

My Dearest Fiona,

I used to think that watching Gwynne die was the hardest thing I'd ever done. To see life ebb from someone you love and be utterly powerless to reverse the decline—indeed, to pray that death will come quickly!—is desperately hard. It is unimaginable. And yet, I was wrong. The hardest thing I have ever done and will ever do is to tell you this: we cannot continue.

I have spent most of the night here by the window, staring up at the sky. I suppose I have been looking for an answer there, in the patterns of the constellations—a different answer from the one I know in my heart is right.

In this valley, on this farm beneath the mountain, there is no place for me—except, I hope, in your heart. I know you know that; I've seen it in your eyes in the past two days. You have a family to which I do not belong. There is no room for me here, darling. You and your family are part of a close-knit community. We could not carry on as we have and not cause harm—to you, to David, to Meaghan, to the entire fabric of your life here. I love and need you with an intensity and a passion so powerful they amaze me. When I leave you, I know the power of that love will break me. But I have no choice; staying here would dishonor you and those you love, and eventually cause you even greater conflict and pain. I cannot do that to you, no matter how much I need you.

This is not a renunciation of our love—far from it. We are, and always will be, two souls united, two beings joined by our hearts, a man and a woman who would travel through eternity together if the constellations of our lives could be altered.

They say the flutter of a butterfly's wings can alter the course of humankind and I believe that. I believe we met for a reason, Fiona, and I believe we will find each other again. Until then, think of me when you look at the North Star—the one true, fixed certainty in a swirling universe—and I will think of you. Know, with all of your heart, that my love for you will be just as reliable, just as bright. Remember what you said in town the other day: I'm easy to find; you just have to look up.

> *I love you—now and forever.*
> *Alec*

Fiona found herself at the kitchen window, as if by standing there long enough she could make the flash of royal blue appear again as it had only a week before. But it did not. She imagined a jagged fissure moving up the lane, splitting the farmyard, and then the house, and then her heart, in two. She clutched her chest as if to keep it in one piece, drifted though the house to her rooms, slipped the letter into a drawer, climbed onto her bed, curled into a ball, and wept.

Meaghan found her there, asleep, an hour later. There was no sign of Alec Hudson. She thought perhaps she understood.

But of course she did not.

december 18, 2005

epilogue

An eternity seemed to pass in a moment.

She felt his warm hands cup her face.

When she opened her eyes again, he was kneeling before her on the stone-flagged floor of the entrance hall.

"Fiona, dear God, I'm so sorry," he said, his face stricken.

"Alec," she whispered.

Alec Hudson rose, wincing as he did so, and drew Fiona to her feet. He wrapped her in his arms and she tucked her head into his broad, flat chest, as she had done before, so long ago.

And, very quietly, she began to cry.

They stood that way for a long time. She had the strange sense that they were fusing. Alec's chest rose and fell irregularly, and she realized he was crying, too.

After a while, Fiona pulled away and looked up at Alec. He had aged more than she might have expected. Then again, she thought, perhaps she had, too. His face was gaunt and deeply lined. But his blue eyes still shone like searchlights. His body felt hard, just as she remembered it.

"Would you like to sit down?" she asked, suddenly at a loss.

"No, Fiona. I would like to kiss you."

Fiona smiled. He leaned down and their lips met. His kisses were as tender and sweet as she remembered, and she lost herself in them. Then, as before, she became insistent, pulling him closer, holding him tight.

Back in the direction of the kitchen, a door slammed and a woman's voice cursed, "Bloody weather!" Moments later, she trooped into the dining room and froze there, transfixed by the scene in the hall.

"Mother?" she said, her mouth agape.

Fiona turned to her daughter.

The young woman, who was very pregnant, stared at them both for a moment, utterly at a loss for words, then plodded toward the hall.

The man smiled.

"Hello, Meaghan."

In a perfect imitation of her mother, Meaghan's hand flew to her mouth, her eyes widened in disbelief, her free hand fumbled for the chair, and she dropped heavily into it.

A moment later she lowered her hand and said simply, "You two were in love."

"Correction," Fiona said, "*are* in love."

"Don't let her fool you with that embrace, Alec; that's how she greets all our guests now," Meaghan cracked, her eyes dancing. "It's done wonders for the business."

"Meaghan!" Fiona exclaimed.

"I don't doubt it in the least," Alec said, for which he earned a sharp poke in the ribs from Fiona.

And then all three of them were laughing.

"But Alec," Meaghan said, "you disappeared."

Alec's shoulders slumped and he looked away, as if across a great distance. His voice, when he responded, was barely a whisper. "It was the right thing to do, the only thing to do . . . it was so hard. I wanted to come back—not just that first day, but every day since . . ."

Fiona turned to Meaghan. "Would you excuse us for a while, darling? We have a bit of catching up to do."

Meaghan nodded and hoisted herself from the chair. She gave Alec an awkward hug, her swollen belly coming between them.

Alec wiped a tear from his cheek. "Congratulations, little mother," he said.

"Congratulations, my foot! As soon as Owen and I figure out what made this happen, we're never doing it again!"

Meaghan lumbered off in the direction of the kitchen and Fiona led Alec through the low oak door to her rooms. She did not stop in her sitting room, but continued though to her bedroom. There, she removed her clothes and then helped Alec out of his. Then she pulled him into her bed and held him close.

"I never stopped loving you, Alec Hudson. I never stopped believing we'd be together again. It had to be; it was meant to be."

"Tell me I did the right thing, Fi."

"It shattered me, Alec; I won't pretend otherwise. I didn't think I'd ever recover. It was worse than a death, because there was always a hope you'd return. Because I couldn't give up that hope."

"I'm so sorry, Fi," Alec said, burying his face in her neck. "So very sorry. It was so hard. It's been so long."

"Sweetheart, you've no need to be sorry. Do you know why?"

She could feel the dampness from his cheeks on her breast as he shook his head.

"Because you did the right thing."

He pulled her closer.

"And in the end, that only made me love you more," she whispered.

They stayed that way, skin on skin, clinging to each other, for a very long time.

It was nearly dark when Alec awoke. Fiona was crossing the room toward him. She had changed and was wearing a form-fitting wool jersey dress in an earthy olive. She climbed up onto the bed facing him.

"How long have I been asleep?"

"A few hours."

"Damned jet lag."

"I'm sure that's what it was, and not that you're an old relic," she teased.

He lurched upright and grabbed her. "Here's what I want to know," he said, pulling her close and running his tongue down her breastbone. "How'd you manage to stay so gorgeous?"

"Clean living and fresh air," Fiona said, pulling away and striking a pinup-girl pose.

"And here's what I want to know," she countered. "What brought you back now?"

Alec smiled. "Could you hand me my trousers, please?"

She looked at him for a moment, head cocked, then hopped off the bed, and brought them to him.

He fished his wallet from a back pocket, opened it, removed a folded piece of paper, and handed it to Fiona.

She unfolded it and recognized it immediately. It was a small notice from the St. Mary's parish newsletter:

> *Meaghan Dorothy Edwards and Owen Thomas*
> *Lewis, both of Dolgellau, were married on 12 June 2004*
> *at St. Mary's Church. The groom is the son of Anna*

*Llewellyn Lewis and the late Raymond Lewis. The
bride is the daughter of Fiona Potter Edwards and the
late David Edwards. The couple will reside at Tan y
Gadair Farm.*

"How?" Fiona asked.

"I subscribe."

"But that was more than a year ago!"

"I know. And David died two months earlier. I read his obituary in the newsletter, too. But when I saw the notice, I thought it would be unseemly to contact you until some time had passed."

Fiona leaned against one of the four-poster's corner posts, crossed her legs, and looked squarely at Alec. "Your problem, sir, is that you are far too concerned with what is respectable. You have cost us an entire year of being together!"

Alec turned away. "After I left you, I had no idea whether you would ever want to see me again."

Fiona smiled at the love of her life. "You must be the dimmest man alive."

"Thank you."

There was a long silence during which the two of them looked at each other with idiotic grins.

Fiona's face sobered. "How long have you come for?"

Alec looked at her, the years of longing etched into his face. "How long will you have me?" he asked quietly.

Fiona threw herself across the bed and into his arms.

"As long as you like," she said, pressing her tiny frame into his. "We have a policy here of never turning away guests."

"How do you feel about forever?" Alec asked.

She looked down at him. "I think that could be arranged," she said with an earthy giggle.

They held each other for a while, each of them absorbing what they'd just confessed. Fiona sat up abruptly.

"What in heaven's name have you been doing all this time?" she asked.

Alec climbed out of bed, naked, and rummaged through the pockets of his sport coat.

"What are you after now?" Fiona marveled at how trim Alec's body was still.

"Your birthday gift, of course," Alec mumbled. "Ah!"

He straightened, returned to the bed, and handed her a small parcel.

She pulled off the gift wrapping and found a slender book. She turned it over and looked at the cover. There was a banner across the top: "The National Bestseller!" The cover was a soft-focused photograph of a gently curving slope, dipping down and then rising again. She was about to go look for her reading glasses when she realized it was a close-up of the small of a woman's back. The title of the book was *Skin Hunger*. The author, Alec Hudson. She opened the book and found a collection of poems. The title poem, the one she'd read years before, was first. There were many more. She was about to close the book when she came upon the dedication page. Surrounded by white space were three small words:

For Fi,
Forever

And again the tears came. Fiona thought they must have been stored up over all those empty years and wondered whether they would ever stop.

Alec took her in his arms. "I'm glad to say that's not been the response of most of my readers."

He felt her laughing through her tears.

"Is this about us?" she asked, sniffling and waving the book.

"It could be if we want it to be."

Fiona pushed the tears from her eyes and stood up. "Put some clothes on, you wonderful, idiotic man; Meaghan's made me a lovely birthday dinner, and you're invited."

"Do you mind if I clean up a bit?"

"Of course not, but be quick about it!"

And with that she fairly skipped out of the room, clutching the little book to her breast.

Alec bathed in the familiar claw-foot tub, shaved, and changed. Someone had fetched his suitcase while he slept.

As he approached the kitchen the aromas were rich and exotic. When he entered the room, he found Fiona and Meaghan, arm in arm. At the Aga, stirring a large pot, was Owen Lewis.

Owen heard him and turned, crossed the room, and wrapped Alec in a bear hug. Alec's heart was so full he could hardly stand it. "Owen," he said, holding the younger man's embrace longer, "I am so happy for you and Meaghan."

Owen stood back and held Alec by his shoulders.

"Welcome home, friend," he said.

Alec sat at the kitchen table and looked around the room he had thought about so often over the years—the beamed ceiling, the limestone floor, the warm wood and cream-colored cabinets, the massive stove. Little had changed. Fiona walked around behind him and ran her fingers through his hair.

"Dinner in moments," Meaghan said, taking Owen's place at the cooker.

"Get you anything in the meantime?" Owen asked him.

"Is there a decent glass of wine in this establishment?"

Owen went to the refrigerator and pulled out a bottle of chardonnay. "It's from Australia; will that do?"

Alec frowned. "Is it alcoholic?"

Owen looked troubled. "Um, yes, I suppose it must be."

"Then it will do!" Alec cried, and the four of them laughed as Owen poured. Alec stood, gestured to Fiona's daughter, raised his glass, and said, smiling broadly, "To new beginnings."

Meaghan's lips quivered and tears filled her eyes. She took her husband's glass of wine, touched Alec's, took a small sip, and said, "For us all, Alec; for us all."

Meaghan had made a fragrant Mediterranean fish stew, thick with shellfish and saffron-infused vegetables.

"It's all your fault," she chided Alec. "You got me started cooking!"

"Did I? Oh good," Alec said, as Meaghan passed around the laden plates.

"I'm not so sure about that," Owen said, patting his belly. He'd put on weight. "Hard to know which of us is having the baby!"

Dinner was a noisy affair, full of laughter and storytelling and catching up. As they finished, Alec rose to clear the dishes.

"You never learn, do you?" Fiona scolded, slapping his hands away.

"That reminds me . . . ," Owen said, dashing out the back door. He returned a few moments later with a large cardboard box. He set it on the table and removed its top to reveal a triple-layer, dark chocolate birthday cake, with the number "50" traced out in butter cream icing.

"It's from Brandith," Owen explained. "We were going to add all the candles, too, but . . ."

". . . it violated the fire code, right?" Alec added.

"Hey!" Fiona cried, hands on hips. "Who are you to talk?"

"I'm fit as a fiddle, I'll have you know," Alec countered. "Never felt younger!"

Fiona leaned close and whispered in his ear, "We'll just see about that later."

Alec lifted an eyebrow and Fiona stifled a giggle as Meaghan passed around slices of birthday cake.

The cake was luscious. Alec learned that Brandith had expanded beyond her shop into catering.

Alec pushed himself back from the table when he finished and accepted a coffee from Meaghan. "I had a thought in the bath earlier . . ."

The three others stopped what they were doing.

"Given your obvious culinary talents, Meaghan, have you considered the possibility of offering not just bed-and-breakfast, but an evening meal as well? After all, there isn't much choice in Dolgellau. You could offer a choice of perhaps three entrees. Maybe even offer wine at a fair price."

Meaghan and Fiona looked at each other.

"We were just talking about that last week," Meaghan said.

"Well then," Alec said, "I wonder if I might apply for the job of sous chef?"

Meaghan looked at him, openmouthed. Then she thrust out her right hand and Alec grasped it.

"Done!" she said. "When can you start?"

"Hang on a bit," Alec said seriously, "there's the little matter of wages."

Fiona wrapped her arms around Alec's shoulders. "It's food, lodging, and all the comforts, just like before," she said.

Alec looked around him, at Meaghan, at Owen, and finally at Fiona. He made as if he was considering the offer carefully. Then he turned, pulled Fiona's face toward his, kissed her firmly, and said, "You've got a deal!

"Now," he added, "where are the cigars and the brandy?"

"Cigars?" Owen said with a laugh.

Alec slumped in his chair. "I cannot believe the depths to which this establishment has sunk."

Then he sat up. "Fi, do you still keep sherry for your guests?"

"Of course I do—or rather we do, since this is Meaghan's business now, too."

"Would you be so kind as to bring some in?"

"Why?"

"Call me a traditionalist."

Meaghan and Owen cleared the table and Fiona returned carrying a tray with a decanter and four small glasses. Alec stood and filled them, splashing only a sip into Meaghan's.

"More toasts?" Fiona asked.

"Perhaps," Alec said with a shy smile.

He stood by Fiona's chair, reached into his pocket, and removed a small box, so small he could cradle it in his palm. It was old and covered in a faded, very pale blue velvet. Embossed in silver letters on top were the words *Tiffany & Co.* He kneeled where Fiona sat and placed the box in her hand.

"This belonged to my mother," he said, barely audibly. "Then it belonged to Gwynne. I'd like it to belong to you, Fiona, if you'll have it."

Fiona lifted the small box and struggled to control her shaking hands. She eased open the hinged top. Inside, shimmering on a tiny silk pillow, was a fiery diamond set in a simple gold band.

She stared at it a moment, then looked at Alec, smiling, eyes filling, her head cocked to one side.

"You certainly don't waste any time . . ."

"We don't have many years left," he whispered.

"Yes, we do, Alec; we have the rest of our lives."

acknowledgments

a reader who knows me well asked of the book you hold in your hands, "Is this a true story?" The answer is no. And yes.

No: this is a work of fiction, which is to say of the imagination, and of the heart. The characters and events portrayed here are creations; they exist nowhere else but in these pages.

Yes: the story is true—as true to the spirit of itself as I can make it, for it is a thing with its own life, and its own truths.

In the telling of these truths, I have drawn upon the help of many generous advisers, to whom I offer my deepest thanks. On matters having to do with all things Welsh, I am in debt to Jane Evans, of the Gwynedd Council office in Dolgellau, North Wales; Helen Davies, of the Welsh regional office of the National Sheep Association; Nick Dawson, the ever-helpful duty manager at the Aberdovey Search and Rescue Team; Jessica Gould, National Botanic Garden of Wales; Kevin Owen, farm policy adviser, National Farmers' Union of Wales; Andy Simpson, press officer, Mountain Rescue of England and

Wales; David Williams, senior warden, Snowdonia National Park; and Dafydd Lewis on the Welsh language. On matters medical, my thanks go to Tom Hornbein, physician, mountaineer, and friend; William J. Powers and Maurizio Corbetta, neurology professors at Washington University Medical School, St. Louis; and the Pesticide Action Network UK for the details of sheep dip poisoning. If there are errors of fact or interpretation, they are mine alone.

I am indebted as well to friends on both sides of the Atlantic who read the original manuscript and made it clear that they should be book reviewers in their next life, especially Cindy Buck, Claire Booth, Martin Mann, Hilary McCorry, Kate Pflaumer, and Lawrence Rosenfeld. In particular, I am grateful to Dianna MacLeod for her support, encouragement, and editorial advice from the conception to the completion of this book. I also want to thank the community of writers and dear friends that gathers almost every Friday afternoon at Ponti's restaurant in Seattle, as well as the waitresses who put up with us; a finer support group one could hardly imagine.

But a particularly enthusiastic bowing and scraping is due to two wonderful souls: Richard Abate, my agent at International Creative Management, who has stuck by me though thick and thin, and Shaye Areheart, my publisher and editor, and one of the most delightful human beings I have had the pleasure of knowing.

Finally, and closer to home, thanks to the people who make life worth living: Hazel, Nancy, Tom, Eric, Ardith, and Baker.

the meaning of home

It all depends on what you mean by home.
—Robert Frost, *The Death of the Hired Man*

*i*n *The Long Walk Home,* when Alec Hudson scatters his ex-wife Gwynne's ashes at the summit of Cadair Idris, he shouts "*Croeso!*" into the wind. It's the Welsh word for welcome. He is welcoming Gwynne's spirit home.

Gwynne was born in California. She'd lived in New York City and Washington, D.C. She died in Boston. Yet when it came time to choose where she would spend eternity, her ultimate resting place, she chose a mountain above a valley in Wales where once she had felt utterly at home.

The idea of "home" has intrigued me for years. What do we mean when we say we feel "at home" somewhere? What is it about a particular place that makes us feel we belong there and not somewhere else? Why do some places just seem *right*?

The word *home* is one of the most frequently used words in every language known to man. Yet defining it is a bit like trying to grasp a greased pig; it's remarkably slippery. Among other things, the word—in English at least—manages to suggest both a physical place and a condition of being. Is home where you live or where you came from? Is it the place that houses your belongings, or is it the place where you belong? Is it a place at all, or is it a state of mind?

The poet T. S. Eliot once said home is "where one starts from." The place where I started from, the place where I was born and spent the first eighteen years of my life, is called Yonkers. It is a large city in New York State that shares a border with, and is virtually indistinguishable from, the Bronx, New York City's northernmost borough. For simplicity's sake and because Yonkers, frankly, leaves a lot to be desired, I usually say I'm from New York. But it never felt like home.

If you look up the word *home* in the *Oxford English Dictionary,* you'll find four densely printed, three-column pages for the noun form of the word alone. But one definition seems to me to get to the very heart—literally, to the emotional core—of what we mean by *home*:

> *A place, region, or state to which one properly belongs, in which one's affections centre, or where one finds refuge, rest, or satisfaction.*

The sleeper here is that phrase, "to which one properly belongs." How would we know the place we belonged if we stumbled upon it? What would it look like?

Almost forty years ago, I stumbled upon the place where I knew, deep in my bones, I belonged. It was England. Now, I'm not the sort of person who believes in past lives, and most of my ancestry is German and Irish. And still, I knew I'd come home. I knew the people I'd never met before and understood their quick-witted sense of humor, knew the landscape as intimately as if I had always lived there, knew the flat English ale I'd never tasted before and loved it, knew how to drive on "the wrong side" of the road without having to learn it. And so much more. Over the years, I'd been content simply to accept these feelings. But then, just a few years ago, it began haunting me. Maybe this is simply part of the process of aging, this needing to know where you belong and why.

So late one spring, a couple of years ago, I shouldered a backpack and spent three-and-a-half months walking some 1,400 miles through most of southern England. I had this idea—no, I had this certainty— that if I slowed down to walking speed and paid very close attention as I loped along, I would be able to identify and understand what it was about this world that spoke to me.

Along the way, I had one or two little epiphanies. You know how magazine articles and self-help books, not to mention Zen masters, tell you that the secret to happiness is to "live in the present"? Well, I don't know about you, but this has always been mystifying to me. But about a week into my walk I realized that "the present" had always seemed to me to be the briefest moment beween grief about the past and anxiety about the future. But when you have no fixed itinerary, and no place you have to be at the end of the day, you live—from the instant you open your eyes in the morning to that blissful second when you close them at night—in the shimmering present. You see, hear, smell, savor every single experience as it happens: the fragrance of wildflowers as you pass, the music of a blackbird in a hedge in the morning, the help-less joy of lambs leaping in meadows, the mystery of a footpath curving through a dark wood, the sweetness of fresh water when you are thirsty, the satisfaction of a pub lunch when you are hungry, the warmth of welcome from people you encounter along the way—and people are always warm to walkers.

And as I walked, I began to recognize other things that made me feel "at home" in this particular place, in a way I never have been in the country of my birth. I noticed that in the market towns and villages through which I passed buildings were never more than three stories high, so the scale isn't dehumanizing, the way it is in most American cities. And shops and houses tend to be clustered together companionably, with breathing spaces provided by small squares, greens, and plazas. They also have what I like to call "public living rooms." In England, it's the venerable institution of the pub. But coffee shops and sidewalk cafés have the same function elsewhere: they're places where people gather to chat or simply watch the world go by. And the places that appealed to me, that made me feel I could fit in, were composed of buildings constructed of local materials—stone, wood, earth. It's as if they'd grown organically from the ground, rather than having been imposed on it.

Places like these seem to have been designed with people—not traffic management—in mind. That was an essential part of feeling at home, and something completely missing in so many American neighborhoods, subdivisions, and entire communities, which feel cold and strangely "placeless."

I was transformed by my walk through southern England, and it won't surprise you to know that, to a very great extent, Alec Hudson's sense of the rightness, of the power of place in the lush, green Welsh valley in North Wales that cradles Fiona's farm, comes from my own experience.

Alec feels that power in the town of Dolgellau, in the valley, and in his love for Fiona. But Alec also understands that he does not yet belong. The earth will need to make a few more cycles around the sun before Alec, like Gwynne, can "come home."

And, in time, it does.

a reader's guide

1. Alec and Gwynne have been divorced for years, yet when she becomes ill he cares for her. Do you know of someone who has been called upon to care for a dying former spouse? Can you imagine yourself in such a situation?

2. When Alec decides to walk to Wales with Gwynne's ashes, what do you think he's trying to accomplish? Have you ever done anything for similar motives? Can you see yourself ever doing something extreme like that?

3. When Alec arrives at Fiona's farm, he is a man of few words. What is it about Fiona that changes him? What is it about Alec that changes Fiona—unlocking her own pain and her own capacity to love fully?

4. Fiona and Alec share a central emotional characteristic: they are both caretakers by nature and upbringing. Because of this, what do they bring to, and bring out of, each other?

5. Fiona and Alec both lost a parent when they were young: Fiona's father drowned, Alec's father drank himself to death. How has each of them been affected?

6. British-born novelist Jonathan Raban has said of *The Long Walk Home* that it is the mountain, "capricious Cadair Idris," to which the

reader must look "for the story's deeper implications." What do you think he means by that? Is the mountain itself a character in the story?

7. Will North admits to being, well . . . a guy. Do you think he succeeds in understanding and revealing Fiona's head and heart?

8. Ultimately, despite the fact that she is married, Fiona and Alec become lovers. Both of them understand that this is wrong . . . and yet believe it is also utterly right. How can that be? And why do we find ourselves rooting for them?

9. Fiona has been caring for her ailing husband for three years. Do you think she should have anticipated his attempted suicide?

10. When Alec discovers David dying on the mountain, he knows that one option is to do nothing. There must be a moment, a fraction of a second, when Alec sees how life would be made simpler by David's death. Given what happens to David—given what happens to Fiona and Alec—do you think he made the right decision?

11. Fiona's daughter, Meaghan, is so close to and protective of her father that she sometimes behaves as if she believes she would be a better caretaker for him than his own wife. Does that ring true to you? How well do you think Fiona handles Meaghan's possessiveness?

12. *The Long Walk Home* is a book about fidelity. Beyond its most obvious form—fidelity to a spouse—what other issues of fidelity do these characters wrestle with? If you were Alec, how would *you* choose? If you were Fiona, what would *you* do?

an invitation to readers' groups and book clubs

One of the real joys of being an author is meeting and chatting with readers in book groups. Sometimes I think I learn as much from them as they do from me!

I'd be delighted to come to your next meeting. Here's how we can do it:

- IN PERSON: If your group is in the Seattle area, or in a town I'm visiting (see my website for events), I'd love to spend an evening with you.
- BY PHONE: If someone in your group has a speakerphone, we can spend an hour or so together wherever you are.
- BY E-MAIL: If it's easier for you, we can meet virtually. Have your group members compile questions, and I promise I'll answer them immediately.

So let's get together. Getting started is simple: just go to my website, www.willnorthonline.com, and send me an e-mail. We'll work it into your group's schedule.

I'm looking forward to hearing from you,
Will